Devouring Raine

BOTTLES 69

Devouring Raine

Zoey Derrick

Cover Design completed by Parajunkee and is copyrighted 2014 by Zoey Derrick. For more information on Parajunkee and to see her amazing work, please visit her page, www.parajunkee.net

Editing completed by Mandy Smith and Lorraine Montuori from RawBooks Editing - They've done an amazing job and I couldn't do this without them - if you need editing services - check them out: http://rawbooksonline.com

ISBN-13: 978-0996259873

The following is a work of fiction - all reference to persons, places or things is strictly coincidental. Some parts (though small)are based on fact or actual events that occurred for the author and are portrayed fictionally here.

For the ultimate Zoey reading experience, here is a recommended reading order of stories (though not required). All books take place in the same "world".

Finding Love's Wings — 1 of 2
Chasing Love's Wings — 2 of 2
One Week — Standalone
Claiming Addison — 1 of 3
Craving Talon — 2 of 3
Redeeming Kyle — 3 of 3
Taming Dex — 1 of 2
Devouring Raine — 2 of 2

About this world...

This world contains celebrities, rock stars, and the agents who represent them - a.k.a. Bold International, Inc.
You will find each of the characters beginning with Cami and Tristan in Finding Love's Wings will carry into the subsequent books.

Books by Zoey Derrick

Contemporary Romance/Contemporary Erotic Romance

Love's Wings Series:
Finding Love's Wings (Audio Coming Soon)
Chasing Love's Wings
—Box Set Now Available —

******

69 Bottles Series:
Bisexual, MMF Menage, Erotic Romance
Claiming Addison
Craving Talon
Redeeming Kyle
—3 Book Box Set Now Available —
Taming Dex
Devouring Raine - Coming July 2015
Defining Calvin Coming October 2015
Loving Eric Coming November 2015

******

One Week (Audio Coming Soon)

Paranormal Romance

Reason Series:
Give Me Reason (Audiobook available)
Give Me Hope (Audio Coming Soon)
Give Me Desire (Audio Coming Soon)
Give Me Love
— Box Set Now Available—

Acknowledgements

My Mom, My Uncle, My Grandma and My Peanut - Thank you for your continuing love and support while I continue on this crazy wild journey of being an author. Without you, I just couldn't do it.

Rachel - My Love - My Best Friend: I'm running out of ways to thank you for everything you do for me. I hope that these little notes continue to be enough, for now.

To The Hype PR, Kelley and Christine - Yea, I'm pretty sure my vocabulary is busted when it comes to the awesome that is the two of you. Thank you so much for everything you do!

To The Z-Team: Without you, I'm pretty sure I'd run out of steam to keep going. The love you have for my stories means so much to me. Thank you for all you do!

My Fans, Friends, and Readers - Thank you for believing in me, for buying my books, reading my books and falling in love with what I do. I hope Raine and Dex are everything you want them to be and more.

Amy - This one was your turn, thank you for being my Beta Girl and for putting up with my unedited monstrosity. You're AMAZING, thank you - from the bottom of my heart!

For Mandy -
For pushing me to raise the bar and teaching me how to
do it better.

chapter
1
raine

"Marry me?" Dex breathes against my lips and I stop breathing altogether.

"You can't be serious?" I say without breathing.

"I think I am." His thumbs rub along my cheeks, the intention is comfort. I can feel that.

"You're insane." I'm finally able to pull air back into my lungs, rational thought returning. "Dex, we hardly know each other. We've...Jesus Dex, we've barely gotten to the point of not wanting to rip each other's heads off."

"So that's a no?" His lips brush mine, I can sense his smile, and I can't help but grin in return.

"It's a, 'I think you've lost your mind'."

He chuckles and his lips land on mine. I'm not entirely sure what was happening in the dressing room that had captured his attention, but judging by the way his fists were balled up and shaking, I can only imagine that there are drugs in that room.

I break our kiss. "Come on you, let's..." He starts pushing me backwards and I grab his biceps for support until he pins me against a wall.

"You're an angel," he breathes and his lips are once again on mine, this time with vigor and desire. My body comes alive when his tongue runs gently across my lower lip, begging for entrance and I grant it. He slides his tongue along mine and my breathing stutters, my head starts to spin and I want nothing short of him taking me up against this wall.

I feel his erection grind into my sex, under my skirt, along my now wet clit. I gasp and moan into his mouth. My hands slide down along his arms to the button on his jeans, desperate to free his cock and slide him inside of me. He chuckles and releases my mouth. I'm left panting, wanting, and desperate.

"You have a bit of a voyeuristic side, don't you, little girl?"

His tone and the term 'little girl' sends shivers down my spine. His hands slide down along my neck, across my collarbone until they gently slide along my bare nipples. Clad only in the silk top of the corset I'm wearing. My breath hitches in my throat and my hips flick against his erection, I moan.

"Shall I put you on display, right here, for everyone to see?" My skin heats, my cheeks flush. He smirks. "You dirty little girl." As he says the words, his fingers clamp down hard on my erect nipples, sending shockwaves of pain and pleasure straight to my core. I know the moment he feels the warmth between my legs when he hisses through his teeth.

In a rough manner, Dex slides his fingers into the top of my corset and backs away from me, bringing me with him. He takes a few steps and reaches for the door knob on one of the dressing rooms, his to be exact, and he steps inside, pulling me behind him.

I watch, almost in slow motion as he closes the door and turns toward me. He removes his hand from my corset and then grabs the top of the undershirt that I'm wearing. He pulls it down. The elastic scrapes across my nipples and they harden further as he exposes my breasts. With both hands, he tucks the material beneath my breasts.

I watch with lust filled eyes as his hands come up to my nipples, taking each one between his fingers and rolling them roughly. My body flinches and I moan. My panties are now soaked beneath the layers of my skirt.

"Please," I moan.

"Please what, little girl?"

I groan at his pet name once again. "I need you," I breathe as his hands grip my nipples tighter, tugging and pulling on them, elongating them. His hands release and my nipples contract back to their normal size and the rush of blood sends a shiver through me.

My eyes find his, hungry and desperate. There is a command hiding behind his features because on instinct, I lower myself to my knees.

"Fuck," he groans as he reaches for his belt. Unbuckling it and removing it quickly. "Give me your hands." His command rocks through me and I raise my arms above my head. Not too far, afraid that I will cover my breasts by the tension on my corset. I lower my eyes to the floor. "Jesus, who has trained you?" he asks softly as he wraps the belt around my wrists. Sending goosebumps flying across my skin.

"No one," I tell him softly. "Honestly, I just know what I want and for some reason that I don't yet understand, I trust you, Dex." I feel the belt tighten around my wrists, pulling my hands together. Though he can't fully secure it, the belt is tight enough that I can't move my wrists.

"Stand up," he all but growls. "We don't have time for what I truly want you to do, but I need my cock buried in your pussy." I stand up and he quickly turns me around, sliding up behind me. "Put your hands around my head," he orders and I reach up, and he slides his head in the gap I've made.

He leans forward, pushing me down as his hands once again glide across my nipples and I shiver. He continues further south, down along my corset covered ribs and to my skirt. His hands make their way under the many layers and he starts to push them upward until he finds my soaked panties. He hisses through his teeth. "Is this for me?"

"Yes, Sir. It's all for you."

I feel a gentle kiss against my shoulder, followed by a wet, warm open mouth kiss, a lick, and lastly, a bite as he shreds my panties in his hand. The sound of the material ripping apart makes me gasp. Then, without warning, his hand is sliding along the seam of my pussy. The action is soft compared to the savage way he shredded my panties and my body begins to quake beneath his touch. "Please don't stop," I moan.

His other hand comes off of my body, forcing my hands to grip his hair and he growls into my ear. I can feel his hand against my ass as he unbuttons his jeans and lowers the fly. Springing his cock free and I feel it bounce against my skirt as his finger finally finds my clit, hard and wanting. He strokes it once, twice and then his hand is gone, I whimper.

Then he lifts my skirts out of his way and forces me to arch just a little further. He quickly realizes that our difference in height is too much and I feel him bend his knees and the head of his rock hard cock is rubbing along my sex. I need him desperately, almost as much as he seems to need me.

With a mind of its own, desperate to find that happy warmth inside my body, his cock lines up perfectly with my dripping entrance and he pushes in slightly.

"Hold on," he whispers and his hands are behind my knees, pushing and bending them as he picks me up.

I squeal until I feel his chest against my back and then, he is sliding in and sliding home. He's holding me, lifting me up as his cock slides into me. My arms tighten around his head and his cock starts thrusting in time to his lifts and drops. "Fuck," I cry out as his cock pushes in deeper than I've ever felt before.

Realizing the reality of him holding me, he stops thrusting and walks forward a few steps toward the couch and he slips his cock out of me. The emptiness makes me feel cold and I shiver as he allows me to stand on the couch. "That's better," he breathes as he repositions me, leaving my arms behind his head. He bends me forward, his hand sliding along my back as he repositions my skirts once more.

Then he is slamming home, hot and hard. I cry out as I feel my orgasm fly to the surface and he starts pounding into me. His hands tighten their grip on my hips and he stills, slowing down his own impending orgasm.

He leans forward and wraps his arms around my chest and he takes a nipple into each hand as he starts to rock slowly in and out of me. "Jesus," I moan and he increases his pace.

In this position, with my arms around his head, I am helpless, I am at his command, only able to enjoy what it is that he's doing to me. He has me pinned down to the point that I can barely move my hips in time to his, until I figure out a smaller rhythm that works for both of us.

"You take it all away," he breathes as his forehead rests between my shoulder blades and I shiver at the gravity of what he's just said. I was his light mere moments ago, pulling him away from the darkness of the opportunity that was before him.

With that thought, I tumble over the precipice I was walking along. Shattering into my orgasm, bringing him with me as he pours himself into me.

chapter
2
raine

Dex's impromptu proposal wasn't brought up again between the two of us. It took everything I had to actually deny him his request. Though, in hindsight, it was the best thing I could have done.

After the concert, we went out, though Dex couldn't keep his hands off of me so we quickly left. Then we spent the next few days in DC before climbing back on the bus to head to Greensboro, which is where we are now, when my phone goes off with an alert. Dex is off talking to Talon about something and I am up on my rack. Victoria gladly moved to Dex's old rack and let us have the two bunk room next to Addison, Talon and Kyle's room. Though Dex and I actually sleep together on the bottom rack, I get work done on the upper one. More head room.

The alert on my phone captures my eye very quickly.

"Has 69 Bottles Drummer Dex Harris tamed his wild ways?" The headline reads and I can feel a little bit of panic rising in my chest as I open the link.

69 Bottles Drummer Dex Harris was spotted Friday night at a local DC nightclub where the band was celebrating their latest concert and there is a woman on his arm. Now, normally this wouldn't excite us except, this is the very first woman Dex has ever touched while walking into and then shortly out of the club. We even captured this image as the door of the town car they were in closed. We looked for them throughout DC over the next couple of days and unfortunately, the only time we saw Dex, he was alone with his bandmates.

Was she just another one night stand or will we actually be seeing this girl again?

I scroll down to the images provided by the article and there I am in all my corset glory. Tattoos on display and all, wrapped in the arms of the sexy drummer that is Dex Harris. The look in his eyes is telling these reporters all they need to know- lust, desire and something else are evident in his stare. The next image is of him and I inside the club, though it's not the best image, you can clearly see me sitting on Dex's lap with my head thrown back laughing and finally the image from inside the car as I all but mauled Dex as soon as I thought we were in the world.

"You're making headlines." I jump at the sound of Addison's voice and I look at her, standing in the doorway.

"I certainly didn't mean to," I say sheepishly and look once more at the pictures.

"I wouldn't worry about it. Maybe it will give them something else to talk about besides me and Talon." She smirks.

"What about Kyle?" I ask.

"Oh, he's there too, but," she shrugs, "we figured it would be less of a media frenzy if it were just him and I versus the three of us. It was actually Kyle's idea."

I nod. "Yeah, I can see that. I knew eventually Dex and I would make headlines, but I guess I didn't think they would jump to conclusions so fast."

She snorts. "That, unfortunately, is all they are good at. Jumping to conclusions. We can put out a press release, if you want."

I shake my head. "I'm still not certain what all this is with him. It's so," I pause, "so, I don't know."

She smiles at me again. "One step, one day at a time, Raine. It will all get easier." She winks.

I try and change the subject with Addison. "How'd you know about the article?"

She chuckles and comes to stand next to the bunk. "Sam," she says simply.

"Who's Sam?" I ask when she doesn't continue.

Addison's smile falls, indicating that I'm only going to get a partial truth on this story. "Let's just say she's a little infatuated with Dex. She met him back in San Diego…"

I put my hand up to silence her and raise an eyebrow. "Do I really want to know more?" I ask.

She shakes her head. "No, probably not."

"Do I need to be worried about this Sam person?" I ask her, wondering if it's going to turn into another Phoenix incident.

"Nope, I've got her under control." She winks and is right back to her lighter self.

"How are you doing?" I ask her.

"Aside from being tired, I'm great. You?"

I smile widely at her. "Never better."

My statement to Addison wasn't entirely true. In reality, I feel like the rug has been ripped out from under me. See that article was exactly what I hoped I'd never see, but it was stupid of me to be naive enough to think it would never come out publicly.

The idea of being Dex's girlfriend is a little scary, let alone the fact that he proposed to me last night before the show. I want to roll my eyes thinking about it. But I can see how the words slipped from his lips. I saved him from doing something extremely stupid so he saw me as his light. Though at this time, I'm not entirely sure how I feel about being that person. Yes, I want to be with Dex, I know deep down that he's the one man that has captured me in his grasp, faster, harder and deeper than any man before, but marriage, now?

I let the thought fall away when I receive an email from Cami regarding Dex and I making headlines. Cami, despite her cool exterior to clients, is a soft, warm romantic at heart. She wants to know whether or not this is a good thing. Yeah, Cami, it is.

Though the headline and the pictures bother me. I've never used social media on a personal level. I've handled a lot of Cami's stuff from time to time so I'm not unfamiliar with it, but I've spent the last years of my life hiding from my family. As far as they're concerned, I'm lost somewhere in the great expanse of the world, or dead. I like it that way. But now, here I am, making headlines with a rock god. Yeah, that will light a fire under their asses if they ever see it.

Then Michael pops into my mind, and Jesus, this is the last thing I need him to see. It would likely be enough to send him off the deep end and I know he's going to see it. Which means, he's going to know where I am, or at least where I was.

I try to shake off the worries by doing some tweeting for Addison and the band. Something she'd asked me to do once in a while and I finish with my emails just before Dex comes back into the room.

"Hi gorgeous," he says with a sweet smile on his face.

"Hi."

"What's wrong?" he asks immediately, sensing my distress, something that over the last couple of days I've noticed him being able to do with ease.

"We're in the papers."

He shrugs, "Good."

"Not good," I tell him. His eyes meet mine, wide and concerned.

"Why not good?"

Then I remember that I never got around to telling him about the Michael incident with my apartment while we were in New York.

"Because I have a psycho ex-boyfriend."

He raises an eyebrow questioningly at me. "Care to explain?"

I purse my lips. "Not really."

He scowls at me. "That's not how this works, glowbug..."

I raise an eyebrow back at him. "Glowbug?"

He shrugs and I roll my eyes. The nonverbal communication in facial features continues for a moment or two until I start laughing. He smiles at the sound and comes up to the bunk, slides between my legs and wraps his arms around my waist. I close my laptop and set it aside as his head rests against my thigh.

I start to run my fingers through his hair and I swear to god, he starts purring. His arms tighten around me.

"Right before Cami decided to send me here," I start to tell him, "I was out with a friend of mine when Cami called me into work. As I was leaving the club, I ran smack into Michael. The conversation turned to confrontation and I ran away quickly. Then, when we were in New York, before the first concert, I received a call from Michael. He was pissed and demanding that I answer my door. Said that 'we needed to talk' and that he wasn't leaving until I came to the door." I take a deep breath, "He started to get aggressive with me on the phone and Rusty stepped in. He called a friend of his with the LAPD and they went to the house and arrested him. After that, my friend Erica was kind enough to go to my apartment and grab some of the more important things and move them out while Michael was in jail. He's out now, I haven't heard anything from him and Erica is checking on my apartment regularly while I'm away."

His arms tighten around me a little more, protective like, and my heart warms. "Why'd you guys break up?" His voice is muffled because of his arm.

"I caught him screwing some chick in my bed, in my apartment."

His head pops up, his eyes meet mine and they're worried. "So what the hell does he want to talk about?"

I shrug. "Beats me. We've been broken up for more than six months. My guess is that he's run out of bimbos and wants me back."

"Do you want..." Before he can finish his sentence I shake my head.

"No way in hell." I smile at him, showing him my happiness and contentment to be right here with him and he lowers his head back to my thigh.

We don't talk, but we stay like that for a few minutes more before he climbs up onto the bunk with me and he lays me down. Wrapping his arms tightly around me, holding me to him. I can feel his erection pressing into my backside, but he never acts on it, and that's okay. Honestly, I've never felt so warm and protected as I do right now.

chapter
3
dex

"We're going out after the show. Are you coming along?" I ask Raine as I head into my dressing room, dripping wet from finishing our set.

"Sure." I lean down and kiss her forehead.

"I'm going to go shower then I'll be in the greenroom."

She wiggles her eyebrows at me. "Want some company?" she asks softly.

I can't say no to her when she's cute like this, and I don't verbally answer her. I simply slide my fingers between hers and bring her toward the door. I can sense her excitement as I open the door and usher her in.

Despite my sweaty, stinky nastiness, she lets go of my hand and pushes me back against the door. She reaches up on her toes and I raise my head and smirk. She pouts. "What do you want, glowbug?"

"Your lips, dammit," she huffs, but doesn't deflate.

"Oh really? And just what do you think you're going to do with my lips?"

I feel her hands slide up under my shirt, along my stomach, toward my chest and her hands are warm and soft against my sweaty, cooling skin. "I'm going to kiss them."

She continues pushing my shirt up toward my head, indicating that she wants to remove it from me and I'm tempted to tease her a little longer. What can I say? I'm a glutton for punishment and torture apparently. I grab her wrists through my shirt, stilling her hands and she pouts prettily at me. The look makes me smile wide. Once I know she isn't going to move her hands, I remove mine and take her face between my palms and tilt her head in my direction. Her breathing falters at my touch and there is that now familiar jolt that passes between us. Her mouth falls slack as I tip her head back further. "I don't deserve you," I breathe as I claim her mouth with mine.

Fire, desire and lust ignite in my veins. This is what I was trying to hold onto for just a little longer. Letting my need for her grow into a burning flame that I can't extinguish without her touch. Her lips are soft, her tongue is hard and pressing into me with desperation. The same desperation I'm feeling for her.

She claimed me for her own. She's doing all she can to remind me that I do actually deserve her, which I still don't see. I may never see it, but I decided in D.C., when she pulled me from taking steps toward destruction, that she was what I needed, that she was the light, the sunshine, that would pull me out of the tunnel I lived in.

My breathing stops and my head starts to spin. I pull back from her lips, desperate to catch my breath and I bring our foreheads together. "What are you doing to me?" I breathe out.

"I could ask you the same thing," she whispers softly as we both work to slow our breathing down.

"Come," I command her and bring her with me toward the bathroom inside the dressing room. Somehow, I always seem to get the nicest room. Probably because I am usually the only one who requires a shower after the show. This facility is by far the best we've been in with a large glass enclosed shower and I have visions of Raine pressed against the glass while I take her from behind.

Instead of me taking control, a shiver of excitement runs up my spine when she reaches into the shower to turn on the water. She tests it a few times, determining that the temperature is right, so I start to pull off my t-shirt.

Before I can remove it, her hands stop me and she takes over. Stripping me of my shirt before she falls to her knees to untie my boots. She helps me shed them, and then she focuses her attention on the buttons of my jeans. I watch as her tongue darts out between her lips as she takes in the bulge before her eyes. "It's all for you, glowbug."

Don't ask me where the hell the nickname came from. Maybe it is my way of reminding her that the light she brings to my life is strong and I can't resist her. Or maybe it is just my imagination coming up with the easiest nickname. But it fits her and she's smiled every time I've used it.

She makes quick work of my buttons, ripping them open, exposing the base of my shaft. She wastes no time as I watch her tongue gently stroke along the shaft as she works to lower my jeans from my waist. She's smiling as my cock pops free and she nuzzles against it. "Fuck," I groan when she wraps both her hands around the shaft of my now rock hard cock and begins to stroke both hands up and down my length.

Her eyes look up at me through her lashes and the look is so unbelievably fucking sexy that I nearly explode right there. "Suck it, please god, suck my cock." I practically beg her and she smiles a wicked little grin at me.

I watch as her tongue dances and teases around the head of my cock while her hands continue to stroke me up and down. She rubs the head of my dick around her mouth, leaving a warm trail around the head. I take her head in my hands, allowing my fingers to slide into her hair. I keep going, pulling her hair into a ponytail with one hand and I hang on tight, pulling her head back slightly as her tongue takes a fat wet swipe along the underside of the mushroom head. "Suck it," I command, gripping her hair tighter.

"Yes, Sir," she moans as she wraps her lips around the head of my dick and I shiver. Coherent thought disappears into her mouth.

"Jesus, fuck," I groan out as I start to thrust my hips in time with the strokes of her hands, sliding further and further into her mouth with each pass. Her tongue is heaven and hell rolling hot and wet across my shaft.

Then I can feel the back of her throat and I try to pull back but she holds hard and steady, pulling me back into her mouth. She moans again when my cock touches the back of her throat and the vibrations are enough to cause my eyes to roll into the back of my head. I look down at her after I've recovered and she is begging me with her eyes. "You want me to fuck your mouth, pet?" I ask her and she shivers, groans and nods all at the same time. "Fuck."

I grip her ponytail tighter in my hand and I cup her face with my free hand. She pulls her hands back and opens her mouth wide, giving me plenty of room to maneuver in and out of her mouth. I start to move, slowly at first, testing the waters with her. I've never fucked her mouth like this before and though I am desperate to do so, I don't want to push it beyond the limits of what she's capable of.

After a few more pumps I watch as her hands go to rest on her thighs and her eyes glaze over, full of lust. "Do I need to stop?" I ask, afraid that I've pushed her to the point that she's checked out on me. She shakes her head no as best as she can with my cock in her mouth. "You're so fucking gorgeous," I tell her as I continue sliding into her mouth. Her tongue begins to dance along my shaft and she starts to moan. "Show me your tits, baby girl."

She quickly complies, lifting her shirt and lowering her bra, bringing out her beautiful tits for me to look at. "Play with your nipples," I command her and she complies quickly, rubbing her nipples between her fingers and moaning around my cock. "Jesus fuck, I'm gonna come," I groan and she tugs on her nipples, moaning louder. I feel her head start to push forward and back as I fuck her mouth. She's eager and it takes me only another few strokes and I explode, the orgasm rocking through me and I buck into her mouth as spurts of come slide down her throat and she moans when she pulls harder on her nipples.

As I come down from my orgasm, I release her hair and extract myself from her mouth. I watch as she adjusts her bra and then lowers her shirt. I'm even more confused when she helps me remove my jeans. "Shower, bubba," she tells me as she steps out of the way for me to pass. I reach for the hem of her t-shirt and she stops me.

"What's wrong?"

She smiles. "Nothing is wrong. You need to shower and get dressed."

"But I want you to join me," I tell her.

"And mess up my hair and makeup?" She snorts a laugh that is really infectious and I smile too. She points toward the shower with her head.

"What about you?" I press into her, lifting her chin with my hand so she can look at me, and with my other hand I try to slide it down her pants, into her panties and against her clit. I get about halfway there when her hand wraps around my wrist.

"I'll get mine," she says, "but you have to get moving." She winks at me and manages to untangle herself and leave the bathroom before I can protest.

chapter
4
raine

I'm pretty sure you're wondering why I just walked away. The answer is simple; I wanted to reward him for a night well done. Among other things, but in reality, it was the time. He didn't have it. He needs to be in the greenroom, especially if the guys want to go out tonight. I knew that if I stayed in there, I'd have gotten in the shower, he would have given me the best orgasm I could possibly hope for and I would be left to the dressing room to reapply makeup and redo my hair, letting everyone know that we got it on in the dressing room. Okay, not that I mind, or give a shit, but one thing I've noticed is that I don't see Addison changing clothes and redoing makeup after a concert. Now on the bus, that is a whole other story to tell. Sheesh, those three certainly cannot get enough of each other. As I watch them now, I can see just how much love flows between them. The way that Kyle practically dotes on Addison and the way that Talon loves on both of them any chance he can get.

I'm having a hard enough time handling Dex, I can't imagine two of him. But then again, Dex is...well, he's amazing.

The concert tonight in Greensboro was a huge success. They played three songs over two encores because the fans demanded it of them. That demand is both a blessing and a curse as far as Dex is concerned. He works so hard while he's on stage. It's amazing to me that he doesn't just climb onto the bus and pass out after his shows. Though I imagine, for him, it's an adrenaline rush and a high unlike anything else he's experienced, including drugs.

After about twenty minutes of the doors being open into the greenroom to greet fans, Dex saunters in; a sad smirk on his face. I can tell he's happy but yet something is bothering him. I'm disappointed, though I have no reason to be, when he heads straight toward the couch where Mouse and Peacock are sitting instead of coming over to me. I watch from the corner of the room as one chick after another comes up to him and the guys. I notice more than a few of them are overly flirty with Dex and sometimes, he is too. I want to scream in frustration at him, but I bury my feelings about it as best as I can.

Yes, we're fucking. Yes, we're sharing the same little room on the bus, but with the exception of his slip of the tongue and his little marriage proposal, we've yet to honestly commit to one another. At least we haven't spoken the commitment out loud.

I close my eyes and roll them. *Jesus, Raine, you're a fucking idiot.* I scold myself internally. *Why do you always do this to yourself? You fucking give people an out, though they shouldn't have one. Just because he hasn't 'asked' you to be his 'girlfriend', I'm pretty sure you've committed yourself to him and him to you.* I continue to beat myself up internally. Trying to talk myself down from the frenzy I've managed to get myself into. But the images of New York, of him wanting me one minute and then going back to having some harpy on his lap are hard to erase.

I sneak out of the room. I need to clear my brain, give myself a minute to think, and I can't do that with all the talking and noise that's going on in the room.

I manage to slip past everyone and right out the back door with a nod to Troy as he's standing guard at the door. When I exit the back door, the bus is only about twenty yards away and I'm desperate to get to it and into my little room before I completely break down.

"Jesus can still save you." I hear a male voice come from behind me and I freeze. "Jesus is ready to take you back, Lorraine."

My blood freezes in my veins and my body begins to shake. There are only three people on this god forsaken planet that call me Lorraine.

"He wants to accept you back into the fold of his arms and his worship. Come back to him and you shall be saved."

The voice is too high, too young, too…

I finally manage to get my feet working once again and though I want to run for the safety of Leroy and the bus, I can't. I finally manage to turn myself around.

There's no one there…

I squint against the two spotlights above the building that illuminate the lot for the buses but I can't see anything.

"Are you ready to accept God back into your life, Lorraine?" I hear the voice again, this time it's coming from the left and I turn.

"Who the fuck are you?" I scream.

All I hear is a distant chuckle and then footsteps, heavy ones.

"Raine?" a deep voice says and I turn, defensive, ready to strike.

"Whoa girl, it's just me. What's wrong?"

I tremble before Leroy as he grabs my arm. "Come on, let's get you on the bus," he says softly and I follow behind him. He unlocks the bus door and ushers me inside.

"You didn't hear that?" I finally find my voice.

"Hear what?" His face is soft, understanding, but yet confused.

"Never mind," I whisper softly. "Thanks for letting me on the bus."

He gives me a sad half smile. "Want to talk about it?" he asks and I shake my head. "Alright, I'll be outside if you need me."

"Thank you, Leroy."

"Anytime," he says as he steps back off of the bus.

I shiver as the adrenaline reaches a crescendo and I head back toward my room.

As soon as I'm there, I hop up onto my bunk and curl myself into a ball as tremors consume me.

Why the hell would anyone I know be here?

No one's here stupid, you're the only one who heard anything.

Why would I conjure that shit up? Out of everything else I could have imagined, why that?

Because you haven't been this close to home since you left, how many years ago? Talking to Dex about your past has dragged it all back up again.

How would anyone in my family even know I was here, where I was or that I would be here?

I let the thought drain off as reality strikes like lightning…the article.

chapter
5
raine

Dex Harris Mystery Woman Confirmed

That was the headline for today's news.

The article went on to state "the woman seen with Dex in D.C., was in fact Raine Montgomery, Bold International, Inc. employee, former assistant to CEO Cameron Enders."

The source remains unnamed, but I am certain it wasn't Cami who released it, and that article was printed today. Still doesn't solve the problem of how in the hell anyone from my little Podunk town in North Carolina could have or would have seen the article in the first place.

I was so consumed with whatever it was that happened outside of the arena last night that it didn't dawn on me until the band returned to the bus that Dex never came and got me. In fact, he climbed into his rack without saying a single word to me. I then spent the next hour crying softly in my rack. Beating myself up for thinking that this was really going to work between Dex and I. I wanted to wake him up, scream at him, yell at him, but the fight in me had gone.

I tried to do some internet research on my parents, to see where they may be, but like most people of their generation, social media doesn't exist for them. Though they still have the same old phone number listed and the same address.

That's when I find it. Andrew Kressley Montgomery, my brother, is on Facebook. I couldn't see much of his profile because it was private, but he made sure that I could see he'd taken after my parents on the religious front.

After that I went looking for some of the people I graduated from high school with, some who were actually friends with Andrew. Though I could see most of those profiles, there wasn't anything to indicate they knew about me being in the papers. Not that they would give a shit.

The town that I come from is small. Everyone talks and I'm pretty sure that should I ever show up there, everyone would know who I am in a heartbeat, despite the ten years since I left.

Eventually, sometime around eleven, I give up my search for any information I can find pertaining to Andrew, or my parents.

I slam my laptop closed.

"What gives, glowbug?" Dex asks from below me.

"What gives? Seriously, you want to ask me that now? After last night?"

I hear him get up off of his rack. He's wearing a pair of thin black boxer shorts, and nothing else. The tent is impossible to miss.

"What the fuck did I do now?"

I fold my arms, feeling stupid and childish. "Forget it."

"No, damn it. What the fuck did I do?" He all but stomps his foot.

"Nothing, Dex, that's the problem, you did nothing."

"You're going to have to do better than that, sunshine. This don't work that way."

"Dex, I'm not sure this," I gesture between the two of us, "is working between us. That's the problem. You walked into that greenroom last night and flat out ignored me. I watched you flirting stupidly with the girls who were overly flirtatious with you. Then when I leave, I swear to god, I have an out of body experience that freaks me the fuck out and I came here." I sit up a little straighter. "Then you proceed to go out with the guys without even so much as a second thought about me. So yes, Dex, I don't think this is working."

I watch as his body deflates. "I never forgot about you. In fact, I knew right where you were and I was waiting patiently for you to come over. I watched you leave the greenroom and I couldn't follow after you. Then when we were done I tracked down Beck to find out where you were. He told me that you'd freaked out about something and ran off to the bus. I didn't know what the hell to do, Raine. I figured I'd done something wrong again, but I had no clue. I thought maybe it would be best if I just let you be."

I don't say anything, realizing that I was rightfully beating myself up over nothing, and that what Dex was doing was absolutely nothing wrong. "I have no claim to you, Dex. I didn't think that I had the right to just come over and climb on your lap," I say softly and he unfolds his arms and takes the step toward me.

"What makes you think you have no claim on me?" he asks as his hand comes to brush hair from my face. I shrug and lean into his touch.

This is what his touch does to me; it obliterates everything I'm feeling or think I feel when it comes to him. When he touches me, he's the only thing that matters. He consumes my mind, my body and soul. He devours me whole. "It's so stupid," I mutter.

"What?" he asks me as he places gentle pressure on my shoulder to capture my attention and bring my eyes to his.

Jesus, I feel so stupid. "You've never asked me out," I say sheepishly, feeling like a high schooler begging her first crush to commit to her.

He smiles wide. "I didn't know that I needed to. I guess I just thought it was implied." He leans forward, cupping my face between his palms. His height gives him enough leverage to lean over and let his lips brush against mine. "Raine Montgomery, will you be my girlfriend?"

His lips land on mine before I can answer him. The question, though asked simply to satisfy me, sends my heart soaring. I wrap my arms around his neck, holding him to me as hard as I can. Trying to indicate that I want him to come up here. Finally he breaks the kiss. "I told you it was stupid," I mumble.

"You haven't answered my question." His hands release me and I grab his wrists before he can get too far away and I place them against my chest and his eyes light up with desire and lust.

"Yes," I moan as my subtle hint is taken and my nipple rolls between his fingers. "Ah fuck."

He releases one nipple as he moves my laptop to between the mattress and frame of my rack, then he pulls back my covers to reveal the barely there thong I was wearing last night. His breathing stops and his arms hitch themselves under my legs, pulling me down my rack, spreading me wide so that my pussy is right in his face.

I hear him sniff and watch his eyes roll into the back of his head. "This, sweet glowbug, is my own personal heaven." He groans as I feel him tug my thong to the side, exposing my clit and wet sex. He waits barely a heartbeat before his tongue is searing wet and hot between my folds. I moan. His hands grab hold of the thin straps and he begins pulling the material. I lift my hips, thrusting my pussy onto his face and he groans, sending vibrations over my sex and I can feel an orgasm building.

His mouth comes away as he pulls my thong out of his way, down my legs and finally off. All while his tongue licks and laps at my sex. When he's done tossing my thong aside, his hands immediately go to the hem of my t-shirt, pushing it up higher until it will move no more. I position myself on my elbows so that I can pull the shirt out from under me, then finally up and over my head.

He groans and my nipples pebble into tight peaks and I slowly cup my breasts, playing with my nipples as he slides two fingers into my waiting pussy. I can feel the tiny spasms my sex has as it sucks his fingers in deeper. It only takes him a moment to find my sweet spot and he starts sucking on my clit. Pulling it into his mouth and massaging it with his tongue.

"Fuck, Dex." I stop myself from screaming out my desperate need for him. His fingers continue flicking against my g-spot deep inside and his tongue dances expertly over my clit.

I roll my nipples between my fingers and my orgasm threatens to consume me whole. My legs start to twitch with each flick of his tongue against my hard clit. His hand is buried in my cunt and I know he's trying to make me come all over his face and it is going to work.

My hands come away from my tits and I thrust them into his hair, holding him hard to my sex as I grind myself against him. "Oh fuck, oh fuck," I moan out as my orgasm consumes me completely. My whole body shakes with my release as Dex's fingers replace his tongue, rubbing feverishly against my clit and the two fingers inside find a record pace as I hear the wetness of my orgasm spraying past his fingers.

I feel his pace slow to a more sensual rhythm and my body twitches as he milks my release.

chapter
6
raine

When I finally start to have coherent thoughts following my orgasm, I realize that Dex hasn't stopped licking and fingering me. I want to push him away, but soon realize the reason he hasn't stopped. "Sorry," I mutter as I unlock my fingers from his hair, holding him to me, but he doesn't stop. In fact, he picks up the pace in double time. "Fuck me," I groan as I feel another orgasm quickly making its way to my sex. "Dex, stop." He shakes his head and continues sucking my clit into his mouth and he moans. I realize now why.

His other hand has disappeared and I can feel his shoulder moving as he strokes his cock in time to his thrusts into my pussy.

"Wouldn't it feel better inside?" I ask him and he nods, but doesn't stop. It takes me another heartbeat to realize that I don't want him to stop what he's doing and I thrust one of my hands back into his hair, grinding against his face in time to his licks and thrusting of his fingers.

It doesn't take long before I am exploding in another orgasm. This time though, it's a little less intense and I can sense his disappointment. "Why do you like it when I squirt all over you?" I manage to ask him, breathless, as I come down from my orgasm.

He finally relinquishes my clit and slowly extracts his fingers from my pussy. "Because," his hot breath caresses my sex and I shiver, "I know that it's real and because there is something about the way you taste when you come on me that I can't get enough of."

He smiles then and I fight the urge to roll my eyes at him. "You're such a man," I giggle and he smirks.

"Can I do something?" he asks, innocent and shyly.

"Anything," I say without a second thought and his face lights up.

"Scoot up, put your arms above your head, rest them on the rail." His voice has that air of command and I shiver at what that might mean.

I quickly comply and I lay my wrists across the bar at the head of my rack. He goes about looking for something, though I am not sure what. I can feel his short chest hair brush across my knuckles as he comes to stand between the racks and the closet. "Close your eyes," he orders and I comply, screwing my eyes shut tight so I'm not tempted to look. "Lift your head," he tells me and I do. That's when I feel something slide over my head and over my eyes, a blindfold.

My breathing hitches. "We good, glowbug?" he asks softly.

"Yes," I breathe.

"Relax for me." Again his voice is soft, comforting.

That's when I feel something soft wrap around one wrist then the other, intertwining around my wrists and securing them together, then finally securing them to the railing of the rack. "Still good?"

"Yes," I whisper, barely audible and goosebumps rise across my body. My nipples pebble as I realize that I am at his mercy, his to play with as he sees fit. A sliver of fear creeps into me as I don't know what it is that he is going to do to me and I'm worried.

"I just want you to feel me," he whispers gently into my ear and then I feel his lips feather light against my own. "Just savor me," he says right before his lips land solidly on mine.

My entire body comes alive. My inability to touch him frustrates me and I fight my bonds, but they are going nowhere. My inability to see him causes my lips to tingle with each press of his lips against mine. After a few beats with just his lips, I feel his hand up near my wrist, its light, but slightly rough from his calloused fingers. The sharpness of his dry fingers and the warmth of his touch are almost too much and my legs scissor together, fighting for relief but finding none.

His hand continues a fiery trail down my arm, inside my elbow, across my bicep and down to my shoulder. His touch remains light against my skin, but there is fire and goosebumps in his wake. He releases my lips from our kiss. Anticipation and excitement over where he will go next with his mouth causes me to shiver. At the same moment his slow moving hand comes to circle my nipple. He circles it once, twice, then continues in an outward spiral, never actually touching the tight peak. Instead, his other hand joins in on the action, repeating the same process on the other breast. My nipples remain painfully hard. Threatening to snap the barbells in half because they are so hard. "Fuck," I groan out as his hands disappear completely. The rack groans beneath me and I hear his knees snap as he climbs up, then I feel him repositioning my legs between his, forcing me to close my legs.

The pressing of my thighs together is almost what I need to reach the orgasm that is fighting to the surface. He straddles me, holding my legs hostage beneath his own and I feel the head of his cock brush directly over my clit. "Fuck," I cry out and my back arches. I feel him chuckle slightly. "You're the devil," I nearly growl at him.

"Oh glowbug, you haven't seen anything yet." The menacing tone in his voice tells me that he's telling the truth and I shiver. His hands are back on me with their feather light touch once again, this time, along my hips. I can feel him slowly sliding toward my sex, painful centimeter by torturous centimeter. I writhe beneath him. I can feel his fingers drawing closer to the small smattering of hair I have directly above my clit, but just before his fingers tickle into the curls, he turns north toward my belly button and I groan in frustration as his hands slide further up.

Once again his hands are circling my nipples, slow and steady until he starts to circle the swell of my breasts. The sensations are too much and I can feel my arousal sliding down between my legs. When his hands move further toward my shoulders, he leans forward. Pressing the tip of his cock directly into my clit. I cry out.

Then without warning, his hands are gone and I feel his dick pressing harder against my clit. Then I feel him adjusting his dick, sliding it further south, right into the V between my thighs and pussy. Then I can feel the head of his cock playing at my entrance. I know he realizes it too the moment his breath hitches as he makes contact with the wet warmth of my pussy opening.

He continues pressing into me and I can feel the veins of his cock sliding along my clit. This isn't going to last long before I'm exploding once again.

I feel him lean forward, both by his position on my legs and the thrust into my sex. It's spreading me wide, nearly to the point of being uncomfortable. Then the bed dips near my head as he positions himself. "We good?" he asks and I nod. He takes my queue and starts to move in and out of me. After a couple of thrusts, I feel him shift again and the blindfold is removed from my eyes. "I need to see you." He says softly as his lips meet mine and I blink against the light in the room. Once my eyes are open he pulls back. "Hello beautiful." He says with a smile. "How does this feel?"

"Good," I groan. He keeps up his pace for a few more thrusts and his dick rubs against my clit, sending all kinds of new sensations radiating from my core. I am near orgasm and when my legs start to tremble beneath him, he knows it. His pace increases marginally but I can tell he's holding back on me.

"Come for me," he says and he thrusts a little more deeply into me, tipping me over the edge. I fight against my bonds as I'm desperate to touch him. The bite of the binding is just enough pain to rocket my orgasm higher.

He brings me down slowly, then shifts his leg over mine, helping me spread my legs. Once he has the leverage over me that he wants he lifts that free leg, driving into me deeper as he presses my leg toward my chest. "Jesus," he groans as he realizes just how deep he's gotten inside me. I can feel the head of his cock against my cervix and the tickling of his balls against my ass tells me that he's deeper in me than he has ever been.

"Dex," I moan out as another orgasm is building hard and fast. "I need you to come with me." He nods his understanding as he thrusts harder and faster into me until he explodes, tipping me once more over the edge and deeper into the emotional rabbit hole.

chapter
7
dex

I reach up and gently undo her bindings. When she's free, I gently massage her wrists and she groans her satisfaction.

When I'm done, I pull the blanket up and over us and then wrap my arms around her, snuggling into the safest place, the only place I want to be. "What did you mean, earlier, about the out of body experience?" I ask the question that's been scratching the surface for the last hour.

"It's stupid really."

I tilt her head toward me. "Nothing is ever stupid, I'd like to know," I tell her and she gives me a small smile.

"When I walked out of the arena last night, someone was out here, but I couldn't see. Leroy didn't hear him either. He was saying all kinds of weird shit and he..." she pauses and looks away, "he called me Lorraine."

I raise an eyebrow at her, "Lorraine?"

"It's my birth name. I dumped the Lor when I moved to California, trying to maintain my anonymity and start over, I figured that was the easiest thing I could do. My friends, in high school, had all called me Raine and my parents hated it. So naturally..."

"You wanted to do something you knew they wouldn't approve of," I answer her unfinished thought.

She nods at me and finally our eyes meet again. "I keep trying to convince myself that it wasn't real. That no one was really there, but I can't come up with a logical reason why my brain would dig up something like that."

"What did they say?"

"Told me that Jesus was willing and ready to accept me back into his arms."

I stiffen.

"It's the same bullshit my parents would spout constantly. They were those crazy street corner types that would stand outside bars and haggle the drunks into believing Jesus could save them from their sins of alcohol."

"Yikes," is all I can manage to say.

She smirks and rolls her eyes at the same time, it makes me smile. "Which again is why I left. After what happened, living with them wasn't an option, aside from them actually kicking me out of the house. Even if they'd welcomed me home when I was released, it would have been worse than hell on earth. I'd already endured that before my attack, so anything on top of that was going to be far worse. I knew where I stood when I got home from the hospital."

"How so?" I brush her hair behind her ear.

"All my stuff was thrown out in the yard. It had been there for a few days and it had been raining. Luckily, the one thing my parents had managed to do was let me work. I'd had a few thousand dollars saved up from working since I was sixteen and shortly before my attack my stipend from school had come in. I wasn't rolling in dough by any means, but I was able to purchase a backpack and a few outfits before climbing on a bus for California." She pauses to take a deep breath, "Greensboro is closer to home than I've been since I climbed on board that bus."

"How would they have known where to find you?" I ask.

"That's why I can't wrap my head around someone actually being there. Leroy said he didn't hear anything and the voice was pretty loud. There was the article, and my picture was in it, but I am far from the mousey brown haired girl that left North Carolina ten years ago. My name wasn't mentioned in that article, though it's out now and confirmed who I am. I'd imagine it would be a matter of time before someone figured it out. But again, they're not the type of people that read articles on the internet or even in the types of papers that have rock star news in it."

She looks up at me. I kiss the tip of her nose and she smiles. "I'm sure it was nothing to worry about," I tell her, though I can't say I'm not concerned about it and I vow to talk to Mills about it before tonight's show.

"Will you share a room with me when we get to Nashville?" she asks me.

I smile. "I thought that was implied."

She smiles back at me. There is something in her eyes, something telling, something that has been lying just under the surface between us for some time now. I snuggle into her. "I love you," I breathe out. The convictions of the words I've spoken rock through my body and I've never felt so right about something in all my life. "You're all I want to be with, you're where I belong. You're my sunshine," I whisper against her forehead then kiss her gently.

When I pull back and look at her I see her eyes are filled with unshed tears. I cup her face in my hand and she nuzzles into it. "I love you too," she says, her voice is heavy with emotion.

"Why are you crying?" I ask her softly as my thumb wipes away an escaped tear.

"Because..." she sniffles, "it all seems too good to be true, Dex. Like I'm going to wake up from this dream any minute and I will be back in my LA apartment, still working for Cami, still doing the mundane day job, not riding on a bus toward Nashville with the sexiest man I know."

I playfully pinch her nipple, hard.

"Ouch!" she squeaks and I chuckle.

"Not a dream, glowbug."

Her eyes dart to mine, then her hand cups the back of my neck and she pulls me into a hard, deep kiss. My semi turns hard as stone in an instant.

"I want to make love to you," I say between her kisses. "But not here. I want you alone in our bed, tonight. Just you and me."

She nods and kisses me again. The passion is there, the fire ignites and I know that I need to be inside of her.

I know she senses it too when she rolls toward me, hitching her leg over my hip and my cock immediately finds the warm slickness that is her pussy and he jumps, causing her to moan into my mouth. "I need you inside me," she moans out.

"I can deny you nothing, glowbug." I use my free hand to line up the head of my cock with her warm entrance and gently slide inside. She uses the leverage she has with her leg over my hip to slide down further on my cock and I growl as I take her lips with mine. "Home."

Her hand fists into my hair, holding me to her, kissing me harder. Her teeth graze against my bottom lip and I can't help but push her onto her back and climb on top of her, my dick never leaving his happy place in the process.

Her wet heat is slick and I slide in and out easily. "Fuck, you feel so fucking good."

Just then she clamps down on my cock, then releases and clamps down again. "Your little fucking squeezes drive me insane," I growl and take her nipple into my mouth, sucking hard as she squeezes my dick again. I release her nipple with an audible pop. "Keep that up and I'm going to explode." She squeezes me again and I grit my teeth, fighting the rising urge to come. I slow my pace and she gives me a wicked smirk.

I bite her nipple, she squeaks then lets out a hot rush of air as the sensation registers. I bite her nipple again and she doesn't squeak this time, but she stops breathing momentarily. Deciding it's time to leave my mark, I lick up a little, above her nipple, and I bite into her breast, hard and I feel her orgasm explode all over my cock and I pound into her, hard and fast. I start sucking and licking on the spot I bit into, trying to soothe the burn of the bite and with each pass over the sore spot, her pussy clamps down a little harder, making it nearly impossible for me to move. When I release her breast, she releases my cock. I smirk, then look down at the angry red welt and teeth marks I've left on her breast and my breath hitches.

"Fuck, Raine, I'm sorry..."

Her finger comes to my lips to silence me. "Do it again," she breathes. Her eyes are glossy, full of lust and desire and submission. Sex and pain are really two things that work with this woman and that makes me want to explode. "Only wait until you're ready to come." *Hrmm, she's topping from the bottom.*

I nod. She has this uncanny ability to submit to me like some of the best trained subs I've ever seen, and yet she has the ability to flip a switch and turn me into putty in her palms.

I begin licking and nuzzling her other nipple, sucking and nibbling against the barbell and tightly pebbled peak. She moans and I can feel her orgasm building in the tightening of her pussy around my dick. I am so fucking close, but I need her to be there too. I bite down on her nipple and she cries out. Her legs start to tremble and I know she's close, oh so fucking close. I increase my pace, I'm right there.

I move off of her nipple and bite down hard against the soft flesh and she explodes around me, bringing me over the edge as I explode inside of her.

chapter
8
raine

"Jesus, bubba," I scold as I stand before the mirror in the bathroom of our room in Nashville. I just finished my shower, okay, *we* just finished our shower.

Dex comes to stand behind me at the mirror. He wraps his arms around my stomach and rests his chin on my shoulder, looking into the mirror at my naked form. "I'm so sorry, I got carried away," he says with a smirk that tells me he's not really sorry.

I'm staring at two gnarly looking, matching bite marks on my tits, just to the inside of my nipples. I gently touch them and they sting, but the pain isn't exactly unwelcome. "No, I like them, they're just, jeez, they look so angry." I smirk. He didn't draw blood, so there aren't any scabs or anything like that, but his teeth have definitely left their impression on my skin. Inside the marks are red and blotchy from the sucking.

Dex raises his chin and releases me, then gently turns me around and he leans down and he kisses each of the angry welts. Each kiss is followed up by gentle soothing licks and another kiss. "Is it wrong that I like seeing these on you?"

I smile at him and he kisses me gently. "No, I like seeing them too. They make me feel marked, claimed."

"Well, you are most certainly claimed, taken, off the market, and all mine," he says with a gentle cup of my cheek. I lean into his touch. Gone is the assholian I met when I first arrived in New York and he's been replaced by someone else. Almost as if he's had a complete mind and heart transplant. I want to trust that it's real, that he really has changed, but I also know how hard change can be. Some men are capable of being tamed, others struggle with it and I worry that he will eventually struggle.

"I need to get ready."

He smiles. "Wear something sexy."

"No," I tease. "I'm going to wear a burlap sack." I laugh.

"You'd still be sexy." He kisses my forehead and leaves me to get ready for the show tonight.

dex

My phone rings and I don't recognize the number, but answer it anyway. "You got him," I say into the phone.

"Hey man, it's Derek."

"Ah, hey. It was great seeing you at the show last night."

"It was great to come to the show, make sure you tell whoever it was thanks for hooking us up with the tickets. Cotah was so excited after meeting you guys in Phoenix."

"Oh I'll do that. I'm glad you and her had a great time."

"Listen, I was calling because of what we talked about last night."

"Oh, yeah." I look toward the bathroom and step out of the bedroom into the small sitting area. "Did you find anything out?"

"I did. I was able to get in touch with the owner. He said that he can let you guys in before opening tomorrow night. Give you a chance to take a tour."

"Oh shit, that's amazing, thank you, Derek."

I hear him chuckle. "Don't thank me yet."

"Oh?"

He laughs, "No, nothing bad. It's actually one of our favorites and I was wondering if you'd mind if we joined you tomorrow night?"

"Oh hell no, come on over. Would love to pick your brain a little more."

He chuckles on the other end. "Is she serious about it?" he asks me, completely serious.

I look into the bedroom. "Yeah, she is. She's fucking amazing at it too. I'm shocked she hasn't been trained."

I can sense his smile. "Some women are just natural at it. Cotah was. Though eventually we hit a few spots where some training was involved. I brought up tomorrow night with her, because we talk about everything. I have a few surprises for you, if you're open to it."

"Absolutely. Where should we meet?"

Derek and I finished our conversation and planned out our afternoon. Raine had run off before they arrived and I am not entirely sure if she knows Derek from work. He is technically one of Cami's clients. I'm a little leary about how Raine is going to react to my plans, but I think it will be important to her. At least I hope so.

Once I'm done texting what I'm going to need from Mills tomorrow night, which is anonymity more than anything, I finish getting ready for the show tonight.

"Come on, glowbug, I gotta get going. Are you coming with me?"

I barely finish when she steps out of the bedroom. "I'm good to go," she says as she comes into view.

My knees wobble. "Jesus fuck," I grumble.

She's wearing a blue plaid lace up corset lined with studs. I can see the top arch of my bite peeking out of the top, it's sexy as fuck to look at. She's wearing black leather pants and a bullet belt that sits on her hips, but what turns me on the most is the simple square studded collar around her neck and of course the black pumps on her feet. There is no shirt under her top so parts of her midriff and sides peek out between the top and the top of her pants.

My cock grows hard against my jeans as I look her over. Her hair is down and brushed to one side and her makeup is black around her beautiful ice blue eyes, making them glow. Aligning nicely with my nickname for her. "You're so fucking gorgeous, glowbug," I tell her and she blushes then twirls around. The leather pants are tight, hugging every curve and dimple of her ass and it is taking everything I have not to smack it.

Instead I walk up to her, wrap my arms around her and grab hold of her ass cheeks through the leather and she groans as she grips my biceps. I grind my cock against her crotch and her breathing hitches. "Even he approves," she giggles.

"Yes, he does. Now let's get the fuck out of here before I peel these pants off of you." I kiss her lips and she giggles.

"Later, bubba."

I smile. "That nickname makes me sound like a redneck."

She giggles. "I know, but it fits."

I scoff playfully at her. "I am not a redneck."

"No, but your big, burly and sexy as fuck." She gives me a wicked smirk. I intertwine our fingers and pull her to the door. I press her against the back of it. Raising her hands over her head and pinning her to the door with my thigh between her legs. My cock jumps in my jeans as my lips crash hard and desperate into hers. Her breathing hitches and she moans into my mouth. She grinds her crotch against my thigh, searching for relief and finding none.

I break our kiss with a smirk. "You're going to kill me."

"That makes two of us," she says, panting and fighting for the air I've stolen from her. My head is spinning from the dizziness she causes me each time I kiss her.

I slowly release her from the back of the door and back away, making sure she's steady as I go.

chapter
9
raine

For Nashville being the country capital of the US, the fans are insane and the concert is probably one of the best I've seen them perform so far. 69 Bottles is at the top of their game right now and nothing can bring them down. I hung out backstage with Addison and Kyle during the show, much like I've done every show.

Addison is always so nice and sweet and because I'd gone to the arena early with Dex, she and I had a chance to discuss a few things about promotion and sponsorship that she was working on. It seems as though after New York, her relationship with Talon and Kyle has grown even stronger, yet there seems to be some very comfortable distance between them.

"Why is that?" I asked Addison before the greenroom starts.

"One of the things we learned when Kyle left was that we were so invested in each other that we'd forgotten that we needed to be ourselves too. When Kyle left, I was devastated, unable to function except when it came to work because that was the only thing I had outside of them. So we realized that it was important for us to find other things that we needed to do on our own, or with just two, versus the three of us," she tells me with a smile.

"Has it helped?"

She nods and smiles wider. "It's made us even closer. Though we miss each other like mad when we're apart, like right now, it makes it all the better when the three of us come back together. I don't go out with them every night, mainly because I don't have the energy, but also because it's important for the guys to spend time together. Also, Talon had pretty much left the rest of the band to fend for themselves, not that they aren't capable of that, but I imagine they were suffering right along with the change in our relationship status. I've noticed that they all seem to be back to the way they were when I first joined the tour. With one exception." She winks at me then.

"Dex?"

"Yeah, but you see, Dex is truly the wild child of the group, so while the guys are missing him, they understand better what he's going through. Like last night," Addison tells me.

"What happened last night?"

She laughs. "Dex was a bit of a log. I could tell that he was really missing you. He kept looking around, hoping you'd show up. When you didn't or when he didn't find you, he deflated a little bit."

"I didn't intentionally ditch him, but he never came looking for me either," I tell her sadly.

"I know. I tried talking to him about it, he just said that something had upset you and you'd run off. He thought it would be best to give you some time to cool down." She gives me a knowing smile. "I agreed with him, which is probably why he stayed with the rest of us until we all left."

"Why?"

"Did I agree with him?" she says with a raised eyebrow and I nod. "That's easy, because sometimes, when we're upset, we do really stupid things, say stupid things, argue unnecessarily and if he fucked up again, it wasn't going to do either one of you any good to fight about it."

I give her a sad smile.

We talked a little while longer before the guys started coming in. I knew Dex would be further behind, as usual. This time, taking his cue from last night, rather than hiding in the corner, I sat down between Kyle and Peacock. They both nudged shoulders with me at the same time, practically squishing me and I laughed. "About time you joined us, short stack," Peacock says playfully.

I look at him and scowl. He puts up his hands defensively. "I'm not that short." I hear Addison and Kyle laugh behind me.

"No, you're not. In fact, you're not short at all, but you're shorter than me, so that makes you a short stack." Peacock laughs. "How are you holding up?" he asks me a little more seriously.

"I'm doing pretty good. You?"

He sighs, "I'm looking forward to a couple days off."

"I can imagine. Any plans while you're here?" I ask and Peacock looks toward Mouse and I can see him deflate slightly. I lean into him and whisper, "When the time's right, he'll come around."

His eyes dart to mine. "I'm beginning to think it's a lost cause."

"You can't help who you fall in love with, Eric, trust me," I say lovingly thinking about Dex. "Sometimes it just takes longer for the other person to realize it."

"Yeah, maybe. I don't know, sometimes I think I'm chasing the wrong person. Then he does or says something to me that makes me think otherwise."

I lean into Peacock's shoulder. "I know we haven't really had a chance to talk, but I'm all ears, anytime."

He chuckles and I can feel it more than hear it. "That is if I can get you away from him." I feel him shift under me and I look up. Dex is standing there with a playful look on his face.

He leans down toward me as I sit up. "He bats for the other team, glowbug. I'm pretty sure you're missing some equipment."

"Hey, they make toys for that," Kyle says over my shoulder toward Dex and I catch Addison's beet red expression as the words tumble from Kyle's mouth. I make a mental note to ask Addison about it, one day. Though I'm assuming he's referring to a strap-on.

Peacock's arm comes around my shoulders and he leans into Dex. "I'd take her over your ass any day, Dex."

We all bust up laughing just as Mills opens the door to the greenroom. Dex looks at Peacock. "So would I, brother." He winks at Peacock then grabs my wrist, pulling me off of the couch, out of Peacock's grasp and into his arms. He kisses my forehead before trading places with me and planting his ass on the couch between the guys and he pats his thigh. I hold up a finger and walk over toward the bar. I grab him a beer, open it and grab myself one too.

When I turn back around the room is filling with fans, but there is something in the corner that catches my eye but it's gone before I can actually look at it.

I walk back toward Dex who has eyes only for me, despite the hoard of woman streaming into the greenroom. I go to hand him his beer and he grabs my wrist, pulling me onto his lap. He's smiling widely at me as he takes a beer from me. "Thank you, princess." I hold my beer up to him and he clinks his with mine.

"Anytime." I smile and take a sip.

I stayed on Dex's lap the whole time we were in the greenroom. He was constantly squeezing my ass or rubbing my back, reminding me that he was there and a couple of times I'd brush my hand along his crotch, seemingly on accident, and his breath would catch with each contact and it would send little tiny shocks of pleasure straight to my sex. Winding me up for what I hoped was going to be a beautiful night between the two of us.

"We're going to go to Lower Broadway," Mouse says to the group.

"Hell yeah," Talon and Kyle say together.

"What do you say, Dex? You two coming too?" Mouse asks.

I look at Dex who looks at me. I smile wide and nod. Dex smiles too. "You got it, brother."

Shortly after that, we're packed up and ready to leave the arena. When Dex and I climb into one of the cars he turns to me. "Are you sure you want to go?"

I smile, "I've always wanted to go."

"We're here a few more days," he tells me.

"Do you not want to go?" I ask. I'm not upset, just unsure why he'd not want to go.

"No, I do, just making sure you want to go."

I climb onto his lap and grab his face. "I promise to not get too drunk." I smile and kiss his lips.

After a beat he replies, "Better not. I'm dying to be inside of you. If you weren't wearing those pants, I'd be buried in you right now." He growls at me and I wiggle my hips against the erection that's straining his jeans. "You're the devil." He huffs as his lips land on mine once more and the car drives off toward Lower Broadway and an entire row of bars and country music nightlife. The heart of Nashville.

chapter
10
raine

When we arrive in the area, the night is hopping with people. It's a Friday night, would you expect anything less? "Whatever you do, do not leave my side; accept no drinks from anyone but me or one of our guys."

His tone is concerned. This isn't the first time we've been out together since hooking up, but this is the first time I've ever gotten a lecture. I try to figure out what's changed. "I won't."

"Promise me?"

I look at him with my eyebrows scrunched together. "I promise. Dex, what's wrong?"

He gives me a sad smile. "Nothing, I just don't want to see anything happen to you."

I cup his cheek. "I'm a big girl."

"So was Addison," he says softly but with concern.

I cock my head at him. "Is that really what this is about?"

"Forget it, just please, don't…"

"No, Dex. We talk, remember? Is Addison's attack in Dallas what you're worried about?"

He shrugs.

I try to let it go and continue walking with the rest of the group until he grabs my wrist and pulls me back into him. He tucks a stray strand of hair behind my ear. "I'd lose my mind if anything ever happened to you," he whispers. I can barely hear him over the noise of the crowd around us.

"Okay, Dex. I promise." I give him a smile, at least the best I can manage. His sudden concern and protectiveness is a little strange, but I am certain there is a reason behind it. He kisses me softly and quickly and we're off again, following behind the rest of the guys.

Lower Broadway is like little Vegas, with lights, bars, streets and sidewalks lined with people, cars trying to make their way through the masses. Drunk people attempting to walk through the crowd. It's almost comical and by the time we reach a bar, I've forgotten about Dex's strange mood shift and I'm ready to have some fun. There's a band performing on the stage, and they're pretty good. They're singing a Blake Shelton song and I start to dance between Dex's thighs once he's seated at a high-top table. They managed to pull together three of them, giving everyone a place to sit, well, everyone but the bodyguards who've scattered themselves around the room.

I catch Dex out of the corner of my eyes as I'm dancing between his legs and he has a wicked little smirk on his face. "What?" I say with a wide smile.

"You're so fucking cute when you dance." I giggle and go back to dancing as the band finishes up the song.

Within twenty minutes we've managed to flag down a waitress and place a drink order and lucky for the guys, the kitchen is still open. Though they serve mostly appetizer type foods, their menu is pretty extensive and they've ordered just about one of everything.

The band on stage takes a break and we all start talking about the tour, life, Addison and how she's been feeling, all that good stuff. Tonight is the first night I'm actually noticing that she's having a great time, really into the evening which tells me that some of her energy might finally be coming back.

When the band returns to the stage, the lead singer does some talking. "We're gonna slow it down a little," he says into the microphone and I hear the familiar strings of Lee Brice's Hard to Love. I grab Dex's hand.

"Come on, bubba," I tell him and pull him off of his chair.

"Where we going?"

"Dance with me."

"Oh no...there's a reason my sexy ass sits behind the drums."

"Bullshit, come on." I laugh and drag him with me.

"I mean it, I really can't dance."

I smile. "Then just hold me."

He smiles in return and wraps his arms around me as we move slowly to the music being played.

The moment is sweet and for the first time in I don't know how long, I finally feel like I belong somewhere and that place is right here in Dex's arms. I've never felt like I do when I'm near him regardless of who I've been with.

No one has ever put as much effort or concern into my well-being the way that Dex did tonight.

"Thank you," I say as I look up at him.

"For what?"

"For protecting me."

He smiles and kisses my forehead. "That's what I'm here for, glowbug."

"No one's ever done that before," I tell him.

"Well then, I'm glad I'm here to do it now." His arms squeeze me tighter as we slowly dance to the music.

When the song is over I tell him, "Thank you for dancing with me."

He smiles. "Thank you for dragging me out here."

"Who's ready for a little dancing?" the singer says into the microphone.

I look at Dex and slip off my heels. I point toward the stage. "You see that spot over there?" He follows my finger and nods, as I bend down and grab my shoes. "Remember my cowboy boots?" He nods, confused. "Take these and go watch." I point again to the empty spot. He raises an eyebrow but takes my shoes. I grab the hair tie off of my wrist and pull my hair up just as the drumbeat picks up for Blake Shelton's Footloose. Oh man, I'm in trouble. I haven't done this in a long time. I shake it off and start clapping with the rest of the crowd that has surrounded me. There are cheers and excitement and Dex's eyes light up.

As soon as the music starts, I'm off with a vine to the right.

67

Country music has never been high on my list of music choices to listen to but watching Raine out there dancing away to Footloose is like a whole other world and one that I've apparently been missing. I see now why she handed me her shoes. There is no way she could have done what she's doing in these things. I notice, past Raine, all the guys at the table, including Addison, are climbing their chairs, trying to catch a glimpse of what's happening. I point at Raine and their jaws drop watching her dance back and forth around the floor. Then she's turned around, facing in their direction. I can tell she's slightly embarrassed because she puts her head into her hand, but doesn't miss a beat.

Fuck, this is probably one of the sexiest things I've ever witnessed.

She continues dancing, spinning and facing multiple directions. One thing I do find kind of funny is that everyone on the floor with her is either in boots, tennis shoes or cowboy boots and jeans. My girl is the only one wearing a corset and leather pants with glowing blue eyes and brightly colored hair. But out there, it doesn't matter.

When the song ends, the guys start cheering and hollering in her direction and I'm clapping awkwardly while holding her heels by the straps.

She giggles as she comes over to me. "That was very impressive," I tell her and she lights up at my compliment.

"Thank you." I hand over her shoes and she drops them to the floor and I offer her my hand so she can put them back on. Once she's done she stands up and wraps her arms around my neck. She's still breathing heavy as I wrap my arms around her and I can't help the butt cheek squeeze. "You're bad," she tells me in my ear and I lift her off of her feet and carry her back toward the table.

When we get there I set her down and the guys are all laughing and telling her how awesome she was. Addison insists that Raine needs to teach her how to do that. "In a few months." I watch as she winks at Addison and I sit back down. Raine comes to stand between my legs again and I rub her back.

When our food finally arrives, Raine grabs a chair and we all dig in. The conversation, though yelling is involved, flows like it always has and I have to admit, this is probably one of the best nights out we've had in a while.

That is until the lead singer of the band comes back onto the microphone. "In honor of the Bridgestone Arena concert tonight." All seven of us freeze. Mid-chew, mid-bite, mid-sentence.

"Shit," Talon says as the band starts to play 'Your Eyes'.

"Do we leave?" Mouse asks.

"Fuck that... let's see if they're any good," Kyle says.

"I agree. Then we can shock the living shit out of them," I say.

"Unless they already know you're here," Raine says.

"I don't think they'd play it if they knew we were here," Talon says back and I can feel the bodyguards getting a little closer. Talon pushes them back. Not to draw attention to the fact that the band whose song they're covering is sitting right in the bar.

When the lead singer starts to sing we all kind of look at each other and shrug. It's not awful, but it's certainly not us.

"I have an idea," Raine says and everyone kind of leans in.

She sets out telling the guys her idea and we all think she's insane, but agree. She quickly disappears back to where it was that I was waiting for her. Talon, Peacock,

Mouse, Addison and myself all stand up. Kyle heads off to the other side of the stage. We're videotaping this shit.

The five of us make our way through the crowd surrounding the dance floor. We spread out as to not draw attention to the mob making its way toward the stage.

I find Talon and Mouse, who then finds Peacock, and we all nod. Stepping onto the dance floor at the same time, walking slowly but deliberately toward the stage, attempting to time it properly with the end of the song. Which we manage to do.

chapter
11
raine

I watch through the screen of my phone as Dex, Talon, Mouse, Peacock and Addison make their way through the crowd on the dance floor. I'm desperately trying to stifle giggles but it's hard. They look like walking trouble. But they time it perfectly. Just as the band rounds out the song, the five of them come to stand in front of the stage.

"Holy shit," the lead singer says into the microphone and some of the audience laughs, the other half look around confused. The guys in the band all laugh. I switch from the guys who are standing there with their arms crossed, attempting to look pissed off, but they're holding back their laughter, to the guys on stage. I watch as the lead singer stumbles to find the right words. "I...crap, we um, we didn't know you guys were here," he finally manages to sputter out.

You could hear a pin drop in the crowd.

Finally the guys all burst out laughing. Talon approaches the stage and reaches up to take the singer's hand. "Nice job, man," he tells the singer as their palms meet.

"Ladies and gentlemen, 69 Bottles," he says into the microphone and finally the reality of what's happened registers on the crowd and they erupt into cheers. Some people are confused, which doesn't surprise me. "Gentlemen, want to join us on stage?"

"Nah, man, we've done our work for tonight," Talon tells them.

The singer moves the microphone so I can't hear what he's saying. Then I see Talon nod and the band on stage climbs down. They shake hands and what-not.

"Raine," Dex says, ushering me over. "They want pictures."

"Of course."

Once they're done taking pictures with the band, they go back to playing and 69 Bottles slowly makes their way back to the tables, stopping for pictures with fans. When we get back to the tables, our bill is there and I snatch it off of the table, slipping my card inside before anyone can protest. "Seriously, woman, that's not your job," Dex whispers in my ear.

"No, but this way you guys can get out of here. I'll be right behind you."

"I'm not leaving you," he tells me, his conviction is sweet.

"Leave Casey, just go. Get out of here. We will be right behind you." I turn and lift up on my toes, kissing his cheek. "Just go. Otherwise we'll never get out of here."

"Casey," Dex barks and Casey comes over, Mills on his heels.

"Casey, stay with me. Mills, get them out of here before we cause a bigger scene. No doubt social media is blowing up."

Mills nods and gathers up the guys and Addison.

I kiss Dex one more time. "Go. Please."

He gives me a sad smile, but follows my command and leaves with the guys. I take the folio to the bar to pay it faster. Once the tab is settled, all three hundred dollars of it, Casey and I leave the bar.

"Where are they?" I ask as we step onto the street.

"Headed for the cars. They need to move away from this area otherwise people will find them. In fact, I'd recommend calling an end to the night, but that's not my call."

"I agree," I tell Casey as we walk quickly back to the cars. They're all standing around outside and Dex lights up when he sees Casey and me approaching.

"Let's call it a night," I tell Dex. Then I look past his shoulder to the rest of our group. "I know you guys want to stay, but-" My phone interrupts and chimes once, twice, then a third time. I pull it out, looking at the alerts.

"That's our cue to go, guys," Addison says.

There is some moaning and groaning from the guys. "Look, it's out that you're in the Lower Broadway area, that means that people will be bar hopping just trying to find you. We can find another part of town or call it a night. Either way, it's up to you guys, but I imagine that if you stay, your night is going to be met with fans and madness."

The guys groan again and everyone starts to climb back into the cars. "Let's go to the hotel," Talon tells Mills who nods in agreement.

"I'm sorry," I tell Dex as we climb in. "Outing yourselves to the band was my idea."

He kisses my forehead once we're inside. "True, but it was fun as fuck. Besides, the guys all went along with it, so don't feel bad."

"Well, I do."

He gently pulls the hair tie from my hair and he watches as my hair cascades down my back and over my shoulders. His eyes light up with desire. "Don't, glowbug. Yes, it's annoying that we can't go out without massive crowds, but tonight was a rare night where an outing wasn't planned, so we were able to eat and enjoy our evening." He wraps his arm around my shoulder as the caravan takes off. "Besides, Nashville is a celebrity hub. I'm surprised we weren't recognized before we outed ourselves. There are celebrity watchers at just about every bar here."

"I know, but still. Maybe tomorrow night we can get away with it again."

"The guys might be able to," he tells me.

"Why the guys?"

"Because, we have plans tomorrow night."

I turn to look at him. "To do what?"

"Have dinner with a friend."

"Oh." I can't hide the concern from my voice. "Who?"

"A couple friends of mine. They were at the concert in Greensboro, but..." He lets the thought fall off.

"So they're coming to Nashville?" I question.

"Something like that."

Unfortunately I don't get to press him too much longer because we arrive back at our hotel and pile out of the cars.

"Don't worry, it will be fun," he assures me as we wait for everyone to join us before heading up.

We stand around chatting for a bit. Dex smokes a cigarette. I'm not a fan of it, but I'd rather him do that than something else. "Is something bothering you?" I ask him while we stand there.

"No, not really, just a bad habit," he tells me with a smile before taking a couple more drags and putting it out.

Beck and Casey follow us into the hotel and up to our floor.

As soon as our door closes, Dex has me pressed against the wall. "I've been dying all night to peel these pants off of you," he tells me before capturing my mouth and raising my arms over my head, causing my breasts to loosen in my top and slide up.

He continues kissing my mouth, then down along my jaw, to the collar around my neck and then to the swell of my breasts. "Dex," I cry out.

"What, sweet girl?"

"I need you," I breathe out and he releases my arms, taking my hand in his as he escorts me into our bedroom.

As soon as we're there, I push him down on the bed and climb on top of him and kiss him with excitement as his hands begin to tug on the strings holding my top together. I pull back to catch my breath. "Leave the collar and shoes on," he tells me and I smirk.

His fingers brush along the choker around my neck. "You like that?" I ask him.

"Oh, you have no idea," he tells me. His voice is soft and full of emotion. "It's probably sexier than this top, or the pants. I'd like to see you wear one all the time."

The idea of being collared sends a shiver up my spine. I know that a collar can come in many forms, not an actual collar like what I'm wearing right now, though I wouldn't mind one of those, just not all the time. I shiver again, my nipples hardening further.

"That idea turns you on, doesn't it?"

"Yes," I breathe.

"Yes, what?" he says with a mischievous tone in his voice.

I shiver again. "Yes, Sir."

His finger brushes over my cheek. "Good girl." His voice is soft, comforting.

"Dex?"

"Yes, glowbug?"

"You asked me about training before."

"I did. I was curious why this comes so natural to you."

"I certainly haven't been trained, but I'd really like to be," I tell him and his eyes light up. "It's just something that feels right, natural to me. I'd really like to find a way to train."

He smiles. "I'm really glad you said that."

I cock my head at him, "Why?"

"Because I'd like to learn for myself and train you as well. I think it's a great dynamic that just might work for us and I'd really like to give it a try."

I lean down and kiss his lips. "So would I."

"But tonight, tonight I want to make love to my sweet girl," he tells me as he finishes unlacing my corset and then pushes it off of my shoulders. Then he surprises me by removing the choker he'd asked me to keep on.

Once the corset is off, he flips me onto my back and he slide between my legs, rubbing his erection right into my crotch before pulling back and removing my belt, then my shoes, then finally undoing the button and zipper on my pants. He begins the removal process and there is a rush of cool that sends goosebumps all over my body. He continues to help cool me off by blowing cool air across my legs as he tugs them downward and finally off of my feet.

"So fucking gorgeous," he tells me as he slides back up my body after removing his t-shirt.

His lips land on mine in a passion fueled kiss that sends a new wave of pleasure through my body.

chapter
12
raine

Dex's passion fueled kisses continued down my jaw, along the curve of my neck and onto my shoulder. With each passing kiss I was growing wetter and more aroused than I was the kiss before. He slowly made his way to the swell of my breasts, placing gentle kisses against his bite marks that still bared the angry red teeth marks. There was a little pain to accompany his gentle kisses and then finally he consumed my nipple.

I spread my fingers into his hair, holding onto him, not wanting him to stop as I writhed beneath his touch with the subtle flick of his hips into my sex. "Ahh," I cried out as his cock brushed right along my clit. I tightened my hand in his hair and he growled at me. His eyes met mine. Love and desire exploded between us. "I need to feel you," I breathe. My voice soft and full of all the emotion I'm seeing in his eyes.

He releases my nipple. "But I'm not done yet," he whispers with a hint of disappointment.

I smile at him. "I adore your willingness to want to please me, but right now, what will please me most is you sliding inside of me. Please?" I whine and he smirks. He kisses me on my breastbone, right between my breasts and directly over my heart before he rears up.

He makes quick work of his button flies and pushing his jeans down to his knees. I watch as his cock falls free, hard as stone and bouncing with his movements as he sheds his pants. My mouth waters and I lick my lips. Desire to take him into my mouth overwhelms my need to have him buried inside my pussy. I sit up, reaching for his cock.

"Nu uh, nope." He shakes his head and pulls his hips away from me. "If I can't make you come with my mouth, neither can you." I look up at him through my lashes and pout. "Now that is quite possibly the cutest face I've ever seen, but it's not going to work. Roll over."

Ah, there's that commanding tone I love so much. I dutifully obey him, then wiggle my ass, taunting him. He smacks my right cheek playfully and I groan, but still. I feel him shift on the bed, then he pushes on one leg, silently asking me to spread wider for him and I do.

He scoots closer to me, his cock running along the crack of my ass and I shiver with anticipation.

Then I feel his hand softly rub along my cheek, right where he smacked me, then up along my spine, pushing down, asking me to arch my back. "Head down, glowbug." I do as he's asked me to, pushing my ass higher in the air and arching my back. His hand continues along my back, climbing higher, toward my shoulders, tracing some of the lines on my tattoo, making me shiver and my nipples harden. He leans over me and I see his big beefy hand ball into a fist and push into the mattress near my head. His other hand moves my hair out of the way and I feel him start to kiss along my shoulder.

I turn to melted butter on the bed as he continues kissing and licking his way down my back, along my spine, gradually kissing the dimples on my ass cheeks. "Please, Dex," I beg. "I need you."

The spreading of his lips, the short warm breaths against my back and the shaking of his chest against my butt is all I need to feel to know that he's chuckling. "What's the matter glowbug? Don't you like foreplay?"

"I fucking love foreplay, but we've been 'foreplaying' all damn night. I'm dying, I'm desperate, please for the love of my fucking pussy, give me your cock. Slide your cock inside and fuck me, make me fucking come all over your dick."

His breathing stops. "I fucking love it when you talk dirty to me."

"Fuck me, Dex, now," I demand and without any more preamble, he lines himself up and he slams into me.

Stars and white fireworks ignite as my eyes slam shut. My body erupts with my orgasm, my pussy clamping down hard on his shaft. "Fuck me," he growls and immediately fights the tightness of my sex, pulling himself back out and pushing back in. In and out, bringing new heights to my orgasm.

"Fuck, Dex!" I scream as he continues sliding in and out of me, his pace increasing, his thrusts gaining momentum and strength. "Fuck! Fuck! Fuck!" I cry out as my orgasm finally begins to subside. Bringing me back to building toward another orgasm.

Dex's arms wrap around my torso, his hands splayed wide. "Come here," he whispers as he slows his thrusts. I feel his hands pulling me upward, up toward him. I relax and go with him, my back arching; his cock sliding in deeper. Pressing deeper than he has ever been before and I shiver. Out of instinct, I wrap my arms around his neck, arching further and pushing my breasts out. He begins moving inside me, slowly sliding in and out of my depths.

"Ahh," I cry out.

His hands begin to roam over my stomach, one hand heading north and cupping a breast, the other goes south until it slides along my clit. The contact causes my entire body to tremble and my eyes to close tight.

He continues pumping in and out while his hand strums along my clit. He pulls my nipple between his fingers and begins rolling it and pulling it, hard. The tiny stabs of pain melt into pleasure and I feel my orgasm climbing toward its peak once again.

I release one of my hands from around his neck and slide it down to my other breast, pulling my nipple and turning it over.

"Does this feel good, baby girl?"

"Yes," I breathe.

"Play with your clit, make yourself come all over my cock," he whispers into my ear before sucking my lobe into his mouth and nibbling on it. His breathing is short hot bursts. The sensation is new and I know just how much I'm affecting him.

I slide my hand down my stomach as his hand comes up. He replaces my hand on my other nipple and he pulls, stretching and rolling them. My finger slides along my clit, and south, along the shaft of his cock as it's entering me. My goal was his balls, but I can't reach, so I settle for using my palm against my clit and my fingers along his shaft.

"Fuck," he growls as he pulls harder on my nipples, increases his pace then licks and kisses along my shoulder.

"Give it to me, Dex. I want to feel you explode inside me," I huff.

"Come on, glowbug, I need to feel you first," he says and his pace increases.

I abandon rubbing along his shaft in favor of my clit. I begin rubbing feverishly against it. "I'm there," I scream.

Dex grabs the arm on the back of his neck and pushes me onto the bed, forcing my orgasm higher, giving him his ultimate goal of me exploding everywhere as he pounds into me.

"Fuck! Fuck! Fuck!" he cries out as he empties himself into me.

My body tingles with the warmth, that feeling you get deep in your gut when you know, no matter what, the person inside you is the right person, the person you have no choice but to love. You're soulmates, bound by destiny. Fighting it no longer seems an option. He is it, he is my one.

chapter
13
raine

The reality of my realization rocks through me harder than anything I've ever imagined in my life. Being with Dex is unlike anything I've ever experienced before. I've never felt this way about anyone, let alone been able to actually act on my emotions.

He spoons in behind me, bringing the covers with him and wrapping his arms around me. "I love you," I breathe and his hand begins to gently rub along my stomach.

He kisses my neck, then my shoulder and back to my neck. I turn my head to face him and he plants a warm, gentle kiss on my lips. "I love you," he says before kissing me a few more times and settling in.

It doesn't take but a few more minutes before Dex's breathing becomes soft and even with sleep. I am exhausted and far from wide awake, but my revelation rocks me.

Of all the people in the world that I could fall in love with, it's Dex. He's not perfect, in fact, he's far from it, but I've noticed his softened demeanor since we were in DC. Since we spilled all our secrets, laid them bare for one another to absorb or reject.

In a way, I'm no more broken than he is or no less. Though we have our own demons that are buried beneath the surface, we've both managed to deal with them in ways that we can understand. I've never had an addiction, smoking, drinking, drugs, gambling, nothing. So I feel like I don't fully understand the struggles he goes through and I'm sure he can't quite understand my own demons.

For having been raped as my first sexual experience, you'd think it would turn me off of sex altogether. You'd think that pain could not exist with pleasure, but for me, they hold the same wheelhouse. Dex is no different. The way he handles his addiction and mishaps is punishment, whether by his hand or that of a tattoo artist. But I've also noticed that there seems to be fewer struggles for him since I came into his life. Maybe it's enough… for now.

Sometime in the early morning hours, I finally managed to fall asleep, but not before realizing how drawn to me Dex really is. If he rolled away from me, it wasn't long before he was draped all over me again.

When I finally manage to open my eyes, the bed is empty and my heart sinks. I look around the room and I can sense he isn't here. I roll over to look at the clock. Shit. It's two thirty in the afternoon. Next to the clock is a note.

It has to be Dex's handwriting because it is sloppy and hardly legible.

Gone out, I didn't want to wake you. Be back around three then we're going out.
P.S. Be naked, just like you are, when I get back.

I can't help but smile at the note.
I stretch and climb out of bed and head for the shower.

In the middle of toweling off I hear the door of the suite beep with someone entering the room. "Glowbug," I hear him call.

"In the bathroom," I holler back.

I hear the rustling of a couple of bags in the bedroom then he comes to stand in the doorway behind me. I can feel his eyes on me, and I know he's watching me, so I drop the towel to the floor. I hear him hiss through his teeth. I smile wide and turn around, facing him. The marks are better today but still there and still they bring me a strange comfort.

"Fuck, you're gorgeous," he groans. "Thank fuck you're all mine."

"All yours," I agree softly.

He makes no move to come closer to me, so I walk toward him.

"You're the devil," he says as I wrap my arms around him.

He brushes the hair out of my face and smiles at me. His smile steals my breath and I can only stare at him. His eyes are alight and excited. "I have something for you," he whispers.

"Oh?" I raise an eyebrow at him and he chuckles.

"We're going out tonight, remember?"

"Just us and your friend or is the band coming too?" I ask as he takes my hand, leading my naked ass into the bedroom.

"Not with the boys," he says cryptically.

"Oh? Where are we going?" I question.

"It's a surprise," he tells me with a fire in his eyes I don't understand.

"Alright," deciding he's not going to tell me, "whatcha got, bubba?"

His face lights up as he goes over to the three bags on the bed. I notice that one of the bags says Jimmy Choo and I feel my heart begin to beat hard and heavy in my chest. A little excitement mixed with trepidation. How much money did he spend?

He opens up the non-Jimmy Choo bag and pulls out something in a charcoal grey. "Tonight is nothing fancy," he says softly. "But it is about being comfortable. So..." He opens up what he's holding in his hands.

"Wow, Dex, that's..." I reach out to touch it. It's knit and soft. It's a charcoal grey dress, with long sleeves, the shoulders are cut out and the dress dips into a v-neck, the back dips by the weight of a hood. I grab a sleeve and notice that there are thumb holes in it. "I love this," I tell him and he smiles wide before laying it down on the bed and going into the bag again where he pulls out a black, sheer bra. I blush. He smirks. Then he pulls out a garter belt, lace topped thigh highs and a skimpy sheer thong to match the bra. "Did you really buy me underwear, bubba?"

He blushes and nods. "What? I couldn't help myself." He lays the undergarments down on top of the dress, though it's overkill for that kind of a dress. Depending on the fit, everything would show through.

He goes into the next bag, again, not the Jimmy Choo bag. From that bag he pulls out a spaghetti strap cotton maxi dress that is low cut with a band under the breasts. It's varying shades of black and grey. "That's gorgeous." He lays that down on top of the other dress then he pulls out another item. A sweater, full length, with a deep hood and a single clasp in the center, right below the bust. "Oh, I like that too," I tell him and he smiles. This doesn't come with underwear and I couldn't wear a bra with it, unless it was one with clear straps. Though I don't think I'd need one.

"Dex?"

"Yeah, glowbug?"

"What's in the last bag?" I say with deep hesitation.

He, on the other hand, smiles wide. Pulling the bag toward him, he opens it and pulls out a box. Fuck me, he bought me shoes. Jimmy fucking Choo shoes. He hands me the box. "Uh uh, nope, I can't do it, Dex. It's too much."

His face falls and I immediately regret it.

"I'm sorry…it's, I…oh how the hell do I say this. I've never spent more than sixty dollars on a pair of shoes in my life…"

His smile returns lightly. "You didn't buy these, I did." His confidence is returning.

"Jeez, I know, but…"

"Please just look at them? If you don't like them, I will take them back."

I fold my arms over my chest and look into his eyes. I can't say anything for a moment and he beats me to it. "There comes a time in a woman's life where she needs to let someone pamper her, someone take care of her, someone who treats her like the queen that she is. Raine, this is your time."

Tears well in my eyes and I can't say anything.

He sets the box down on the bed and comes to stand in front of me. He cradles my face in his palms and he tilts my head up so that my eyes can meet his. "I won't push this stuff on you, I won't be upset if you don't accept it, but if I have it my way, these won't be the last gifts that I buy you."

"It just throws me off balance. I know that you have money, probably tons of it..." He starts to interrupt and I silence him with my finger. "But you have to understand that I have struggled, I have scrimped and saved pennies from the bottom of my purse for emergencies. Dex, I have lived off of ramen noodles and hot dogs. I have struggled for everything that I have and let me tell you, it isn't much. I have done everything on my own for so long, and I have never had anyone buy me anything remotely close to what you've purchased today, let alone myself. The only reason I have half of the clothes I have for this tour is because I was given a clothing budget from Bold, dinner last night was on Bold's credit card. Dex, I have maybe two-thousand dollars in my bank account and the only reason I have that is because I have a housing allowance that is paying my rent while I'm away on tour. I am poor, I am broke and this...It's so much, too much." I blink back the tears that are threatening to overwhelm me.

Dex rubs his thumbs under my eyes, capturing the strays.

chapter
14
dex

"It was not my intention to make you feel uncomfortable. I really just bought a few things that I thought would look amazing on you. I can tell by your reaction so far that you do like them. Raine, if I could, I would spoil you every day, but I know that's not what you want me to do. These are little gifts from me to you and believe me, these are more for me than you." I give her a playful smirk. "I understand how accepting lavish gifts can be hard for you, but these are far from lavish. These are simply to make you feel special tonight, to make you think of me when you wear them."

I watch as her face softens and the unshed tears dry up.

"I am capable of giving you so much more, and I want to do just that."

"You give me so much already, Dex. Just being you, being around me, making me feel like I'm the most important person in the world."

"You are the most important person in my world and all I want to do is make you happy. If taking this stuff back will make you happy, I will do just that," I tell her and I mean what I'm saying. The last thing I wanted to do was upset her today. I didn't think that buying her a couple of outfits, a pair of shoes and a new handbag would do this to her. It never occurred to me that she wasn't used to being lavished on. Or that she never pampered herself. But more importantly, I learned something new about my glowbug. She is stronger than I could have ever imagined her to be.

"No, please don't take them back," she whispers.

I smile at her. "I won't. But I need you to understand that this won't be the last time I buy you things."

She gives me a half smile. "I understand and I will try to be a little more excited next time." She smiles wider. "Can I see the shoes?"

I chuckle and kiss her lips. "Of course."

I release her and reach for the box. I hold it out to her and she removes the lid. "Holy crap," she squeaks. "Those are fucking sexy," she says, our conversation forgotten. I have a feeling we just might be back here again one day, but for now, I will take her enthusiasm.

The shoes are a black and silver suede strappy number that have a wedge heel. Now don't go getting all 'oh he knows his shoes' on me, that's what the woman at the store told me. I just thought, like Raine, that they were sexy as fuck. "So you approve?" I ask, raising an eyebrow. Her excitement is telling me that this is okay.

"I do. They're amazing."

"Good." I smile and kiss her forehead. "One more thing."

"Dex," she scolds.

I laugh. "Close your eyes, princess." She complies and I pull out the handbag from the Jimmy Choo bag on the bed and hold it up in front of her. It's some black leather looking thing with a short strap. Shut up, I'm a guy, I don't do the whole purse thing. "Open your eyes," I tell her and she does.

She's shocked and she covers her mouth. "Do I even want to know how much that cost?" she says behind her hand.

"Probably not, though I'm not sure I know." I give her a half smile. "I noticed the one that you had was kind of beat up and that you really don't carry it often. I thought maybe you'd like something new. I found one in Louis Vuitton…"

"Don't you dare," she scolds me again. "That is something you would have taken back," she tells me and I nod. She's right, the one I saw was about half this size and three times the money, not that I wasn't ready to pay for it, but I'd already purchased this one.

She finally takes the bag from my hand and looks it over. "This is gorgeous, Dex."

"You like it?" I say like a little boy and she giggles, then sets it on the bed. She's still buck naked, mind you, as she throws her arms around my neck, and pulls herself up to wrap her legs around my waist.

"I love it." She plants a chaste kiss on my lips. "I love you," she tells me and my heart skips a beat.

"I don't think I'll ever get used to you saying that," I tell her and I kiss her. After a beat or two, I work to coax her mouth open and succeed, sliding my tongue in along hers. Warm and wet. My cock jumps and it's going to take everything I have to stop this from going further. Her hands slide into my hair, holding me hard against her lips as my breathing grows ragged.

She pulls back. "We don't have time," I softly say against her lips. "You need to get dressed, glowbug."

She pouts at me, but nods.

"There will be plenty of time later," I tell her as I set her down. "Now, go get ready." She kisses me briefly one more time before heading toward the bathroom. "Oh, and princess?"

"Yes." She turns back toward me. "Leave your hair down tonight, please?"

"Yes, Sir." She smirks and my cock jumps once again.

"No, we'll be fine," I tell Mills on the phone. "No, if the guys are going out, you're going to need all the help you can get. Keep the guys. I don't know where we're going, but we'll be with Derek."

"I need to at least know where you'll be," Mills says through the phone.

I tell him where we will be for dinner. "We're going to a private club afterward."

"I don't like the sounds of that."

"Mills, please don't press it. There is more security in this club than you or your men can provide. It is exclusive and private. The kind where you need a five million dollar bank account to get in."

"Alright," he relents. "Just keep her safe."

I snort into the phone. "Do you seriously believe I would let anything happen to her?"

He sighs. "No, I don't imagine you would."

"Thanks, Mills."

"Yup, call if you need anything."

"Done," I say and we hang up and I return my phone to its holster on my pants.

"A five million dollar bank account?" I hear Raine say softly and I jump, standing up and turning around.

"Shit," I breathe as I take her in. She's wearing the charcoal grey dress. Her hair is down, like I asked and cascading over her shoulders. I can see her nipples through the top, not horribly, but... "I can see..." I point with a smirk.

She laughs. "It's your bra, bubba," she tells me. "It's sheer, incapable of hiding anything. Do you want me to put one of mine on?" she asks and I gently shake my head no. "I didn't think so." She smirks. "Now, five million..." She doesn't finish her earlier question.

I give a shake of my head as I'm contemplating how to explain this to her. "That's not entirely accurate, but all members are required to go through a strict background check, pay dues and such before they are admitted into the club on a probationary basis."

She gives me a puzzled look. "I haven't provided any of that."

I cut her off, "We're going as guests of registered members. So we're alright. But it is tight on security and because of its exclusivity, I don't need or want our guys hanging around with us tonight."

"Alright," she says without hesitation and I go back to looking her up and down. She's added a couple of bracelets over her one wrist. I love that the dress has built in thumb holes so that it goes almost all the way down her hand. "I can't wear your garter with this dress," she tells me and I know my face falls. "It's too form fitting, I could see every line."

"Are you at least wearing the thong?" I ask, curious. She shakes her head, then begins to lift her dress, showing off the shoes I bought her, then her shapely gorgeous legs and finally as the dress crests her thighs, I see nothing. "Oh fuck," I growl and I charge at her. "That is the sexiest fucking thing I've ever seen." I pin her against the door jamb and run my finger along her cheek. "You're so beautiful," I tell her, but I behave myself with a soft chaste kiss. "You ready to go?"

"Almost, I just need to grab my purse," she tells me with a smile on her lips before I release her. She goes into the bedroom for her new purse and when she returns, I offer her my elbow, all gentleman like before we leave the suite.

chapter
15
raine

Dex, in a button down black shirt, open at the collar with the sleeves rolled up, revealing his tattoos, and black jeans and shit kickers is, yep, it's panty melting, if I were wearing any.

He escorts me down to the lobby. I notice he's looking around as he leads me into the bar area of the hotel. "Oh, there," he says while pointing a toward one of the darker corners. We approach a very handsome, long brown haired man and a very pretty blonde. Dex continues leading me until we're standing at the table with them.

"How's it going, man?" Dex asks the guy as they shake and the man stands up.

"Good. How are you?"

I watch Dex light up. "Excellent." Dex then turns to the woman, releasing me. He leans over and kisses her cheek. "Dacotah, it's great to see you again."

"Likewise," she says back softly.

Dex takes my hand again. "Derek, this is Raine. Raine, I'd like you to meet Derek Hunter." When I look at Derek, something about his look sends a thrill up my spine and I suddenly feel the urge to lower my eyes. Then realization dawns on me.

I extend my hand to Derek who promptly takes it. "The pleasure is mine, Raine. I've heard so much about you." He kisses the back of my hand, all gentlemanly.

"You have?" I say surprised.

"Cami speaks very highly of you. We've even spoken on the phone a few times."

"Oh…oh, you're…" I take a deep breath, trying to settle myself a little bit. "You're Cami's friend Derek?" I finally manage to say.

Derek smiles, his demeanor softening. "I am. Cami and Tristan are great friends of mine. But I am being rude. This lovely lady is Dacotah, my girlfriend and my submissive."

My eyes lock with Derek's, then to Dex, then finally, remembering my manners I turn to Dacotah. "It's a pleasure to meet you," I say and it's not a lie. I've never met another submissive before and now all of a sudden everything clicks into place and makes sense.

I watch as Dacotah looks to Derek who nods, then she looks back at me before wrapping her arms around me. "It's great to meet you too," she says with enthusiasm. "Derek hasn't stopped talking about you," she whispers conspiratorially into my ear. I smile. Suddenly eager to get on with this night but in the same, I can't take my eyes off of Dacotah.

"Would you guys like a drink?" Derek asks.

Dex squeezes my hand and draws my attention back to him and Derek. "I'd love one, please."

"Perfect," he says and we tell him what we'd like to drink. "Cotah," Derek says with a firmness similar to what Dex uses with me from time to time. I watch as Cotah promptly gets up, rounds the table and kisses Derek on the cheek with a wide smile before going to the bar with our drink orders. I stand there, dumbstruck.

"Sit," Derek says and Dex immediately grabs for a chair, pulling it out for me and I take a seat near where Dacotah is sitting with Dex closer to Derek. "You're right, Dex," I hear him tell Dex.

"I told you." Both men look at me.

I flush. "What?" I say without thinking.

Derek smirks. "Dex told me that he thought you were a pretty natural submissive and I have to agree with him."

"Oh." I blush and lower my head, my hands wringing together. I bite my lip. Confusion and a feeling like I've been shut in the dark courses through me and I don't like the idea one bit.

"Raine, can you please look at me?" Derek asks nicely and I look at him. "You're intimidated by me, aren't you?"

"Yes, Sir," I say automatically.

"Please don't be," he says gently and with a smile. "I don't mean to scare or even trigger your submissive side, but I guess there are certain things that I do, without realizing it, that come across as Dominant. So please, forgive me. Tonight is very informal, but I'd like to help you and Dex. If you're interested, after tonight that is."

"What's happening tonight?" I ask, looking from Derek to Dex and back again.

"I wanted to surprise her," Dex says quickly and Derek chuckles.

"Well, first, we're going to have drinks here, then we're going to go out for dinner. After that, I'd like to take you to a place called The Box," Dex tells me.

"What's The Box?" I ask.

It's Derek that answers simply, "A BDSM club."

I gasp and a shiver runs up my spine. Not in fear, but utter excitement. "I've never been to one before," I tell both Dex and Derek.

Just then Dacotah returns to the table, kissing Derek before taking her seat. I watch as he reaches over and takes her hand. "The waitress said she would bring them over for us," Dacotah tells us.

"Great, thank you, Cotah." Derek then kisses her on the cheek and she glows. Then he whispers something into her ear. I watch carefully as a switch flips with Dacotah and she lights up a little.

"Thank you," she says to Derek and I can't help the puzzled look on my face.

Derek smiles at me. "Cotah and I have a lifestyle relationship. She is my submissive twenty-four seven. However, on nights like tonight, for now, the majority of her rules are turned off."

"Rules?" I ask curiously.

"I am allowed to talk without permission," she says with a bright smile. "I can basically do whatever I want, talk, be friendly, be normal." She shrugs. "For lack of a better way to describe it. Though there are still certain rules in place because everything I do reflects back on Derek."

"Jeez, it all seems like so much," I mutter. My confidence is raised a little when Dex squeezes my hand then pulls it onto his thigh.

Before anyone can say anything else, the waitress arrives with our drinks. "Thank you," I tell her before she leaves.

"How you wish to live the lifestyle is up to you and your partner," Derek says. "There are any number of ways you can work a Dom/sub relationship. In fact, there are no guidelines. It's more about what pleases you and your partner. I, for example, enjoy a lifestyle submissive. One who is rewarded for the things that she does and her behavior while doing them. We live by the Dom/sub rules twenty-four seven. Except on nights like this where we're out with friends or out with people unfamiliar with the lifestyle and especially for business related functions. To them, we're boyfriend and girlfriend. Much like right now. Though we're discussing the lifestyle, I think it is important that you be able to discuss any questions you have with me or with Cotah."

"Thank you for that," I say as I take a sip of my Cosmo. I look over to Dex, who has been quiet since we've been down here. I'm not entirely sure what to say at the moment and I need to find a distraction, but unless it involves asking more questions, I'm not sure what to do or say.

Dex helps me with that. "How long have you and Dacotah been together?" He naturally asks Derek the question, which is fine. I watch as Dacotah lights up then blushes, probably remembering something about how they met.

"Almost a year," Derek says before taking a drink of his beer. "We met in Vegas last May." Cotah blushes again and I wonder if there is a way to flush out that reason.

"Vegas of all places," Dex says.

"How'd you meet?"

Cotah giggles, "An indecent proposal." That's all she says and now I'm fully intrigued.

"Is this like a romance novel come to life?" I ask and Cotah giggles again.

"You could say that," she says with a big smile. She looks up to Derek who has a huge smile on his face too.

"That wasn't exactly my finest hour," he says with a laugh before leaning over to kiss Dacotah.

Dacotah looks at me. I can see her becoming more animated with each passing moment as she leans into me. "He practically stalked me around Vegas until he finally managed to get me alone over breakfast." She blushes. "Over that breakfast, he asked me to spend the week with him. No strings attached."

"Oh my god." I giggle.

"And how'd that work out for ya?" Dex asks Derek.

"Well, I knew about three days into it that I was falling in love with her. Then she made me chase her all over the country to find her." He playfully scowls at Cotah who blushes with embarrassment. "I found her at Cami and Tristan's in Phoenix." He squeezes her hand and winks at her. There is a love connection between the two of them that I am beginning to see more frequently in Dex's eyes.

"Dacotah…"

"You can call me Cotah," she says and I smile.

"Cotah, so you know Cami and Tristan?"

"I didn't, not until that week in Vegas. Derek took me to one of their charity events. I fangirled over Tristan, Derek laughed at me, called me crazy, then the next day we had lunch with them. Cami and I hit it off pretty well. We became pretty good friends and she invited me to Jaden's first birthday party, which is where Derek found me again." She nods in Derek's direction.

I giggle. "The We Are One Event?" I ask and she nods. "I was at that event. Running around like a maniac, but I was there."

"Oh that's too funny. I'm surprised you haven't met Derek before today. He's been in Cami's office several times since she took over."

I shrug. "Honestly, he looks familiar, but so much of the time I was running around that office like a mad woman." I shrug and take a sip of my Cosmo.

"Yeah, you've always been pretty preoccupied," Dex chimes in and I look at him. "Sweetheart, I've seen you in that office a few times and never once did you pay me any attention."

I nearly spew alcohol threw my nose and the three of them laugh. "That you know of. The same could be said for you, mister." I bump shoulders with him.

With the funny banter between the four of us, our night slides into a normal friendship style, talking about work, business, the band, the tour, and all that fun stuff. We left shortly after finishing our drinks for dinner. Derek took us to a nice, not overly fancy place to eat before we played a game of musical cars. Derek had said that he wanted to be sure no one was following us. After the roundabout and twenty minutes, we arrived outside of The Box.

chapter
16
raine

I can kind of see where The Box gets its name. The building is exactly that, a box. Though it looks like a more run down warehouse on the outside, with the exception of the rather ornate looking doors we're standing before now. I watch as Dacotah shifts her stance, and I can watch as her submissive side comes back. She and I have already exchanged phone numbers, vowing to talk frequently. She'd told me to call her with any questions but that she herself is still learning the lifestyle and learning what she likes and hates about it.

Derek, with a massive duffle bag thrown over his shoulder, punches in a code. "We're here before the doors officially open. Master Orik, who you're going to meet in a moment, is the owner of The Box. He's going to go over a few rules for the two of you. If you decide you want to stay after the doors open, he's going to need some information from the two of you, for security purposes. But I can assure you, anonymity is important and required." He opens the door and ushers us inside.

We step into a rather dark reception area. There are a couple of chairs and a podium that stands in front of curtain covered doors.

Derek continues, "Most of the people who come here have alternate names that they use. For example, I am Orion, Master Orion or Sir Orion." His eyes light up when he tells us his club name. I watch as Dacotah smiles. "Depending on who is here tonight, you may recognize a couple of them. The Box is an exclusive club that caters to the wealthier side of Nashville, including celebrities."

"Oh goody," Dex says a little sarcastically and I want to punch his shoulder.

"Oh believe me," Derek says without hesitation. "No one in this club talks about its members outside these doors. It's against the rules for one and for two, speaking about the club, or its members, puts the entire operation at risk, which can include the closing of the doors. One thing you will quickly learn about those in this lifestyle is that there is no judgment on anyone's part and odds are, outing one member means that the person doing it has just as much if not more to lose as well."

"He's absolutely right." A deep baritone voice says from behind Derek. "Sir Orion." The burly man that accompanies the voice comes to shake Derek's hand and Dacotah bows her head and clasps her hands in front of her.

"How are you, Master Orik?"

"Fabulous. Are these your friends?"

"They are. Dex, I'd like you to meet Master Orik, owner of The Box and our tour guide for this first little bit."

Dex releases my hand to take Master Orik's. "Pleasure to meet you, Master Orik."

"Likewise. If I must say, before we enter the club itself, that I'm a huge fan."

Dex chuckles. "I can't take this mug anywhere, can I?" The men all laugh.

"No, probably not, but I assure you, I will be the only one saying anything about it. And who is this beauty next to you?"

"This is Raine." Dex gently places his hand behind my back, giving me some encouragement. I'm sure he can sense how nervous I am. I extend my hand to him.

"It's very nice to meet you, Master Orik," I say politely.

"Likewise Raine." He releases my hand. "Welcome to The Box. If I'm remembering correctly, you and Raine here are interested in the lifestyle?"

Master Orik does not address me, only Dex, which I can tell since he's yet to acknowledge Dacotah is protocol, so I keep my mouth shut. "We are. More interested in learning about the dynamics and of course I'd like to learn about some of the tools of the trade as well."

"Absolutely." Master Orik smiles at him.

"I've been to a couple of clubs before, learned some, but hardly enough to make a BDSM relationship with Raine completely safe. I know she's never been to a club before."

"Excellent. Orion here is a pretty good teacher, though I understand you live in LA?"

"We do," Dex replies.

"There are some wonderful clubs out that way. I'd love to get you some information on a few of them. In fact, there is another club with the same type of clientele as I have here, and owned by a good friend. We'll get you hooked up."

"I belong to that club too," Derek chimes in. "It's not as good as The Box, but it's comparable."

"Wonderful," Master Orik says. "Before we can go in, I need a few things from the two of you, if you don't mind."

"Not at all," Dex answers quickly.

After handing over our driver's licenses to have Master Orik complete a form and then finally signing a confidentiality agreement that states we will not discuss the club or its members outside of these four walls, Master Orik walks toward the curtain.

"The reception area here is where everyone checks in for the evening. All members are on a master list and the list is used so that we know who is here at any given time. In general, no one's real names are used. Or only their first names preceded by their titles. Once they're checked in, they're allowed to enter the club. There are a few of my dungeon monitors here already as we open in a little over an hour and they're going about their duties. Dungeon Monitors are here for everyone's protection. The submissive, should she safeword while doing a scene, are immediately protected by our DMs. The situation is assessed before the submissive can be released back to her Master or Dominant. They're also here to protect Dominants and the other people within the club. Most of the time, they are in the shadows and are hardly noticeable. They themselves are either Dominants, submissives or switches."

With that, Master Orik pulls back the curtain, and beyond it there is a slight blue glow of black lights. He ushers us through the curtain and my breath catches in my throat as I take in the sight before me. The room is massive.

The floor and walls are black and lining the room are various apparatuses from St. Andrew's Crosses, to tables, frames, and benches. In the center of the room there are several tables in front of what appears to be a bar.

"We do not serve alcohol, but we do offer a variety of juices and waters. Can I get you anything?" Master Orik asks and Dex meets my wide eyes. I shake my head.

"No, thank you," Dex says and Derek declines as well.

"Master Orik?" a gentleman calls from the other side of the room.

"Excuse me." Master Orik dismisses himself.

Derek turns to us. "What do you think?"

"It's big," Dex says. "Probably the biggest I've seen."

"It is, probably one of the biggest in the country. Orik expanded a few years back. His clientele was growing and so was the demand. He was forced to limit the number of people to first come first serve or a sign up, so he expanded. We don't get a lot of time tonight because of the club being open, but if you guys would like to stay, and watch..." He doesn't finish his thought and Dex looks to me.

"I'd love to stay," I tell him and Derek lights up.

"Good," Derek says before he slides the bag off of his shoulder and hands it to Cotah. "Take this to our room." He leans down and kisses her cheek. "You know what to do."

"Yes, Sir," she says with enthusiasm.

She disappears toward where Master Orik disappeared a few moments ago. "There are private rooms back there. You can rent or purchase one for your personal use. If you want to stay, Cotah has agreed to being put on display, to give you guys a chance to see how we play."

"Oh she doesn't..." I start to say and he stops me with a look.

"If there is one thing I've learned about this lifestyle, Raine, it's that you can read about it all you want, you can watch all the bad porn you desire, but nothing compares to seeing the real thing in action. You may not get another chance to see this for yourself. So, if you don't mind, we'd like to show you and Dex."

I nod and give him a small smile. "I'd like that."

"Good. Now, since Orik is occupied, I'll show you a few more things while Cotah gets ready." He turns and leads us toward the bar area, then makes a left. "There are no gender roles in this dungeon. He points to two different doors. One says Dominants, the other submissives. "Dominants and submissives are both male and female, inside the room are private dressing/changing rooms and restrooms along with lockers and a common area." He goes toward another hallway that is lined with curtains. "This is an aftercare area. For club members who do not rent rooms, they're allowed to use these for their aftercare purposes." He stops in front of one of the pulled back curtain doors.

I look inside the room and there is a bed, about full or queen size, along with a nightstand and a doorway that appears to have a bathroom and standing shower inside. One of the common things I've noticed throughout the dungeon and now in here is that there are bowls of chocolates everywhere and I wonder what that's all about.

"Each night stand is actually a fridge with water and Gatorade in them. One of the most important things that can happen after a scene is aftercare, and hydration is important. The chocolate is a sweet, and if you've never tried eating chocolate after sex, you should." He grins. "There is just something about it that is blissful."

"I've heard of that," Dex says with a smirk. "She could have used that a time or two."

I shoulder check him. "Hey now." Both men laugh.

Derek ushers us back into the dungeon area of the club and Master Orik returns. "Where's Cotah?" he asks Derek, which surprises me because he's paid her no attention so far.

"She's changing. They'd like to stay and they're going to watch us scene."

"Excellent idea."

"Will Cherry be here tonight?" Derek asks.

"She's up in my office right now. She's being a brat."

That doesn't sound good.

Derek smiles and shakes his head. "You know she only acts like that to rile you up."

Master Orik laughs. "I know and I fucking love it. I'll let her come down later. She's do for a good punishment. Maybe I should just tie her to a chair and make her watch Cotah."

"Now that's an idea," Derek says.

I squeeze Dex's hand and I'm longing for a few minutes alone to talk to him. To ask him how he's handling all this, but I can tell by the way his eyes are lit up that he's observing as much information as Derek can throw at him tonight. A thrill runs up my spine.

chapter
17
raine

"Raine, will you come with me?" Derek asks me and I turn to Dex who smiles and nods.

I stand from the table we occupied a few minutes ago and follow Derek toward the private rooms.

"How are you handling all this?" he asks me once we're out of ear shot.

"I'm already in love and I haven't seen anything yet."

He smiles at me. "What makes you so interested in the lifestyle?"

"If I say I've read too many books, does that sound too cliché?"

He chuckles. "No, not really. Books can be a good gateway, but I know of several books that do a bad job of portraying the lifestyle."

"I agree completely. I've read a few of those. I tend to stick to those written by authors who are active in the lifestyle. It makes them easier to understand because they do a better job of explaining it. But in all honesty, I think a lot of it stems from my willingness to let it all go at the pleasure of someone else. But I also think that I have a Dominant side to me as well."

"Do you see yourself in that role?" he asks.

"I can, and in a way, I enjoy that side of things too. Dex also has a submissive side to him as well."

"That will make for an interesting dynamic between the two of you."

"How so?" I ask.

"Well," he pauses in front of a door, "sometimes it can be a struggle to let go when you really want to top. Other times it is hard to top when you really want to be on the bottom. Which are you more interested in learning first?" he asks me with honest curiosity in his voice.

"The bottom," I tell him with conviction.

"Why?"

"Because I like the way Dex makes me feel when he takes control. I love the way I feel when I am at his mercy. It's empowering and enlightening. I want to please him."

He smiles. "That is a great place to start. Now, I'm going to ask you a few personal questions."

"Okay."

"Safeword?" He raises an eyebrow at me.

"Kit Kat."

He chuckles. "Hard limits?"

"Feces." I watch him shudder.

"No argument there. Anything else?"

"Without knowing, I can't say for sure. I'm open to trying anything and…" I hesitate to tell him the next part. He raises an eyebrow, expecting me to continue and my inner submissive kicks in, "I love pain." I reach up to the V of my dress and pull it wide enough so that he can see Dex's marks.

"Oh, ouch," he says.

"It was a heat of the moment thing the first time. I begged for the second."

"We're going to get along just fine." He smiles. "I'm going to open this door. Cotah, being the good girl I know she is, will be on her knees, facing the wall. She will be naked except for a pair of boy shorts. Does that bother you?"

I shake my head.

He opens the door. He was right. She is kneeling in the corner, her back to us, her head lowered and her palms are resting on her thighs.

I watch Derek as he admires her. There is a gloss that fills his eyes as he looks upon his sub. There is a loving adoration that is coming off of him in waves as he steps toward her. He unbuttons his dress shirt as he goes, removing it before he reaches her and tossing it over the back of a chair. When he comes to stand next to her, he gently rubs along her head and she comes alive, leaning into his touch. "Well done, pet," he tells her.

There is a level of intimacy that comes with what I'm watching that I almost want to turn away from.

"Raine is in here with us. Nod if you understand." I watch as she nods twice. There was no hesitation in her nod and I take comfort in that. "Rise up and present your wrists."

I watch as she rises to her feet and she turns to face him. I notice now that the necklace I'd seen her wearing earlier has been replaced by a black leather collar that has a loop hanging from the center of it. A shiver slides up my spine as envy and jealousy rock through me. What I wouldn't give to be in her shoes right now. Only with Dex leading the charge.

She presents her wrists to him and he reaches onto the chest of drawers and pulls one of the four cuffs sitting atop it. He makes quick work of securing it to her wrist, then checking its tightness. I shiver. He repeats the process for the other wrist. When he's done he brushes his hand gently along her cheek. "Spread for me, pet," he says and she widens her stance, then places her hands behind her back, bending and grabbing the opposite elbow.

Derek lowers himself to the floor, bringing the two other cuffs with him, and quickly secures them around her ankles. Then he rises to stand before her. The look in his eyes is back to the loving admiration I saw earlier as he cups her chin in his hand and lifts her face to look at his. "Open your eyes," he commands and she does. I watch as she visibly melts. Much the way I do when I look at Dex. Then Derek kisses her, hard and full of love, passion and desperation. She moans into his mouth when he pulls back. The loss nearly insufferable to her.

He reaches for the last thing on the desk and the noise it makes as he picks it up sends another thrill through me as the chains clink together. I watch as he clips the end into the loop on her collar and she instantly lowers her chin, her eyes downcast. "Come," he commands and he starts walking toward me. I step out of the way so that he may pass. "Ready?" he asks me.

"Yes," I breathe out and he smiles a knowing smile at me.

I fall in behind him and Cotah as we walk back toward the dungeon. There are a few people inside now as the club is opening to its members. I quickly spot Dex, but I wait to be dismissed from Derek before going over to him. He turns toward me and says, "Grab a chair and Dex. I'm going to take Cotah to that cross." He points to a table where the duffle bag is sitting now. He'd fetched it right after we sat down, before he took me back to claim Cotah.

I smile at Dex as I approach. "Hi sexy," I say to him.

"What was that all about?" he asks me, no menace in his voice, just honest curiosity.

"He wanted me to watch Cotah as she presented herself to him."

"Oh, and how was that?"

"Erotic as fuck," I breathe out.

"Really?" His voice is skeptical.

"Yeah, I wanted to be her." His expression falls. "Not for Derek, in fact, all I could picture was doing what she was doing, only doing it for you," I tell him softly and he relaxes. "There isn't anyone I want to explore this with more than you, Dex. Believe me. I trust you," I tell him and kiss him gently on the lips. "Come on, grab your chair, Derek wants us closer."

"Alright."

We grab our chairs and walk toward Derek and Dacotah as I watch her standing there, the leash dropped and her head lowered as she stands before the cross while Derek pulls some things out of his bag. We put our chairs near the table. Derek nods, and Dex and I take a seat. I snuggle into Dex to watch what's about to happen.

Derek finishes what he's doing and I can see various floggers laid out on the table. He walks up behind the cross and reaches around it. Grabbing Cotah's leash, pulling her forward until she is flush against the cross. He caresses her head and whispers something in her ear and she nods. I watch Derek and he unhooks the leash and drops the chain to the floor, then he sets about securing her wrists to the hooks at the points of the cross. Hands first, then her feet. Once she is secure, Derek steps back to admire his sub on the cross.

Out of nowhere someone replaces Derek behind the cross but in front of Cotah.

"Hello Cotah," the man says.

"Hello, Sir," Cotah responds to him.

"You haven't been here in a while, can you please remind me of your safeword?"

"Chasseur, Sir."

"Very well," he says and off he goes.

Derek turns to us and explains, "Every safeword is different. Though red is the standard word, Cotah has chosen her own. But I, along with anyone else in this room, will honor red for her as well."

Dex and I both nod our understanding and Derek turns to the table where he grabs a flogger, it's black and bushy. He brings it over to me and Dex and we both reach out to touch it. It's soft and there are a lot of tails on it. Derek doesn't explain anything about it, just gives us a chance to look at it before he turns around toward Dacotah.

When he approaches her, she jumps slightly, but his hand caresses along her back, comforting her. His right hand begins twirling the flogger in a circular motion and just before it makes contact with her back he removes his other hand and she moans out the moment the flogger makes contact. Derek continues spinning it around and kissing her back with it, then moves it down to her thighs and over and back up. Then he brings the flogger to a halt and he switches sides. He takes the falls into one hand and then pulls the flogger free.

The sound is heavy against her bare skin and I watch with wild fascination as Derek continues to flog her back.

chapter
18
dex

I've barely been able to pull my eyes away from Derek and Cotah since he started flogging her back. He's gradually moved his way from the flogger to a riding crop and then onto a paddle and then had us move before he brought out a bullwhip. With each crack of the whip, I watched Raine flinch at the sound. It is a scary as fuck sound, but Cotah, fuck, I didn't know the girl had it in her. We watch as Derek flicks the whip against her back, against her ass. He'd relieved her of her panties around the time of the riding crop when he'd made her come. It was the most glorious sight I'd ever seen.

He continues with the whip. He's got amazing aim and he's hypnotic to watch.

He strikes the whip again and Cotah cries out, pulling hard against her bindings. "Ahh, ahhh..." She continues to cry as Derek approaches her and whispers something in her ear, talking her down. She settles and then he backs up again and readies to go again. Cotah's breathing is returning to normal as she settles back into the cross. Derek only takes a few more swipes at her before he stops altogether. Dropping the whip on the table and grabbing a blanket before approaching her. He slides up behind her, caressing the bright red welts left behind by the whip then he opens the blanket, covering her.

I watch as he unhooks her cuffs and he catches her in his arms. I watch as she snuggles into him and he kisses her forehead. He nuzzles his face against hers and she raises her head and he kisses her hard. She moans and is practically climbing up his chest. He approaches us and we stand up. He smiles wide. "You're more than welcome to stay, but I am going to go take care of my angel. I've arranged for a driver to take you back to the hotel. If you're up for it, we can do lunch tomorrow."

"I'd like that," I say and Raine agrees.

"Wonderful, I'll call you around ten or so?"

"Perfect. Thank you for showing that to us," I say to him with a little more excitement in my voice than I'd intended.

"You're most welcome. How was it for you, Raine?"

"Amazing," she breathes and smiles at him.

I notice that Dacotah is completely checked out, breathing softly against Derek's chest.

"I have a few more ideas for you guys. Let's talk tomorrow."

I nod. "Thank you, Derek." Raine's voice is soft.

He smiles gently at her. "You're most welcome."

With that he heads back to the private rooms and I turn to Raine. "Should we stay or...?"

Master Orik approaches us before I can finish. "How was your night?" he asks me, ignoring Raine, which is apparently the norm here and for some reason, I'm not sure I like that much.

"It was wonderful." I extend my hand to him. "Thank you so much for letting Orion bring us in."

"Absolutely. We'd like to extend you a full invitation for membership if it's something you're interested in."

"Absolutely," I answer.

"Perfect, I'll be in touch with what we need from you and then we can go from there."

"Sounds wonderful, thank you, Master Orik."

Finally he turns to Raine. "It was a pleasure having you here tonight. I look forward to seeing you again."

"Likewise, Sir. Thank you for having us."

I get the feeling that Master Orik has taken a little more interest in Raine than I'm comfortable with, but I let it go and escort Raine back through the curtains and out the door.

Raine started asking questions as soon as we got into the limo and all I could do was kiss her. Fuck, I am so turned on after watching that. All I want to do is get back to our hotel room and bend her over. But I settle for kissing her. We make out the whole way back to our hotel.

When we arrive, our driver lets us out of the back of the limo and I escort Raine inside. "I can really use a drink or four," I say to her.

"Please," she says and we head into the bar. It's much quieter in here now than it was earlier and we grab the same table, tucked off in the corner.

"So, is that what you want?"

I watch as she shivers. I can't tell if it is a good or bad shiver. "More than anything." She gives me a wide smile.

"Me too," is all I can say.

All night I kept picturing Raine up on that cross, me behind her, wielding the floggers and toys. The crop and whip were the most fun to watch, especially the way that Dacotah's skin would flash red briefly following each strike. The only red marks that stuck around were the whips marks.

I shiver thinking about it myself.

raine

Sleeping with Dex that night was phenomenal, probably the best we've had yet. I know that's probably hard to believe, but believe it.

We went to lunch with Cotah and Derek the next day. We had a wonderful lunch and I know I grew more and more comfortable around Derek as the day progressed. After you've witnessed something as spectacular as what we did, it's hard not to hold the man in high regard. His primary idea was to invite us to their home in North Carolina after the tour was over. He wanted to spend some more time with us and he wanted a chance to show both Dex and I a whole lot more about the lifestyle and of course, more toys and goodies. Dex and I both agreed quickly.

We've arrived in Atlanta and the guys are busy getting ready for tonight's show. Well, they're running sound checks while I finish getting dressed for the show tonight. Tonight I decided to wear the other dress that Dex got me along with the hooded sweater. Though I have a feeling I'll be shedding that sooner rather than later. It's kind of warm back here. Immediately following the show we have to leave for Orlando and the last two shows before the week long break.

The band made the papers after their nights out in Nashville and Dex and I have been photographed more than a few times, but the stories have been favorable. Though the media outlets are starting to call this tour the "love boat" tour because two, previously single, members of the band are now officially taken off of the market. Technically three, but the world doesn't know that yet.

Addison and I have been working really hard on some band sponsorships and some endorsement deals. We even have a couple of potential commercials in the works. It's rewarding to see the band being wanted by various outlets.

I'm nearly done with my makeup when my cell phone rings.

"Raine," I say into the phone.

"Baby, it's Erica."

"What's wrong?" My heart starts hammering in my chest.

"Baby, I'm..." she pauses.

"Reeks, what's wrong? What's going on?"

"Baby, I'm standing outside your apartment, it's been...it's been broken into."

"What?" I say in a huff as I collapse onto the couch. "When? How? Who?" I start bawling as I put my head into my free hand.

"I was here Monday night, and I just came by after work and the patio window has been shattered."

"What's missing?"

"That's just it, baby. Nothing is missing, at least not that I can tell. Everything is still intact. It's just...the apartment's been trashed, baby." She's crying on the other end of the phone which makes me cry harder. I jump when Dex sits down next to me. I didn't even hear him come in.

"What do you mean trashed?" I ask her.

"I will send you pictures as soon as the cops let me back inside. Your electronics have been trashed, the screens are destroyed, including your TVs and your computer. There is paint and spray paint everywhere. He spray painted 'slut' across your living room wall and whore is repeated throughout your bedroom."

I can't talk, I can't... "I'm coming home."

"Like hell you are," she tells me through the phone. "What exactly are you going to do here, sweetheart? We're going to board up the door, the apartment is placing security here, and you only run the risk of actually being here when he comes back. You-" Dex takes the phone from my hand.

"What are you..."

"Who is it?"

"Erica," I tell him.

"Hi Erica, this is Dex."

I can't hear the other end of the conversation. "What happened?"

There is a long pause while Erica tells him what happened to my apartment. I put my head into my hands and cry. I don't know what else to do.

"I'll be sending someone there, someone that will stay in the apartment."

Another pause. "Can you stay there until they get there?" Dex rises from the couch and I lift my head in time to see him punch the door then open it. "Rusty," he shouts into the hallway. "No, Erica, I'll have somewhere there in about an hour, two tops. You don't need to stay in the apartment and if the cops are there now, I imagine they will still be there when someone shows up." Another pause and Rusty comes bounding into the room.

"What's goi..." He catches an eyeful of my raccoon eyes and looks from me to Dex in alarm.

"Nope, we'll take care of it. Thank you for calling." Pause. "Don't fret, I'm taking good care of her." He looks at me with such love and devotion that I can't help but nod. I wish I could find it somewhere in me to smile, but that's lost right now. Dex ends the call.

"What's going on?" Rusty asks just as Mills and Beck walk into the room.

"Raine's apartment back in LA has been trashed. I'm going to go with my gut and say that it was Michael or whatever his name is." I nod at him confirming the name. "Rusty, do you have someone that can stay at the apartment?"

"Yeah, I'll send my guys over there."

"Hopefully it's over and done with, but I'm pretty sure that if it's Michael, he's done all he can do at this point. I'm sure our headlines are what has set him off."

"Motherfucker," I growl.

"Raine?" Mills says and I look at him. I'm pretty sure my stare is blank and hollow, it's how I feel right now. "Do you have renter's insurance?" I nod. "Can you get me the information? I'll get them called."

"What's the point?" I sob.

Dex comes to kneel in front of me. "Glowbug, please don't be like this. The point is, we can get the insurance rolling so your stuff can be fixed and replaced."

"I know...it's just, I don't know if he's done with his games. What's the point in replacing it if he's just going to do it again." I cry harder and Dex wraps his arms around me. "Everything in that apartment I've worked my ass off for, and it's all gone thanks to the rage of an idiot."

chapter
19
dex

"Where's Raine?" Addison asks as we approach her before taking the stage. "Dex, what's wrong?"

"Have Rusty explain it to you."

"Are you and Raine...?" She doesn't have to finish the question.

"We're fine, love. Rusty can tell you," I tell her then kiss her cheek. At one time I took comfort in kissing Addison, mostly to get a rise out of her, now all I want to do is kiss my glowbug, but she's not out here, not yet anyway.

"Alright, I'll talk to him," she replies as I take the stage and climb behind my drums. I've lost most, if not all of my enthusiasm for tonight. That is until I catch something in the corner of my eye on the right side of the stage. I smile wide when I see her standing in my normal line of sight. I blow her a kiss, she catches it then blows one back. That was the endorphin rush I needed.

That little kiss was all it took for me to get through the show. I pull my sweaty ass off of the stage after our encore and right into Raine's arms. "Hi bubba."

"Hi bug." I kiss her hard. After what happened, I have this desperate need to be close to her, and fast.

"Hurry with your shower, brother. We've only got about ninety minutes before we have to be on the road," Talon tells me. "How you doing, girl?" he asks Raine who smiles.

"Better, thanks."

"Good. Mills told me what happened. I'm really sorry, sweetheart," he tells her and she gives him a small smile.

"It's just stuff," she says, though I can tell she's still heartbroken. I'd vowed to fix it and told Rusty as such. No matter the cost, replace it all with something similar or better. He said he'd jump right on it. This way Mills can file the insurance claim and she can keep the money.

"You know," Addison chimes in. "I have extra room in my condo, if you want to have your stuff moved over there. You're welcome to stay with me until you can find someplace new."

"I..." She looks to me, I shrug.

"Not a bad idea. Get your apartment emptied out..."

"Well, from what Erica told me, everything is pretty much trashed. She texted me a little while ago, letting me know that Rusty's friend showed up and was going to stay in the apartment until it could be secured. She said that she would email pictures once she got home. But she basically told me that there is very little there that isn't painted or cut." I watch as her eyes fill with tears.

"Let's talk more on the bus," Addison says and I have to agree with her.

"We have time to sort it out," I say with a small smile then kiss her gently. "Want to come with me or wait in the greenroom?" I ask her.

"Greenroom, if that's okay?"

I give her my sexy smirk. "Perfect. See you in a few minutes," I tell her and kiss her one more time before heading back to the dressing room. Rusty is standing there, and I jump.

"Give a man a heart attack, why don't you."

He laughs. "My friend's at the house, he's sending me pictures now." Rusty turns his phone around. It's a shot of what I'm guessing is her bedroom. The word 'whore' is spray painted over and over again all over everything.

"I'm going to kill him," I growl.

"Ryan says that there is little left to salvage. Her dishes have been dumped all over the kitchen floor, shattered. Her fridge emptied, though there wasn't much in there, all appliances and electronics have been scratched, dented and painted over. I recommend trashing everything and starting her off fresh."

"Yeah, we're going to have to do something. Addison offered her some space at her condo to move stuff and I hate to just throw everything away without her knowledge."

"After Michael had called her in New York, she had her friend Erica go to her apartment and get some stuff. But short of her moving out, I'm pretty sure she couldn't get everything."

"Right. Alright, let me talk to Raine. Erica is going to email her pictures as well. I'll have her take a look at everything and then we can go from there. Mills will file the insurance claim and I'll give you money to replace stuff, but we need to get it out of that apartment. She needs to move."

"Right, but where's she going to go? She's going to have to break her lease."

"I know, I'll deal with it."

"Alright."

"Out, I need to shower."

"Yup."

"Hey Rusty?"

"Yeah?" He turns back toward me at the door.

"Thanks. For everything."

He gives me a smile. "That's what I'm here for. But make no mistake. If that douche goes back to that apartment, Ryan will make him wish he hadn't."

"Good."

Rusty leaves after that and I climb into the shower.

raine

Dex was lightning fast tonight with his shower. He came into the greenroom to find me sandwiched between Mouse and Talon. His eyes light up when he sees me and I have no doubt that mine do too. I'm finally starting to feel a little bit better, but I'm still waiting for Erica to send me pictures. Then again, I don't think I really want to see them.

"Hi you," I say to Dex when he comes to stand over me.

"Hey."

"You look better," he tells me.

"I'm feeling better."

"Good," he says as he grabs my hands and pulls me up, wrapping his arms around me and planting a warm wet kiss against my lips and I can smell his body wash. I run my fingers through his still damp hair and hold him to me a moment longer until someone clears his throat. He growls against my lips and pulls back.

"Hey, it's bad enough we have to listen to you two on the bus, we don't want to watch it too." Dex and I both turn to gape at Talon.

"You're fucking joking, right?" Dex teases him. "I'm pretty sure the three of you take the cake on the loud and proud award."

"Well, that doesn't bother me," Talon snorts and the tension is lifted.

"Yeah, whatever, man. I'll remember that the next time you're pounding away. I'll come pound on your door."

Everyone starts to laugh and I nod to Mills, telling him to open the door. "Sit," I tell Dex and he pants like a dog. I smack his shoulder and he takes a seat.

I go over to the bar and grab his usual beer and one for myself. After opening them and tossing the caps, I turn around and head back to Dex.

Something in the corner of the room captures my attention. Though it doesn't fully register before I drop the beers and they shatter across the greenroom floor. People jump back, my head starts spinning and the next thing I realize is that the floor is rising up pretty fast. "Raine!" someone shouts, but that's the last thing I hear.

chapter
20
dex

"What the hell happened?" I nearly shout as I take Raine from Beck's arms. He managed to catch her just before she hit the floor.

"I don't know, Dex. She just panicked and fainted."

"Don't let anyone out of this room," I bark.

"Already on it," Beck whispers.

"Where's Rusty?"

"I'm here, bro." I look up at him.

"Is he, what's his fucking name, is he here?"

"No, Ryan sent me his mugshot when he was arrested before. He's not here."

"Then what the fuck…" I look down at Raine.

"Come on glowbug, wake up baby." I run my hand along her cheek while Beck checks her pulse.

"Keep talking to her," he whispers.

"Come on, princess, wake up. You can do it. Please." I keep sputtering out things to say, pet names, nicknames, her name until she finally twitches in my arms.

Then out of nowhere she pulls in a deep breath and sits straight up.

"Thank fuck," I growl and she turns to look at me. "Hi you," I say with a smile.

"Hi, wha..." She looks around, confused.

I watch her as realization dawns on her. "I'm going to kill that mother fucker," she all but shouts.

"Who?" Rusty, Beck and I all say at once.

"Andrew." She moves to stand up. I look at Beck and raise an eyebrow at him, then give him that weird frown indicating that I don't know what the fuck she's talking about.

She's on her feet, but grabs on to my head to steady herself. I remove her hand and take it in mine.

The next thing I know, she's charging over me, straight into the corner. Walking toward some wiry looking geek in the corner. We'd all noticed him when he came in, seemingly out of place for a rock concert. I watch as my feisty kitten walks right up to him and smacks him across the face.

Mills wraps his arms around Raine and Casey takes hold of the fucker she smacked. I get to my feet just as Mills, Raine, Casey and the dork start walking out the door of the greenroom. I follow behind them, much to Beck's chagrin. When we clear the doorway, I notice that they keep walking all the way out the back door.

"Let me go." I hear Raine struggling against Mills' hold on her.

"Not until I know you're not going to hit him anymore."

"I'll fucking hit this dirty ass son of a bitch all I fucking want."

I clear the back door and am now standing a few feet behind him.

"Not on my watch, you won't. I won't have you getting arrested," Mills states matter of factly. "Now, are you going to calm down?"

"No, let me go. I'm going to kill that son of a bitch."

"Whoa." I move to stand between her and the guy in Casey's arms. "Look at me," I command her and she settles instantly in Mills' arms. "Why would you kill him?"

"Because that nerdy son of a bitch is my fucking brother."

Red… that's the only color I manage to see. I turn on my heels headed straight for Casey, without even realizing I'm doing it. Then, out of nowhere, my fist connects with his face, hard enough to knock him out of Casey's arms and onto the ground.

"Fuck!" I hear Mills behind me. "Beck, Troy," he barks into his mic. "Leroy," he shouts.

Heavy footfalls come flying across the pavement and the backdoor flies open and all I can do is stare at the son of a bitch on the ground, holding his face. Casey, abandoning the duckweed on the ground, wraps his arms around me. "Fuck off, I'm fine." I fight his hold. "Don't," I snap and Casey lets go. I kneel down, catching my breath as Casey assesses him on the ground.

"Do you need a doctor?" Casey asks him.

The motherfucker spits at Casey's feet and Casey reacts by grabbing a hold of his shirt and lifting him up. "Explain your purpose here," Casey demands as he sets him on his feet. "You're obviously unwelcome, so why have you come here?"

"I came to talk to my sister," he says and I scoff.

"You lost that fucking right ten years ago, Andrew," Raine shouts from behind me.

I turn to Mills. "Let her go."

He does and she comes to stand next to me. "You're no longer my brother, you son of a bitch."

"Such foul language, Lorraine."

"My name is not Lorraine." I can see the fiery anger building in her clenched fists. "What the fuck are you doing here?"

"I came to bring you home."

"You've been stalking me. You were there in Greensboro, weren't you?"

"Jesus is ready to welcome you home."

"Bullshit," she spits and now I can finally see it clear enough. "If Jesus was so fucking great, Andrew, I wouldn't have been raped, I wouldn't have been abandoned by our parents. By you. Do you ever think about that? Does it ever fucking occur to you that they, your parents, are wrong?"

"Mom and Dad want you to come home."

"I find that hard to believe."

"It's true," Andrew argues.

"Really? Then where the fuck are they? Are they here?" Andrew shakes his head. "Did they fucking send you here?" Again he shakes his head. "So you just thought you could show up here and haul me back to Hickory like nothing happened? Like it hasn't been ten years? Did you think that I could stand on their doorstep and they'd welcome me back with open arms? I hate to blow up your delusional bubble here, Andrew, but one, I would never return to Hickory, and two, if I was so fucking important to them, I would have never been thrown out, would have never been left to fend for myself and Jesus fucking Christ…"

"Don't use our Lord's name in vain, Lorraine."

"Fuck you, you fucking moron, get off your god damn high horse and go back to mom and dad."

"Dad's dying."

That was the last thing I expected him to say.

"He's desperate to repent his greatest sins."

Without even missing a beat Raine replies, "Well, he can die with his greatest sin unforgiven. Now get out of my sight. If you ever show up around here again, there isn't a single fucking person out here that will stop me from killing you." I watch as she charges past him. Casey and Leroy are standing between him and her so that he can't get to her and she runs full tilt onto the bus.

I walk up to Andrew. "You ever come back here, come around her, come anywhere near her ever again, if she doesn't kill you, I will. Now run on back to mommy and daddy and tell them that their daughter is dead as far as they're concerned." I turn to Casey. "Get him the fuck off the property, make sure he leaves."

I push past all of them, walking onto the bus in a huff, stomping my way back to our room, back to my woman.

When I round the corner into our alcove, she's standing there, her back to me, sobs wracking her entire body. "Raine." She jumps.

"That motherfucking cocksucker. Who the fuck does he think he is?"

I frown. "I wish I knew."

She sobs out. I reach out to touch her back and she pulls back, turning and plowing into me, her hands in fists beating against my chest. "Shh, glowbug, I'm here. He's gone. Come on, princess, please." I rub my hands along her back, comforting her as she settles into my embrace.

"I've spent ten years trying to forget them, trying to move on from what they did to me, and now, tonight, when I finally feel like I'm capable of letting it all go and moving on, he has to fucking show up here."

"You said he was stalking you…"

"Remember my out of body experience?"

"Yes," I say with hesitation.

"I'm pretty sure I convinced myself it wasn't real. That it was strictly psychological because that was easier to process. Easier for me to deal with, but in reality, I had a feeling it really was him. The last couple of days in Nashville, I kept getting this creepy, 'I'm being followed feeling' but I just thought I was being paranoid."

"Why didn't you tell me? I'm supposed to take care of you…"

"I know, okay, I just thought I was overreacting. I guess I couldn't wrap my head around the idea that someone would go to those lengths to follow me, to track me down, not now, not after all these years." She wipes away the tears and I slide down to the floor, bringing her with me and she curls up on my lap. "When your parents died, were you upset?"

I rub her back. "No, I was relieved. But I had a very different relationship with my parents. They didn't give a rat's ass, yours care too much, to the point of smothering, there's a big difference."

"I don't see it that way," she tells me. "I see it the same. There is such a thing as loving someone too much, which I think they thought they did, but the reality was different. They held me back from so much. I saw that when I got to California and I felt like I grew up fifteen years on that bus. I didn't have a clue about anything. I was so naive to think that I could do it on my own, but…" she pauses as she nuzzles into me, "I figured it out because I had no choice."

"But look at you now, you're strong, independent, loving, caring, but yet you maintain a sense of yourself without getting lost in it. You're probably one of the most loving people I know." I kiss her forehead.

"I'm going to smother you to death."

I wrap my arms around her, holding her tight to my chest. "Impossible." I kiss her forehead again and we say nothing else for some time, until I hear the guys come on the bus and I realize that she's fallen asleep in my arms.

chapter
21
dex

I managed to get myself up off of the floor with Raine in my lap and to lay her out on the lower rack. Once I lie her down, she settles in and I cover her up before kissing her forehead. With her squared away, I head out into the main cabin of the bus. There's a lot of conversation going on.

"Jesus, Dex, what the hell happened?" Talon asks as soon as I round the corner.

I put my finger to my lips, shushing them. "She's asleep," I say quietly. "It was her brother."

"My god, I can't imagine anything that would set her off on her brother like that," Addison says.

I look at her. "I'm surprised she didn't kill him."

"That bad?" she questions.

I nod. "Her family booted her when she was eighteen."

"Fuck, so what the hell was he doing here?" Kyle asks.

"Trying to convince her that after ten years her parents wanted her to come back home."

"Why'd they kick her out in the first place?" Addison asks.

I sigh. I knew someone was going to ask the question. "She grew up in a very strict, very religious household. When she was eighteen, barely in college, she was beaten and raped."

I watch shock cross everyone's features and Addison covers her mouth and sits down. "That's no reason to abandon your child," Addison says as she strokes her hand over her growing bump.

"It is when you're left with no choice but to have an abortion." I jump and turn to see Raine standing behind me.

"I'm sorry..." I start to say and she stops me with a small smile and a shake of her head.

"When the choice comes to your own survival or the loss of both lives...what would you choose?"

I look to Addison who has tears in her eyes, "I would have done the same thing."

"Well, my parents would rather have seen me buried than have an abortion, regardless of the circumstances behind the pregnancy. It didn't matter that I was beaten, near death and raped, a life was a life. When I got out of the hospital and returned to my parents' house, all my personal things were thrown out on the front lawn. I spent less than twenty-four hours in town before climbing on a bus for California. I knew my parents had talked, had told them what I'd done and when you come from a town with the same views and morals, or lack thereof, as my parents I may as well have been walking around with an A on my clothes."

She comes to stand next to me and I wrap my arm around her shoulders, providing comfort and security. "Well, you have nothing to be ashamed of around us," Mouse, of all people, says.

"We have no grounds to judge anyone based on their past, present or future," Talon adds.

"We're family," I declare, and I mean it.

My declaration is met with cheers, laughter and good times. Within another twenty minutes the bus was pulling away from the Atlanta arena and we were on our way to Orlando.

Raine and I stayed up in the kitchen area with the guys and Addison for some time. Raine and Addie even made us all dinner while we bantered and bullshitted.

I realized that we hadn't done this in a really long time and I started to feel guilty about that.

Feeling guilty reminds me of how much things have changed these past few weeks. Before I would have never given a shit, but before this tour started, we were all really close and gradually we've all managed to separate ourselves. Talon and Kyle with Addison, me with Raine, and watching Calvin and Eric now, their dynamic is changing. They treat each other a little differently than how they would have in the past. It causes me to raise an eyebrow but who am I to judge.

Tori joins us to eat.

"Sorry guys, we're gonna stop up here."

"Everything alright?" Kyle asks the driver.

"Yup, we need to pick up a passenger."

"Who?" Talon asks.

"Mills," the driver replies and we all look at each other in confusion.

"Why didn't he just call me?" Tori says, not really expecting an answer.

We travel another ten minutes or so before we pull into a gas station. "Do I have time to run inside?" Kyle asks the driver.

"Go for it, we'll wait for you."

"Thanks." Kyle hops off the bus as soon as it stops and Mills hops on.

"Good, you're still awake," he says to Raine who's sitting on my lap.

"What's wrong?" she asks nervously. Mills looks around, everyone is here. "I have no secrets, nothing to hide," she tells him and he finally decides it's okay to talk.

"Someone showed up at your apartment."

"Fuck, who?" I ask.

"We don't know. It wasn't the same guy that we have previously identified as Michael," Mills says as he reaches for his phone. "Ryan snapped a picture through the window. He was looking around, even hopped your patio and was pushing against the plywood. Here," he says turning the phone around so that Raine can look at it.

I look at the picture, hard. Then a little harder. "That's not a guy," I say, my anger boiling up to the surface. I squint, looking at it a little more. She's familiar, but…

"I'm gonna fucking kill her," Addison barks.

Raine can barely get a word out before Addison is grabbing her phone. She presses a couple of buttons. Then holds it to her ear.

"Jess, it's Addie."

Jess… Jess… I notice Peacock sits up a little straighter, paying more attention now. "No, no I'm fine, yes, they're fine too, listen, I need you to do me a huge fucking favor, like right this minute." There's a pause. "I need you to go to my condo. I will call and tell the doorman to let you into my apartment. I need you to let me know if you notice anything wrong, missing, damaged or...yes, no, yup. Alright, yes, call me once you're there...okay, thank you Jess." She hangs up.

"Mind cluing the rest of us in on what you know, love," I growl at her.

"That, in the picture," she gestures to the picture in Mills' hand, "That's Sam."

chapter
22
raine

Dex practically dumps me on the floor in his attempt to get up. "Dex?" I squeak as he stomps off of the bus.

"Who the hell is Sam?" I turn to Addison. There is a loud noise outside then something hits the side of the bus.

She sighs. "Dex met her in San Diego, she was a friend of mine who came to the concert. She and Dex met, she threw herself at him and...well...he took her bait."

"Oh! Oh...So she's the one that destroyed my apartment?"

"We don't know that yet," Mills answers my question.

"Shit," I say as I stand up and go as quick as I can, flying down the steps, and off of the bus. Dex is walking away from the bus. A billow of smoke in his path. I run as quickly as I can toward him. "Dex."

He throws his hands up and keeps walking.

"What's going on?" I hear Kyle as he approaches. He's carrying a couple bags of stuff from inside the store.

I nod in the direction of the bus. "They'll explain it. I have to go after..." I don't need to finish my sentence before Kyle nods, walking away and onto the bus.

Dex has stopped at the edge of the parking lot. I move quickly to catch up to him. "Don't come any closer."

"That's not how this works, Dex, you know that."

"Well, now it does." He hangs his head.

"What the fuck does that mean?"

He doesn't answer me and I make moves towards him. "Stop," he commands. His voice has that power over me and I stop dead in my tracks.

"Don't do this," I breathe. "Don't shut me out. We talk about this, Dex."

"If that cunt is responsible for your apartment, I will never forgive myself."

"We don't know that, bubba, we don't know if it was her, or Michael, or someone else entirely. Why are you being like this? I'm not mad at you, even if she's the one responsible for it. We both have pasts, it's a part of who we are, there's nothing we can do about it except move forward." I take a step toward him and he doesn't stop me so I take another step in his direction.

He turns on me, throwing away his cigarette as he charges toward me. His hand splays wide over my face, fingertips sliding along my features. "I'm poisonous. I will forever fuck up everything good that comes into my life. I refuse to fuck you up too." He side steps me and walks back toward the bus.

"Dex!" I shout after him, but he keeps walking. "Dex!" I cry out and he ignores me. "Damn it, Dex, what the fuck are you doing? Are you fucking insane? If you think this changes anything about how I feel about you, you can go fuck yourself," I shout at him. He finally slows and stops, hanging his head.

I back up to the curb he was standing at and sit down, wrapping my arms around my legs. I can't stop the uncontrollable sobs that are tearing apart my body, my heart and my soul.

Dex never came over to me. In fact, he walked on board the band's bus and packed a bag before climbing on board the crew's bus. He didn't say a word to me, or to anyone else in the process. I climbed into my rack and curled in on myself.

When we arrived in Orlando, I got a room by myself. Addison tried on numerous occasions to talk to me. I'm sure she, better than anyone, could understand what I was going through, but I didn't want to get into it. When I told her I wasn't going to the show, she didn't press the situation any.

I decided, after Dex moved buses, that I needed to give him some space, some time. He needs to sort through his shit before we can even begin discussing what happened.

Rusty kept me up to date on what was happening with my apartment. I'd finally been shown pictures of everything. It was quite possibly the second worst experience of my entire life. Though the result was better having seen it in pictures versus in person. Mills had filed the insurance claim and the appliances, as well as painting and wall repair, was being handled by the complex. Once the money from the insurance company comes in, I will have to pay them for the damage done. It was after that that Rusty told me he had a crew ready to go in and trash anything that was damaged, destroyed or otherwise unusable. Which, from what Ryan had told him, there wasn't much that was going to be salvageable. I told him to trash everything.

I cried myself to sleep that night.

In the course of twenty-four hours, I've lost my apartment, I've lost my boyfriend, I've lost everything I've ever worked for.

Friday morning, I booked airfare back to LA. I told Addison that there was too much going on back home, with my apartment and everything that I needed to head out early. She assured me that it was no problem and that she'd send over the details on the flight to Denver after the break. Around noon, I called Cami and filled her in on everything that had happened with my apartment, with Sam and of course with Dex. I told her that I would be leaving for the airport in a couple of hours. She tried to talk me into staying, but agreed that I needed to deal with my stuff back in LA and the sooner I could deal with that, the easier it would make it to return to the tour in twelve days.

Mills refuses to let me take a cab to the airport. Telling me that with everything that has happened, he wants me to be escorted there. I didn't have it in me to argue with him about it. Despite the fact that most of the band and crew had gone to Disney early this morning, Mills was making arrangements. I don't know if Dex went along and I didn't ask either. It's been nearly two days without a word from him and I think I know where I stand with him. Not that it makes it easy, in fact, it takes all the energy and strength I have to put on a brave face long enough to make it into the car and to the airport.

dex

"Come on, Raine, open up. Please."

I keep pounding on the door, eventually I'll annoy her enough that she'll answer. I've fucked up, yet again, royally. Though I doubt an apology from me is going to be enough to set things straight between the two of us.

Pound, pound, pound. "Come on, glowbug, please, open the damn door. I need to talk to you."

The hallway is empty. Everyone has gone to Disney, including the crew. I texted Kyle who said that Raine hadn't gone along, so she should be here. "Please, Raine, open the door." I bang my head against it before turning around and sliding my ass down the door to sit in front of it. She can't go anywhere without running into me and it doesn't stop me from bouncing my head off of the door every few minutes reminding her that I'm still sitting outside her door.

"Dude, wake up."

"Wha...oh crap,"

Raine...

I stand up and turn around, before I can knock Beck stops me. "She's not in there."

"Where the fuck did she go?"

"You don't know?"

"What don't I know? Beck..."

"She went home," he says stoically.

"Home?" I breathe, confused. "When?"

"Her flight left twenty minutes ago." I deflate. "What the fuck did you expect, bro? After what happened Wednesday night, did you honestly think she'd stay around here? Her house has been fucking destroyed, by one of your cunts, mind you, and you want her to stick around while you walk around with your head up your ass."

I slam Beck into the wall. "You don't know jack fucking shit."

"Really? Because we've all fucking seen it, Dex. We witnessed what you did Wednesday night. I'm pretty sure she told you that your past doesn't matter to her and you fucking pushed her away. All she ever fucking did was love you and look at what you've done."

Rage and the urge to knock him the fuck out courses through me until I realize that he's fucking right.

The elevator chimes and I make a dash for it, standing off to the side while the guys step off. Before it closes, I slide in and push L. "Dex!" a bunch of people shout as the door closes and descends into the lobby.

chapter
23
raine

"Hi, you must be Ryan?" I say to the strange man standing in my apartment.

"Hi Raine, yup, I'm Ryan." We shake hands. I got over the shock of my apartment from having seen the pictures. Though my kitchen is barren of appliances and my furniture is piled in the middle of the living room. The paint appears to be gone from the walls and the apartment smells like fresh paint.

"I don't know how to thank you for staying here," I tell him, fighting another emotional crying jag. It's all I pretty much did on the plane ride home.

"It's no problem. I haven't been able to stay here the last two nights, because there are no appliances and the water is shut off. Security is keeping an eye on the place. They have a guy walking or biking past every twenty minutes or so and then at night they have one stationed here inside. I hope you hadn't planned on staying here?"

"No, I'm going to check into a hotel after I talk with the complex about my lease."

He nods his understanding. "The furniture in here wasn't touched too bad, your bedroom is another story. We've gotten rid of just about everything in there. I imagine by tomorrow it will be empty for you."

"Thank you so much for all you've done."

He smiles widely at me. In another world, I may have found him attractive, but I can't even begin to fathom that idea at the moment.

I take a few minutes and wander around my now bare apartment. Ryan leaves with me, locking the door and we nod to the security guy. Ryan flags him down so that he can introduce me to him and the guy is nice enough and tells me that he'll pass along the information to the rest of the staff.

I walk around to the leasing office and end up spending more than thirty minutes with the manager. They don't want to let me out of my lease without a fuss. I told them that it's unsafe for me to live there anymore and that I have police reports and documentation to back that up. When I tell her that the apartment will be available by tomorrow, it gives her enough time to re-rent the apartment before next month. She also tells me that my security deposit will be returned because the damages have already been paid for.

"Who paid for it?"

She looks in my folder. "A gentleman by the name of Mills."

My heart sinks. "He didn't have to do that," I whisper. I vow to send him a text message after leaving here.

We talk for a couple more minutes and I tell her that I will hand in the keys by Monday morning.

After leaving her office, I sit in my car and text Mills.

Raine to Mills: Thank you for covering the appliances in my apartment. I will pay you back as soon as the insurance money comes in. X Raine

Mills to Raine: I didn't pay for it, Dex did.

"What?" I breathe.

Raine to Mills: Your name was on the information they have?

Mills to Raine: My name is on most dealings with the bands finances. It's part of what I do. Glad you made it home safe. How's the apartment coming?

Raine to Mills: Oh, well thank you for taking care of it. Apartment is nearly empty, Ryan isn't staying anymore, can't, no appliances or running water. Should be empty by tomorrow. Turning in the keys on Monday.

Mills to Raine: Where will you go now?

Raine to Mills: *shrug* not sure yet. Need to find a new apartment.

Mills to Raine: Addison's offer stands.

Raine to Mills: I'll think about it, thanks again.

Mills to Raine: I know you're hurt and upset, but I feel it's important to tell you that Dex is missing.

Raine to Mills: WTF as of when?

Mills to Raine: about half an hour after your flight took off. We know he's here in Orlando, but unsure of where.

Raine to Mills: Keep me posted.

Mills to Raine: Will do.

I throw my phone on the dash and take off out of the parking lot. It's four o'clock so I head for the office.

When I arrive, I take the express elevator up to the top floor. When I round the corner I can see Cami in her office.

"I was wondering if I'd see you today. Sit," she says and I take the seat in front of her desk while she gets up to close the door. "How are you?"

"A fucking mess," I tell her honestly.

"I can imagine."

"I need to discuss an advance on my salary."

"No discussion needed. What do you need?" she asks as she takes a seat.

"I need to move. I need to buy all new furniture, clothes, things like that." Tears well in my eyes, the breakdown that I know has been coming threatens and in front of my boss. "I have no idea how I'm going to pay it back, but…I don't know what else to do."

She stands and comes around her desk, bringing a box of tissues with her. She sits on the edge of her desk and holds out the box to me. I pull a couple of Kleenexes from the box and wipe my eyes.

"You've been around me long enough to know that I look after my own, regardless. If you keep going the way you are with what you've been doing with 69 Bottles, you'll be able to pay it back in no time at all. But until then, I'll deduct twenty-five dollars a paycheck."

"Cami, I…"

"Hush." She gives me a smile, "I'd do it for anyone who works in this building. Use your credit card. I'll authorize all your charges and we'll pay for them. I've made reservations for you at the Hyatt downtown. It's one of their studio rooms so you'll have a kitchen and it's close to shopping and dining."

I start to cry a little harder.

"It's reserved through the Wednesday you're supposed to leave for Denver. After that, we'll go from there. Do you have your car?" I nod. "Okay, so you're good on transportation and when you find an apartment we'll get what you need for your deposits, provided you can't use the credit card to do it. But right now, I want you to go, get yourself checked in, get your clothes to the laundry, and take a deep breath. It's all going to work out. One tiny step at a time."

"I don't know how to thank you."

She smiles at me. "Like I said, we take care of our own." She reaches onto her desk for something, and comes back with an envelope. "I was hoping you'd come by." She hands me the envelope. It's not full, but it's not thin either. "There's two thousand in cash…"

"Cami, I can't…"

"You can, and you will. Use this for food, gas, take care of your last minute bills for your apartment, whatever it is that you need."

"That was all paid for by my living stipend, I don't need this much cash."

She waves it off like it's nothing. "Just keep it. You never know when you'll need it. Payday is next week, by then you'll be good. Living in a hotel can be expensive." She runs a hand through her hair. "Believe me, I know." She winks.

I try to smile.

"Come here," she says and I stand up. She hugs me hard. "It will all be alright, believe me." She squeezes one more time then lets me go. "So what's going on with Dex?"

I shrug, "Honestly, I have no idea. He hadn't talked to me since Wednesday night and I left without saying good-bye. I haven't heard from him since then."

Cami and I talked a little more before she dismissed me around five to go home to Jaden and Tristan. But not before inviting me for dinner. I declined, saying I wasn't going to be good company.

When I climbed back into my car I fought the breakdown that was threatening me. I needed to keep it together just long enough to get checked in, get the door shut and then I was free.

I drove, painfully slow, through LA rush hour traffic to get to the Hyatt.

"Raine Montgomery."

"Oh yes, we were expecting you." She moves quickly in getting my keys for me and telling the bellhop with my luggage the room number. He takes off before I do for my room.

I sign the check in slip and she directs me to the elevators for my room.

Almost there.

As I reach my floor and round the corner the bellhop that had my luggage is coming toward me with an empty cart. I palm him a twenty and thank him before disappearing into my room. The minute the door shuts, I fall against it and slide down into complete and utter darkness.

chapter
24
dex

Alcohol…
Drugs…
Alcohol…
Pain…
Pain is the best medicine.
Pain cures more than it causes.

The hum of the tattoo needle fires up for about the hundredth time since sitting down in this chair more than two hours ago.

Alcohol was my goal.

Tattoo shop across the street…that's where I ended up.

The place was clean, the portfolios were nice, the dude exceptional and more than capable and willing to put me in the chair.

I've decided that there is someplace far more sensitive than one's ribs. The breast bone, collar bone and neck. I knew that there was a reason I'd been saving this spot. But until I walked in here, I had no idea why.

As I watch him go to work, he's wrapping up. Nearly done. Soon the endorphins will take over and I'll be able to walk out of here.

She left.

She packed her stuff and left.

Do I blame her?

Fuck no.

I put my head back against the chair and close my eyes.

I can still see her, curled up, arms around her legs, sitting on the curb. I knew I needed to go to her, but I knew then that I'd damaged things. I'd hurt her, I'd upset her. I needed to pull my poisonous ass away from her before I completely shattered her. But in reality, I poisoned her more by walking onto that other bus. I realized the moment my head hit the rack that I wasn't where I wanted to be, only where I thought I wanted, thought I needed. What I needed then and need even more now, is the reason I'm in this chair.

My phone buzzes with a text, probably the thousandth one I've received since sitting in this chair. Fuck 'em, whoever they are.

I hiss through my teeth as he cuts in a little deeper, running over already torn up flesh. I soak it up. Let the pain radiate outward, out across my body, to my fingertips and toes.

The doors on the elevator open.

"Jesus, what the fuck happened to you?" Beck scolds me.

"Not a fucking thing."

"Then what's with the…another one?"

"Fuck off."

"Which one was it this time?" he asks.

"Raine," is all I tell him.

"No drugs?" he asks, a little shocked.

I shake my head. No, my glowbug deserves better than that, but I keep that part to myself.

"Are you sober?" he asks.

"As a fucking rock. I just want to sleep," I tell him as I swipe my card key and my door beeps.

"She's back in LA," he tells me as I step over the threshold.

"Good," I say and I shut the door in his face.

I pull off my shirt, then peel back the bandage, just enough to look at it one more time, then cover it back up. I shed my jeans and boots before collapsing onto my bed. Holding onto the pillow, wishing I was holding on to my girl instead.

Three o'clock Saturday, my phone rings.

"Hey bro," I say into the phone.

"What's going on?"

"My life sucks," I say simply.

"Want to talk about it?"

"Not particularly. What's up, Derek?"

"Well, I know you guys are on break next week, right?"

"Yeah…?"

"Well, I have to go to Vegas next week for work. Cotah is coming with me, I'm wondering if you and Raine would want to join us?"

Shit, uh…

"I own the penthouse on top of the Cosmo." he interjects before I can come up with anything.

"Good god."

Derek laughs. "I have a private playroom. You know, if you and Raine want to work on some things."

Just hearing him say her name makes my heart hurt. "Yeah, about that…"

"I already know. The girls have been talking. Well, enough for Cotah to deduce that Raine was back in LA and your ass is stuck in Miami. What do you have…two shows down there before you can bail?"

"Yup," I grumble into the phone.

"Are you going after her?"

"You bet your sweet ass I am."

"Good, my plane will be ready at Kendall-Tamiami Executive Airport starting at 11 p.m., on Sunday night. When you get there, it will take you to Los Angeles. I'll have a car there waiting for you."

"Why?" I choke out.

"Because, I ran after Cotah once and it was the best fucking decision of my life. But before I could go after her, I had to fly my ass all the way to Paris first. So, if what I saw between the two of you is true, you're crawling out of your fucking skin right now because you can't do a fucking thing about it."

I run my hand through my hair. "That's an understatement," I admit to him.

"I also happen to know, because Cami is one of my closest friends, that she is staying at the Hyatt downtown in room nine-twenty-one. When you're done there, and you're done realizing what an idiot you are, drive your happy ass back to the airport and my plane will bring you guys to Vegas."

"Fuck. You have to at least let me pay you back."

I hear him chuckle. "We can discuss the details later."

"I need one more favor from you," I tell him.

"You name it, you got it."

"I bought a ring, in Nashville."

He chuckles. "I'm all ears," he tells me and I launch into my plan.

"What are you waiting for?" Talon asks me.

"I have got to shower for god's sake. I'm drenched," Addison laughs at me as I stand there all flustered and completely uncoordinated.

"There's a shower on the plane," Talon points out.

I shiver. "Fuck that shit. A stationary bus is one thing, but a moving airplane, fuck that." I smile.

Tonight's show was fucking amazing. They closed up the VIP list for tonight so that I could bail out as soon as possible. Everyone is anxious to get out of here tomorrow morning. They're flying back in the label's plane. I am flying back on Derek's jet.

I shiver with excitement and anticipation. I'm ready to see my glowbug. I miss her like crazy.

When I get into the bathroom, I look at my chest. The lines are still red and puffy, I went shirtless tonight since I tried with a shirt last night and though I soaked up the pain, it was too much with the drums and I shed it quick. I hoped and prayed Raine wasn't stalking me on YouTube. I didn't want her to see it before I really had a chance to show her myself.

I shower faster than is humanly possible and I'm dressed in record time. Grabbing my already packed bags, I say bye to the guys and Addie before Beck and Casey whisk me off to the airport.

As Derek promised, his plane is standing by, ready to take me back to LA.

chapter
25
dex

Ryan to Dex: She's arrived back at the hotel. She's turned in her keys.

Dex to Ryan: Thank you for keeping an eye on her.

Ryan to Dex: Anytime.

raine

Knock, knock, knock…

I walk to the door, turning the handle I open it, expecting to see a bellman with my laundry.

Instead, standing there, bracing himself against the door with muscled, t-shirt clad arms is Dex. My mouth waters seeing him again.

He doesn't give me a chance to say or do anything before he's coming at me, pushing me back until my back bumps into the wall of the entry way. His hands cup my face, holding me steady. Tears well in my eyes, his eyes too are full. Without a word, his lips land on mine. Stealing my breath instantly. The fire ignites in my veins. My hands wrap around his neck, pulling our bodies together. I can't pull him close enough to me. I'm practically climbing his body as mine melts into his. And I sob.

His thumbs wipe away the tears that are spilling freely down my cheeks as he pulls back. "Hi glowbug," he whispers. His voice is shaky and broken.

"Hi bubba," I tell him back.

All anger, angst, washed away in a single kiss.

"I'm sorry," he breathes against my lips before kissing me again. "I never wanted to hurt you." He kisses me gently. "I never imagined my past indiscretions would haunt me like they have. First with Kate in Phoenix, now you and Sam. Jesus, Raine, you deserve so much better than me. You don't need to deal with my past, not ever."

"Shut up," I tell him. He stares at me. "I knew what I was getting myself into in New York. I knew by DC that it didn't matter, that I could and would handle anything you could throw at me. By Nashville I was head over heels. When I went after you that night, I knew. I knew that seeing Sam in that picture was the definition of fucked up for you. You felt like you betrayed me, like you owed me something more than you could possibly ever give me. Dex, I went after you because your past is your past. If we let it ruin whatever future we may have together, then we've learned nothing from it. You accepted my being raped." I watch as his eyes close and tears drip down his cheeks. "You accepted the fact that I was broken inside. I accepted your addictions, I accepted your past, I accepted the fact that you have a long list of women who've preceded me, but I also knew then, like I know now, that I am the first and only woman who's ever made you want to be a better man, made you realize that your addiction doesn't have to rule your life and more importantly, I know that I'm the only woman who you've ever loved."

"Only you," he breathes out before his lips land once again on mine. "I need you. I went to your room Friday. I sat there banging on your door for hours. No one had told me you'd left. By the time I'd found out, you were gone."

"I know," I tell him.

"You know?" he cocks his head at me.

"I chatted with Mills after arriving back in LA. He told me that you'd run off and that you'd been gone for a long time, but that he knew you were still in Orlando, just not where."

"Did you know I was coming?"

I shake my head. "No. I thought you were a staff member bringing back my laundry."

He smiles.

"How'd you get here anyway?"

He just smirks and doesn't answer. His answer is simply to kiss me again, only to have it broken by a knock at the door. "That would be my laundry," I say with a smirk as I step out from underneath him, opening the door. "Thanks," I tell the gentleman on the other side of the door. I slide him a tip and close the door. Dex takes the laundry bag from my hand and replaces it with his own as he leads me into the suite.

He sets the bag on the little table in the kitchen. "That can wait." he says as he turns back to me. "Is it really this easy?" he asks me.

"What do you mean?" I ask.

"Do you really forgive me for what I did?"

"There's nothing to forgive, Dex. I knew you needed time. I was more than willing to give it to you, but..."

"Then why'd you leave?" he interrupts.

"Because I needed to deal with my apartment and," I shrug, "I was starting to believe that we were really over. After being handed my own keys, I just assumed that you needed distance from me. But then you never came to talk to me, you never so much as bothered to check and see if I was okay. No texts, no phone calls, no nothing. What else was I supposed to think, Dex?"

He brushes a stray hair from my face, then he repeats the splayed hand routine, allowing his finger tips to touch my face lightly. I melt.

"It was honestly all too much to handle. Between my apartment, Andrew, then the whole Sam thing, Dex, honestly I thought I was imploding. If I didn't try to get some order back into the chaos that had become my life, I was going to lose it completely. The only thing I knew I could take care of was my apartment. Talking to you was impossible, I didn't know how to do it and I certainly wasn't going to push it if you weren't ready."

"I'm sorry. I should have put you on a plane before the Atlanta show. Gotten you back to LA to deal with your apartment. I tried to just take care of it all myself, but I realized so much of what I was doing was without your opinion, your consent, had I asked, maybe it wouldn't have been such a burden on you."

I back away from him and sit down on the bed. "I know you paid for the appliances and repairs to the apartment," I whisper.

'How'd...?"

"I asked the leasing manager. She said that someone named Mills had paid for it. When I thanked Mills, which is how I found out about you knocking on my hotel room door, he said it wasn't him, that you'd done it," I tell him. "I was angry at first, but then I realized why it was that you were doing it."

"Why was that?"

I smile at him. "You were trying to take control, trying to take the burden and worry out of my hands."

"I felt it was my responsibility to handle it, especially after seeing that picture of Sam."

I smile at him again. "It was in that moment that I realized that there was nothing to forgive. I figured one of two things was going to happen." I tell him, "one - exactly what happened, you showing up here, though I'm curious how you found out where I was?" I raise an eyebrow at him.

"What's the second?" He raises his head, a little cocky, so I know he won't tell me his source until I finish my thought.

I scowl at him. "I'd end up on that plane to Denver next week and you'd have no choice but to see me."

He chuckles. "There is no way in hell I'd have waited that long. I'd already booked airfare for this morning when I got a call from a good friend."

I raise an eyebrow. "Who?"

"Derek. He said that you'd talked to Cotah."

"That little..."

"Now now, glowbug, you do understand that in their relationship, she can hide nothing from him, correct?"

I huff, "Yes."

He chuckles, "He'd gotten all the information he needed from Cami. They're both incurable romantics. He chased Dacotah across the globe to bring her back, do you honestly think he'd let us fall apart like that? He waited to call me after he'd made arrangements for his jet to meet me last night after the show and fly me back here. Then he pretty much ordered me to get you and bring you to Vegas."

I look at him with equal parts shock and confusion. "Vegas? Why Vegas?"

He gives me a knowing smirk. "He has business to attend to, he thought we needed a getaway..." He doesn't need to say anything further and a shiver of excitement slides up my spine, causing my nipples to harden.

"What are we waiting for?"

He cocks his head at me. "So eager?"

I laugh, "Maybe a little."

"Well, I have something else in mind first," he says in such a way that I slide to the floor, right off the bed and onto my knees. Contrite and at his feet.

I feel his hand come to my chin, raising my eyes to meet his. "While I value your willingness to submit to me, now is not that time. I need you, not your submission."

I stand up and he pulls me into a strong deep kiss unlike anything I've ever felt from him before and I shiver with anticipation as his hands slide over my now hard nipples. My hands go to his chest, ready to rake my fingernails down but he hisses first and grabs my wrists, pulling them back and releasing my lips.

"What's wrong?" I ask, truly concerned.

He has a knowing smile on his face. He releases my wrists and goes for the hem of his shirt and he pulls it up and over his head.

I hiss through my teeth and fall back on the bed. Stunned into silence by what I'm looking at.

chapter
26
raine

Tattooed on his chest, over his breastbone, onto his left peck, up to his shoulder and a little onto his neck is a massive spider web. The web has bright blue drops on it, like drops of rain. In the lines of the web there are words. I regain my composure enough to stand up and look closer at it.

It says…

It's not about waiting for the storm to pass, it's about learning to dance in the Raine.

"Because you've caught me in your web," he says softly.

I start to cry again. I reach out with my left hand to touch my name gently. "You're everything to me," he breathes before capturing my hand in his and bringing it to his lips. "Before you left, I knew that I was going to do whatever it took to get you back." He lowers himself to the floor. "I mean it this time." He reaches into his pocket. "I never want to spend another minute without you in my life. I will spend every moment earning your love, your trust, your desire, your devotion and your love. I will spend all my time showing you that I am worthy of what's in your heart, in your mind and in your soul. Raine Montgomery, will you marry me?"

He holds up a beautiful ring, with a heart cut diamond set on a platinum band, and my eyes go back to his, glossy with tears. "Yes."

He quickly slides the ring on my finger and stands up. His lips capture mine quickly before he lays me out on the bed and hovers over me. His lips melt into mine and our tongues dance with each other as love, devotion, passion, desperation and adoration pour into me. I kiss him back with all that and so much more. He moans into my mouth before pulling back and kissing along my jaw, down my neck until he comes into contact with my t-shirt. His hands quickly shift to pushing up my shirt. I hiss.

He pulls back. "What's wrong?" I can't help the smirk and the pointing with my eyes downward.

dex

I couldn't wrap my head around what would cause her to hiss, then she directed me downward with a smirk.

"Jesus…" I breathe out. I rear up, quickly pulling down her pants. I look at it, then back at her, then back at the new ink she's added to her body.

A pair of grey, looking like plated steel, drumsticks crossed slightly with a ribbon winding around them. On the drumstick, the word 'bubba' is written, making it looked stamped into the stick. The ribbon wrapped around the sticks is blue, giving it a glowing appearance, and in the center of the ribbon, inside of it, it says one word. "Glowbug," I say out loud.

"You're not the only person who takes comfort in pain therapy," she tells me as I lean down and gently kiss around the sticks that are on her left hip, pointing downward toward her pelvis and nearly reaching her ribs.

While my lips are busy kissing along her new ink, my hands are busy trying to pull her pants off. My desire to be inside of her has just catapulted outside of this universe. She chuckles when I start to have trouble and have to pull away from kissing her in order to get them off. She kicks off her flip-flops just as I pull her pants off of her feet.

I quickly climb back up her body, grabbing her hand and pulling her up so that I can pull her t-shirt off and then finally undo her bra, freeing her perfectly gorgeous tits for my mouth's consumption and I waste no time sucking one of her dark rose colored nipples into my mouth. My tongue flicks along the barbell running through it and she moans.

Her hands are not idle, as she tries desperately to free my cock from my jeans. Once the buttons are undone, I climb off of her and slide them down my legs and kick off my shoes. I stand before her, naked as she is and it's like I'm a virgin. Staring at a naked woman for the first time as I look at her, her hair spread out on the bed above her head. Her new tattoo seems to glow off of her skin, her whole body is alive as she squirms under my penetrating gaze.

She slides up on the bed, centering herself then she rolls over, pulling open the bedside drawer and I wonder what she's doing. That is until she pulls out the cuffs she'd bought. Seeing them sends a shiver up my spine. She stands up and comes to stand in front of me. She takes one of my hands in hers and she quickly wraps the cuff over my wrist. I cock my head at her. "Lay down," she commands me. Her voice, her tone, her everything has me complying with her and I lay down on the bed. "Arms above your head." Again, I raise my arms up and she quickly climbs on top of me, careful to avoid my chest as she wraps the cuff around the spindle of the headboard and then around my free wrist. Locking me to the bed.

She climbs back off of me. My cock is hard as fucking steel, immobile and at her mercy. She goes to the foot of the bed and grabs my ankles, pulling me down the bed. The comforter on the bed slides with me, making the action effortless for her. She smiles a satisfied smile before walking back toward the head of the bed. I watch as she reaches into the bedside table one more time and brings up something. I can't quite see it before she's straddling me again.

"Am I hurting you?"

"No," I answer her.

She reaches and tweaks my nipple, hard. "No, what?"

"No, Mistress," I correct myself and I watch as she shivers at the words I've used.

"Good boy," she says quickly before her hands are in front me, producing a mask, the one I'd used on her on the bus. "Close your eyes," she commands and I do. She puts the mask over my head, covering my eyes and I am plunged into complete and total darkness. "What is your safeword?" she asks.

"Sunshine, Mistress."

As soon as I'm settled, she slides off of me, and the lack of warmth causes me to shiver and a drop of pre-come to slide down my dick. She hasn't left the bed as I am leaning in her direction. Then her lips land on mine. The overwhelming sensation of not being able to see is a lot to handle and I moan into her mouth. She steals her moment to slide her tongue along mine. I feel her hand slide along my stomach, causing me to twitch. She smiles against my lip as her hand rides higher until she finds my nipple, rolling it between her fingers. I moan again and she lets my mouth go.

Being unable to see opens everything else up, including sounds, but she, with the exception of her breathing, is quiet as a mouse. The next thing I feel is a hot wet tongue sliding over my free nipple, near my fresh ink. The entire area is tender and sensitive making me groan with the pain that quickly burns out into pleasure.

She doesn't stop kissing me as she moves around my chest, quickly biting on my other nipple before moving south. Kiss, lick, bite, repeat. My cock twitches again and I feel another spurt of pre-come make its way down my shaft.

"Well well," she breathes and I feel the bed move again and she climbs off of it. I can't hear her move, but I can sense her, somehow, don't ask because I have no clue, but I know that she's standing at the foot of the bed.

"That is by far the sexiest thing I've ever seen in my life," she whines and I want to smile, but I keep my composure.

"Thank you, Mistress," I respond to her. I, unlike her, have seen training in action and though she's a natural at it, we both have a lot to learn.

I feel her tap me on the inside of my knees, indicating that she needs me to spread my legs.

I do and I feel the bed dip between my legs. Then her lips are licking and kissing their way up my thigh. Anticipation is making me crazy. Desperate and wanting to beg her to fuck my cock with her mouth, but I know better.

She bypasses my cock for my stomach. She's yet to lay a single finger on it and I'm dying. I whine.

That's when her warm hand wraps around my balls and she squeezes. "Fuck, I'm sorry," I cry out. She squeezes a little tighter, "I'm sorry, Mistress," I say and she squeezes once again before letting go.

"What do you want, pet?" she asks me. Hearing the term pet makes it nearly impossible for me to hang on to my orgasm.

"You, Mistress."

"How so?"

"I need you."

"Tell me what you want, pet."

"I want you to suck my cock, please, Mistress."

I feel her hands slide along the topside of my thighs, I can't see her but I can feel her warm breath against my shaft. Then without warning, her hot tongue sears along the underside of my dick and I erupt all over the place.

"Fuck me," Raine cries out right before her mouth wraps around the head of my cock and sucks me down. Swallowing the spurts that slide down her throat. I can't stop groaning and shaking as she milks my cock.

Finally when I stop coming, she doesn't stop sucking, determined to keep me hard. It doesn't take but a moment and I'm back to standing at full attention.

chapter
27
raine

Well, that was certainly unexpected. I crawl up Dex's body, still tethered to the bed. I need him inside me more than I need my next breath. I rub my pussy along his cock and he hisses through his teeth as my wet warmth registers. I lean up on one knee, giving me the ability to maneuver his cock and line it up with the opening of my sex. He moans as I slide the head in my wetness, preparing him to slide inside me.

That's when I line him up and slowly adjust so that I can slide down on top of him. The moment the head of his cock breaks through that outer barrier, I shiver. "Ah fuck," I cry out. He gently pushes himself up inside me and it's at that moment I know he's trying to take back his control. It's also when I realize that I won't ever make a very good top. That my place is on the bottom and at his feet. I push myself down and hold him down while I reach up to remove his blindfold.

He blinks as the light hits his eyes and they adjust. I can't help but kiss him in that moment. I reach up to the cuffs and unbuckle one of them. "I need your hands on me, please," I beg him, trying to indicate to him that I need him to take back control. He smiles as his wrist is freed and I push the cuff through the bar.

He brings his arms down and I sit up, taking him in deeper than I ever have before. "Fuck," I moan, arching my back, sucking him in deeper, my breasts are pushed forward and he knows exactly what I need when his hands come up to cup my tits in his hands. His fingers immediately find my nipples and roll them, tugging on the barbells in the process. My eyes roll up into my head as I start to move on his shaft. My hands work to undo the other cuff from his wrist. "I can't top you," I breathe.

"Sure you can, you just don't want to right now," he answers as the cuff falls away and I toss it on the floor. "You see, princess, you needed that. You needed to know that you could control the situation."

"And you needed to know that you could give yourself over."

"Turn around," he orders and that missing shiver of submission slides through me. "Carefully."

In an awkward twist, I manage to get myself turned around and I'm leaning forward, my hands on his thighs for balance. His hand slides up my back, causing a shiver and my back to arch.

"Now, lay back," he says sternly. I push myself up his shaft so that I can make the transition without causing myself pain. I lean back, my hands on his chest and he growls. I pull my hand away quickly remembering his ink.

"I'm sorry."

"Shh, it's alright. Shift your feet, so they're in front of you."

Again in another awkward move I manage to switch my feet around and get them under me so that I can hold myself above his hips. He then moves my hands, causing me to lie back on his chest. I rest my head against the right side so that I'm not against his fresh ink. Then his hands slide up my body, once again cupping my breasts as he gets his feet under him, lifting me up. I steady myself on my feet, giving me added leverage. Once he notices the shift in the weight, he starts the slide of his cock in and out of my pussy and I'm ready to explode. He's so deep, the head of his dick sliding along that perfect sweet spot. His hands continue to work my nipples between his fingers, until one comes away, the one opposite my new ink, and it slides down my stomach, finding that little patch of hair before finding my clit.

His hand on my nipple, his cock pounding into me and his fingers stroking my clit send me soaring over the edge and I explode around him. "That's my girl." His breathing is ragged and harsh in my ear as his thrusting increases inside me until my orgasm subsides and he pulls himself free of my pussy, quickly flipping us onto our sides where he hitches my leg up and quickly slides back inside.

"Fuck, Dex," I cry out as he continues assaulting my sex, bringing me back to the brink of another orgasm.

"My goal is to make you come in every position I can think of right now," he growls into my ear. "And I don't care how many times I have to come to do it."

Shivers of excitement run through me and his hand tugs on my nipple hard at the same moment his finger presses into my clit. My legs begin to shake with his touch. I can't stop it; the orgasm he's working me up to is intense. I cry out.

He pounds into me three more times before I explode, sending my orgasm from my body, his favorite thing to make me do. "Oh fuck!" he moans and his hand strokes at my clit ferociously, drawing out my orgasm that much more as I feel him pouring himself into me.

After a few heartbeats, he slows. My legs are still shaking with my orgasm and he extracts his still hard cock from my body before rolling me onto my back. Then he slides in between my legs. On top of me, looking at me. "There are a thousand and one more positions I can think of, but right now, I need to look into your eyes," he whispers as his cock slips inside me and his lips land on mine.

"Ahh!"

He steals his chance and slides his tongue inside my mouth. I can feel him rubbing along my tattoo and if it weren't for the fact that I'm afraid of scarring, I wouldn't mind the lick of pain. "Dex?"

"Hmm," he says with lust filled eyes.

"My ink."

"Shit," he says as he scrambles onto his hands, barely missing a beat as he slams into me. My eyes roll up. He takes to licking and kissing along my nearly healed, but still purple bite marks. Then he kisses his way over to a nipple that he pulls gently into his mouth. After having tugged and pulled, the softness is a welcome change. I run my hand through his hair and hold him there. Our eyes meet.

The look in his eyes causes my eyes to roll up once again.

"Look at me." His soft command brings my eyes back to focus on him as he takes my nipple back in his mouth. He tugs and pulls on it, stressing it out before letting it bounce back. I watch as his tongue swirls around it.

"That is so fucking sexy," I say as he pounds into me a little harder.

His cock never stops moving as he switches sides, treating the other nipple with the same love and tenderness as the first. I watch him again, this time my orgasm is near its peak and he knows it. His thrusting increases and I wrap my legs around him, holding him to me. "Come for me, bubba. Please," I mewl and he thrusts harder once, twice and finally stilling on the third as he explodes.

Feeling his come filling me sends me over the edge as he grinds out the last drops of his orgasm.

chapter
28
raine

"I'm going to check out of the hotel," I tell Cami.

"Why?"

"Um, Dex is taking me to Vegas to see Derek and Dacotah."

She laughs. "So he did find you."

I look at Dex. "Did you honestly think he wouldn't?" I laugh.

"No, I knew he would."

"Thanks for telling Derek where to find me," I tell her.

"I would have told Dex too, but he never called."

I laugh again. "That's because Derek beat you to the punch."

"Good. Go have fun and don't check out."

"It's a waste of a room."

"Don't worry about it. Just take what you need with you to Vegas and leave the rest there. How long are you guys staying?" she asks.

I look at Dex who shrugs. "I don't know, a couple of days maybe."

"Nah, leave your stuff there. Take what you need and go have some fun. You deserve it."

"Thanks Cami."

"I'll talk with Derek and Tristan, maybe him, Jaden and I can pop over there."

"That would be awesome. I haven't seen J-Man in a while."

"Alright, you better get going."

"Thanks again," I tell her and we hang up.

"She said to leave my stuff here. Just take what I need for Vegas and call it good," I tell him.

"That's fine, I would have paid to keep the room going, you have a lot of stuff here," he tells me as he looks around the room.

"It isn't anymore than I had on the bus, just that it's scattered around. Until a couple of hours ago, I was staying here until next week."

He pauses what he's doing. "Why next week?"

"Or until I can find a new place to live. I turned in my keys this morning. They let me out of my lease." I watch as relief washes over his features. "Because you paid for the appliances, I get my security deposit back, but probably not for forty-five days."

"Your insurance money should be in before then," he says as he sits down on the bed. "I want to help you."

I sigh. "I've already gone to Cami. She's allowing me the use of my company card to refurnish and find an apartment."

"Do you have to pay it back?"

"Yes," I say hesitantly. "Why wouldn't I?"

"Well, what if you just moved in with me?"

I stop and sit in the chair, unsure of what to say.

"Hey, you just agreed to marry me," he smirks.

"Well, there is that."

He frowns. "Do you take it back?"

I smile. "No. It's just," I look at my hand and the ring, "I'm not used to it."

"We've practically been living together for the last couple weeks, sharing a hotel room, a bunk on the bus, how much different would it really be?" he asks.

"Fair point. Can we talk about it after the tour?" I ask.

He stands and walks over toward me. He leans down and kisses my forehead. "That's probably a good idea."

"Why's that?" I challenge.

He chuckles. "Because I live in a tiny ass studio apartment."

I laugh, "You're joking right?"

He laughs with me, "No, I'm not. We settled out here shortly before the tour. I think we all took the first thing we could find because we had like three weeks before the tour started. Talon might still be in his van for all I know."

I want to roll my eyes. "Well, then it's a good thing we're going to Vegas," I giggle and I go back to packing up my bag.

A few minutes later I'm packed and ready to go. "Is everything going to be safe here?"

"No one knows this is where you're staying and you can tell them downstairs that you're leaving for a few days and that you don't need maid service and to contact you if anyone enters your room. These hotels down here have pretty strict security because of their clientele," he tells me with confidence.

"Well, alright then. Let's do that."

Twenty minutes later we're in a rental car that Derek rented for Dex to get him here and back to the airport. "How'd you ditch the crew?" I ask when we're on our way.

He laughs. "I pretty much told them to fuck off. I didn't need an audience and I certainly didn't want someone standing around waiting for me to come out. To be honest, I wasn't sure if you were going to come with me today, or at all."

I give him a sad smile and he takes my hand and puts it on his lap. "I was afraid I'd have to board that plane next week and have to watch you go back to your old self," I tell him, trying to maintain open communication with him.

"I don't think I can ever apologize enough for the way I handled the other night. I would have run after you right away if I could have, in fact, I nearly had."

"You could have just called."

He smiles and looks at me. "No, I couldn't."

"Why?" I ask as he comes to a stoplight before getting on the highway.

"Because I needed to be able to look into your eyes when I apologized."

"Who are you and what have you done with Dex?" I tease him.

"I left him back in New York," he says with a straight face. "I left him the moment I realized I was in love with you."

"In New York?" I can't hide my shock.

"I'm pretty sure I fell in love with you the moment you had that waitress dump that drink over my head." He squeezes my hand on his lap.

"Oh my god," I giggle.

"Then I fell more in love with you the moment your knee connected with my balls."

"You're sick." I laugh a little harder.

"Nah," he looks over at me briefly, "I just figured out what I wanted. What I needed."

"You're gonna make me cry," I tell him.

"Please don't do that. I think we've done enough of that." He smiles with a brief look in my direction before looking back at the road.

About forty-five minutes later, after Los Angeles traffic, we arrive at the airfield and at Derek's plane. "I've never been on a plane this small before."

"This isn't small, glowbug."

"Yes, it is." I can't stop giggling with giddiness. He stops the car. "We're really going to Vegas?" I ask.

"Yup." He takes my hand and kisses it before climbing out of the car. I climb out after him and he grabs my bag. He left his with the plane.

Two and a half hours later we arrive at the Cosmopolitan in a limo. "Mr. Harris, Ms. Montgomery, if you'll please follow me." Dex and I fall in line behind a woman dressed in a skirt suit and she leads us through the sliding glass doors. "Mr. Hunter is expecting you. If you want to leave your bags with us, we'll see that it's delivered to Mr. Hunter's condo."

"Sure," Dex says as he hands over my bag to a gentleman dressed in livery.

"Mr. Hunter is waiting for you in here." She leads us into a back hallway and then finally into a mini ballroom where Derek and Dacotah are waiting at a table for us. I notice that Derek is dressed similar to Saturday night in a dress shirt and slacks and Cotah is wearing a cute sundress of pinks and greens.

"Hi guys," Derek says as he stands to meet us halfway. Cotah follows behind him and I hug her first.

"Hey girl," she says to me. "I'm glad you're here."

"Me too," I whisper back and release her, then Derek wraps his arms around me and Dex says hello to Cotah.

"Good to see you here," he tells me.

"You guys act like you thought I wouldn't come," I tease both of them.

They both shrug and Derek ushers us back to the table. Dex, being a gentleman, pulls out my chair for me to take a seat.

Once we're all seated, it's like we haven't missed a beat since Nashville.

I end up filling them in on what happened in Atlanta, then what happened with my apartment. I notice that Dex gets a little nervous when we're discussing it and I don't quite understand why that is, maybe it's just the memory of seeing Sam in that picture that bothers him the most. Then I notice Derek is a little edgy too and it doesn't seem to make much sense to me, but I brush it off and we move on in the conversation.

chapter
29
raine

"Is there something you guys want to do tonight?" Cotah asks as we finish up our dinner. I glance at my watch, it's just after seven in the evening.

I shrug. "I'm open, Dex?" I look to Dex, he shrugs too. "I guess we're no help. It's been a long few days, I'm not even sure if Dex has slept."

"I haven't, but I'm good." He squeezes my hand under the table.

"Why don't we retire upstairs? It's a great night out," Derek suggests. "We have plenty to drink."

"Sounds perfect to me," I say and Dex agrees.

"Perfect." Derek finishes off his wine and then stands up. "Follow us," he says with a smile and we do.

Once we come out of the hidden hallway, he hangs a left into a small elevator alcove. From here you can see into the Cosmopolitan's casino area. "I've never gambled," I say randomly.

"Never?" Dex raises an eyebrow at me.

"Nope." I smile.

"We just might have to change that," Derek says as he calls the elevator, which arrives immediately. He shows us how to enter in the code and hands Dex a card with the code written on it. "You cannot go anywhere on this elevator without that code or a keycard. The elevator opens into my condo and usually, once I retire for the evening, the elevator is locked by either myself upstairs or from down here if I call down."

The elevator takes off, faster than the one at Bold and I grab the railing for support. "I hate these things," I say, "at least the express ones. I'll sit through twenty floors at the office before I take the express up to Cami's office."

Derek chuckles. "That express elevator has been there a long time. I know Bobby insisted on it."

"You knew Bobby?"

"I did. He was a decent friend of mine. Not as good a friend as Cami and Tristan are, but decent enough. We had a couple of business investments together back when I first got started."

"I miss him," I say, again very random and open.

"That's right, you were his assistant too, up until his passing."

I give a sad smile. "I was. But I have to agree. I have a much better relationship with Cami than I ever did with Bobby."

That's when the elevator comes to a halt on his floor and the doors open. He ushers Dex, Cotah and I into the penthouse.

"Holy crap," I say as soon as I get a clear view of the room, but it's not the room that has my attention, it's the strip. "I've never been up this high on the strip before." Shut up, Raine.

Derek chuckles. "It's quite the view, that's for sure. What can I get you guys to drink?"

"I'd love a beer," Dex says. "Raine?"

I turn to Derek. "Wine would be great, white."

"You got it. Little one?"

"Yes, Sir," Cotah replies to him quickly.

"Why don't you take Dex and Raine onto the patio. I'll be there in a minute with drinks and then we can take the grand tour."

"Yes, Sir."

Cotah heads toward a door I don't see in the glass. "I'll be right there," I tell them and I stay back, following Derek into the kitchen.

"Everything all right?" Derek asks me.

"Two things," I say softly.

He smiles at me, "anything."

"Thank you for getting Dex to Los Angeles, and then bringing us here."

He cocks his head at me. "You're most welcome, sweetheart. I was once in Dex's shoes."

"I know and I don't know how to thank you for what you did."

"You being here is enough. Just relax, enjoy yourself. I imagine being on the road isn't easy, in fact I know it's not. There are months where I'm literally gone twenty-eight out of thirty days. I figured you and him could use some true R and R time."

"Thank you," I say again.

"You're welcome." He finishes pouring a couple glasses of wine then turns and grabs two beers out of the fridge. "You said there was two things?"

"I did. I noticed that you called Cotah little one and out of respect for you, I wanted to ask permission to speak to her."

He smiles very warmly at me then touches my cheek with affection. "You're very sweet to ask, but you don't ever need permission, unless we're upstairs. She is your friend, or at least I'd like to see you guys be friends, and they come with different rules. Cotah knows her rules, and you're free to talk openly with her about anything." He winks at me.

"Thank you for that, Sir." I smile at him and he nods. "What's upstairs?" I ask.

He pulls a Dex and raises his eyebrow. "Dex didn't tell you?" I shake my head. "I have a private playroom upstairs." A thrill runs through me. "You like that idea, don't you?"

"I do, Sir."

"You remind me so much of Cotah when I first met her. Willing and eager. I had to ask her so many times if it was really what she wanted or if she was doing it to please me. You know what she told me?" I shake my head and he smiles. "She didn't verbally tell me anything. She got down on her knees and presented herself to me. I knew then that it wasn't for me, that she enjoyed being submissive, despite knowing nothing about the lifestyle." I grab the two glasses of wine and Derek the beers and he leads me onto the patio. "One thing we learned to do very early on was communicate and to never be afraid of a safeword. She's used hers before, several times in fact, when I've pushed her too far. Sometimes it's easy to call it out of fear of an unknown, when you get too inside your own head, which is what I know happened a few times. But we'd talk it out and try again, many times, not that same night." He pushes open the door. "I learned that when we do scenes together, it is better for me to communicate with her some of the things I have in mind for her and I've learned what punishments work for her."

Dex and Dacotah join us then, listening to our conversation and Dacotah chimes in, "He never tells me what my punishments are unless he wants me to stew on them all day." She smiles at me.

"She's right. Tell them what your least favorite, most often given punishment is, little one?"

She shivers. "Ginger root."

"What's that do?" Dex asks the question I'm thinking.

"Pet?" Derek requests that she answer.

She shivers before doing so. "Peeled ginger root, when inserted in certain areas burns really bad."

I shudder just thinking about that.

"It's a superficial burn," Derek continues, "kind of like rubbing alcohol in a cut. It's very uncomfortable."

"And effective," she adds and I smile at that.

"What's your most common punishment, little one?"

She flinches. "Rice."

"Rice?" I ask. Dex smirks. He knows the answer to this one.

"Dex?" he asks, "Do I have your permission to show Raine what rice means?"

Dex looks at me then at Derek before answering, "Yes."

I kind of panic a little as Derek leads us back into the house and into the kitchen. He reaches into the cupboard and grabs a red box of rice, then proceeds to sprinkle it on the floor. I watch as there's a shift in power between Derek and Dex. "Kneel," Dex commands and on instinct without a second thought, I do.

Right. On. To. The. Rice. "Ow! Ow!"

"Effective," Dex says, but he pets my head and I lean into his touch.

Fuck, this really fucking hurts. I keep thinking over and over, but I do my best to not show it. But then I accidentally shift positions and the rice digs in further. "Ow," I whine.

Dex holds his hand out for me to take. "Up. You're not being punished," he says softly and I take his hand, rising up off of the rice. Brushing it off gently as I go.

"I don't like that," I say with a small smile.

"But it's a great lesson, to keep you in line," Dex says with a smirk.

"Yes, Sir," I say and he wraps his arms around me.

"Why don't you guys go back outside, I'll clean this up," Cotah says without hesitation. I pull myself back from Dex to see an approving exchange between Derek and her. "Can I be honest, Master?"

"Always."

"Since the rice was out, I thought if I cleaned it up, I could save myself from earlier."

"Ahh, and here I'd forgotten about that, little one."

I watch as her face falls and she lowers her head. "I'm sorry, Sir," she whispers.

"I know you are, little one. Clean it up, we can discuss it later."

"Yes, Master." She still has a sadness in her voice, but he approaches her and caresses her cheek.

The moment turns intimate and I turn away, snuggling into Dex.

chapter
30
dex

We all retired to the patio area after Dacotah was done cleaning up the rice. I won't lie, watching Raine react on instinct, not knowing what to expect gave me a hard-on, though seeing her in pain was pretty difficult to witness. Which doesn't give me much hope in the punishment department of this budding dynamic.

"So what's the plan for tomorrow?" Raine asks and Derek and I exchange a look. Thankfully, Raine doesn't notice it.

"Tomorrow, you and I are going shopping," Cotah says with enthusiasm.

"Oh." Raine raises an eyebrow at her.

"Yup, I have a whole day planned out for us. Orion has to work most of the day."

"What about Dex?" Raine asks as she looks at me.

"Oh, don't worry about me, sunshine. I have a few things I'd like to do tomorrow too. You and Cotah go have fun shopping."

After that, Raine gets a little excited but it's quickly wiped away by something, though I'm not sure what exactly.

We spent a good few hours drinking beer and wine while talking near the pool. It was a cool night, but much warmer than what we've been in. Around eleven or so, I can barely keep my eyes open. "Why don't we show you guys to your room?" Derek asks and I nod.

"I'm fading pretty quickly," I say as I rub Raine's back. "It's been a long day."

We all stand, grabbing glasses, bottles, garbage, etcetera before going inside. Once we're done he escorts us down a hallway behind the elevator that we came up in before showing us into a room that is certainly bigger than my entire apartment. In the center of the room is a massive king size bed that looks very inviting. Standing near the bed are our bags.

"Bathroom is here, there are plenty of toiletries and towels, but if you need more, let us know," Cotah tells us and we all say goodnight.

I'm a little disappointed that we didn't get to see the playroom tonight, but that's alright, we have plenty of time for that.

"What's the matter?" I ask Raine as she stands by her suitcase. I approach her, placing my hand on the small of her back.

"I can't afford to go shopping tomorrow," she says and I sit down on the bed, asking her to come to me. She does with ease and stands between my legs.

"You absolutely can, and you will," I tell her, almost as a command.

"No, really Dex, I mean it, I don't have money to go shopping. Whether I move in with you or not…"

I place my finger over her lips. "Listen to me, please?" She nods. "Can you please try to keep an open mind about this as well?"

"Dex, I can't let you…"

"You can and you will. If it hadn't been for Sam's bullshit, you wouldn't need new clothes, you wouldn't need new furniture, and you certainly wouldn't need to stay in a hotel room." She tries to stop me but I give her a glare and she quiets. "Whether or not it was Sam, I still feel guilty about it and I'm going to tell you why." I place my hands on the back of her legs, holding her to me. "Even if it was Michael who did it and not Sam, I still feel responsible for it."

"How?"

"Because, I put you in the spotlight. It's how your brother found you, it's how Michael and Sam found out. I did that. So, tomorrow, I will be giving you my credit card and you will be going shopping." She tries to argue again. "Remember what I asked you earlier today?" I remove one hand and take her left hand and twist the ring on her finger. She nods. "You saying yes to that question means that I get to take care of you. No matter what the reason. If I want to give you my credit card so that you can go shopping, I will give you my credit card, and if I want to buy anything for you, I'm entitled to do just that. So please, don't take that away from me."

She cups my face in her hands. "You don't fight fair," she whispers before kissing me.

I smile. "I never said I would. Now, strip. I want to fuck you."

She shivers in my hands and quickly removes her shirt. Exposing her breasts clad in the bra I'd bought her in Nashville. My hands quickly cup them and begin toying with her nipples while she unbuttons and removes her jeans. She flinches slightly as they rub along her hip where her new tattoo is, but she doesn't let it stop her. I feel her kick off her shoes and then finally pushing her jeans down. The only problem is, she's left her thong and bra on and I'm disappointed. I back off from kissing her and she sways her hips to unheard music. She gives me a little strip tease, though I can still see everything through the sheer fabric of her undergarments.

"That's my girl," I encourage her as she continues to tease me. Finally shedding her bra and in a very sexy show, she removes her thong with her ass right in my face. I grab her hips and pull her back onto my face and my tongue slides inside her already slick cunt. I growl into her pussy and her legs tremble. I don't stop licking and she spreads her legs wider, giving me better access to one of the places I love to devour on her. She tastes so sweet. Just the smell of her cunt alone is enough to get me hard.

I stop toying with her slit after a few more moments. "Now, strip me," I command and she straightens. Her legs are wobbly and I can tell she feels unsteady. After regaining her composure and her stance she tugs on my t-shirt and I raise my arms so she can pull it off. Then she pushes me back onto the bed so that she can unbutton my jeans. Once she's done that, she pulls them off, but not before licking and kissing right along the waist of my pants.

Her mouth is warm and the air is cool, the action sends goosebumps everywhere.

Once she's managed to rid me of my jeans, shoes and socks, she kneels between my legs and I watch her. Her eyes are silently begging me for permission and I nod. She gently takes my cock in one hand, stroking it gently upward. Then she cups my balls in the other as she begins to stroke and play at the same time. I groan.

After a few heartbeats, I watch as she sticks out her tongue and begins licking along my shaft from base to tip. "Fuck," I growl as I fall back onto the bed. I adjust, putting an arm under my head so that I can continue to watch her lavish my dick with her mouth. I gently place the other hand in her hair, encouraging her to continue, to suck me in deeper.

She does not disappoint. Before too long, her mouth is sliding up and down my shaft with ease. She pushes me as far into her mouth as she can and I can feel the back of her throat. I can hear her choking slightly but it doesn't seem to bother her and it makes my dick twitch. "Fuck." I can't take much more of this. She uses the added lubrication from her dripping saliva to stroke my cock with two hands and suck on the head.

When I'm on the brink, I manage to find the strength to stop her. "I want to come inside you, not in your mouth." She smiles and licks a couple more times before letting me go and climbing up my body, her slick cunt sliding along my cock. She moans when my dick caresses her clit.

I roll her over quickly before she can mount me. While I love her on top, I like her better on the bottom.

I pull my hips back, letting my cock slide down her sex until it lines up with her entrance. I tease her with tiny little thrusts, barely pushing in and then pulling back out again. Her back arches under me and she shifts her hips, begging for me to slide inside of her. "Please Dex. Please," she mewls and I smile down at her. I love that I'm capable of making her wanton. Her breathing comes in short spurts the longer I tease the outside of her pussy. I notice that her legs are trembling beneath me.

"Are you ready to come, little one?"

She shivers and pants, "Yes. Please, let me come," she begs me and I nearly come at the sound of her voice.

I pull her hands up, stretching them out over her head, holding her there. She wraps her legs around my waist, once again changing the angle of her hips, I slam into her and she explodes all over my dick.

chapter
31
raine

Dex elicited two more orgasms from me before he had one and we snuggled in and fell asleep. When I wake up, it's nine in the morning and the windows in the room have a gorgeous purple black tint over them, keeping most of the sunlight out, but giving the room an almost black light effect. Dex is still snoring softly next to me and I just lay there watching him.

The last few days have been complete madness, between what happened in Atlanta, followed by my leaving Florida and then Dex showing up at my hotel room, to him proposing to me and us ending up here in Vegas. I stretch, feeling deliciously sore from all of our activities yesterday.

Wanting to let him sleep, I slip quietly out of bed and into the bathroom. Hanging behind the door are two bathrobes and I grab one and head into the kitchen in search of coffee.

"Good morning," I say to Dacotah who is sitting on the couch reading a book.

She looks up and smiles at me. "Morning. How'd you sleep?"

"Like the dead, you?"

She sets her book down and stands up to come toward me. "Excellent. Want some coffee?"

"Oh, I'd love some. Where's Derek?"

She smiles lovingly. "He took off for work around five."

"Jeez, have you been up all this time?"

"Me?" she giggles. "No, I've grown pretty used to his work ethic. He's usually up around four and out the door by five, five-thirty." She grabs a cup for my coffee and slides it over to me, then slides over some creamer. I pour some in and she's ready with the pot. "How long do you think it will take you to get ready?" she asks as I blow across my coffee.

"Just for shopping?" She nods enthusiastically. "Probably forty minutes or so."

"Yay," she giggles. "I was told by Derek that we have a shopping list."

"We?" I ask.

"Yup, apparently there is a cocktail reception tomorrow night, and the four of us are going."

"Oh good lord." I roll my eyes.

She laughs. "They're not so bad, but at least I'll have you to chat with."

"There is that." I take a sip of my coffee and we talk for just a couple more minutes before I slip back into the bedroom. After rummaging through my suitcase for something to wear, I land on a pair of cargo crops, along with a cami and finally a low cut t-shirt to go over it. I pair it with a pair of cage sandals and call it good. It's just shopping, right?

When I come out of the bathroom about thirty minutes later, Dex is stirring on the bed. When I click off the light in the bathroom he wakes up. "Morning, sunshine," I tell him and he smiles.

"Morning." I lean over the bed and give him a gentle chaste kiss on the lips, but he wraps his arms around me and pulls me down on top of him.

"Hey now," I tease and he kisses me again and again. I can feel his erection pressing into my hip. "You're mean," I giggle.

"I'm on vacation," he says back before tugging gently on my shirt, pulling it down to expose the swell of my breasts.

"You are, and Cotah is waiting for me."

I watch as he pouts, then licks and finally kisses against one of my bruises. "Why didn't you wake me?" he asks sadly.

I run my fingers through his hair and his steel grey eyes meet mine. "Because you deserved to sleep in. You'll have the condo to yourself once we leave. Derek's gone to work."

He mumbles incoherently before licking and kissing at my chest again.

"You're so mean to me." I laugh, then fist my hand in his hair, pulling his head up and kissing his lips. "I have to go."

"Can you bring me my wallet, please?"

I kiss him again. "Absolutely." Then I climb out of bed, grabbing his wallet off of the dresser near the door before returning. He's sitting up, but I can tell he's still very groggy. "You should go back to sleep," I say as I hand him his wallet.

"I just might." He rubs at his eyes before opening his wallet and handing me a black and silver credit card. "Have fun shopping." He grins.

"Do I have a budget?" I ask to avoid arguing further about him buying me clothes.

He gives me a wicked little grin. "No."

"Dex," I scold.

"Sit," he commands and I do, facing him. His hand cups my cheek. "There is nothing in this town, short of real estate, that you could buy that will make a dent in my finances."

"Dex," I argue.

"No, listen to me. I do not act like it, I do not spend money frivolously, and I certainly don't flaunt it, but I am not poor, Raine. When I got the money from my parents, after getting sober, the first thing I did was invest it and I invested it wisely. I make more money on interest a month than I could ever possibly consider spending on monthly bills."

"I had no idea," I breathe, shocked.

He gives me a soft, genuine smile. "I would give you the world, if you'd let me." His hand caresses my cheek and I lean into his touch.

"I don't want the world, Dex. Only you."

He kisses me then, warm and passionately. Desire ignites in my body and I want him, need him, but before I can get too lust crazy, he pulls back. "If you see it, you like it, you want it, buy it."

"I'm not wired that way."

"Think of it like this. If you were handed a massive bonus at work, all your bills were paid, what would you do with the money?"

"Put it in savings," I giggle.

Dex laughs too. "A woman after my own heart. Okay, you found fifty thousand dollars on the street, what would you do with it?"

"Turn it in."

He throws his head back laughing in a way I've never seen before. "You're incorrigible, glowbug."

I smile, "I get what you're saying and I will do my best to spend your money."

"Good." He laughs. "Now leave me so I can sleep."

I kiss him one more time before grabbing my purse, the Jimmy Choos he bought me in Nashville, and heading into the living room where Dacotah is waiting, bouncing excitedly.

"What's with all the white formal dresses?" I ask Cotah as she throws another one over the door of the dressing room. "Oh never mind, I like this one." I giggle and so does Cotah, the sound fading as she walks away from me.

I pull the dress off of the hanger and slip it over my head. I fasten the criss-cross halter around my neck and look at myself in the mirror.

The dress is white, knee length that's tapered with several layers. Under my bust is a rhinestone band with silver, white and ice blue gemstones. The same pattern is repeated on the straps that wrap around my neck. "Cotah!" I holler.

"You don't like it?" I hear her disappointment, then I open the door and step out into the open area.

"Nope," I say with a cheeky grin on my face, her face falls. "I love it."

I watch as her face lights up and she starts to clap excitedly. "Good, because it's fucking gorgeous on you." She gestures toward the three-way mirror at the end of the dressing rooms. I can see myself from here and I absolutely love it. I walk toward to the mirror, taking a closer look. I start playing around with my hair, pulling it up, pulling it to the side.

"I need to get my hair done so bad," I mumble as I look at the fading colors.

I watch as Cotah blushes and smirks before turning away. "Cooootaaaahh…"

"What?" She stops, turns toward me and I glare at her. "Oh well fuck, you're almost as good at that as Orion is…fine, fine, fine…we have an entire spa day for tomorrow. Massage, hair, nails, makeup, the whole nine yards."

"You're kidding me?"

She smiles and shakes her head. "It's Orion's tradition, anytime we have a fancy evening, I get a spa day. He says it's my reward for putting up with being his arm candy for the night." She giggles, but I can tell she really doesn't mind being arm candy. "So I told him that it was only fair that I got to bring you with."

I laugh. "Well then, hair problem solved." She laughs and I return to my dressing room, and carefully remove the dress and return it to the hanger before getting dressed.

When I come out, dress in hand, she's browsing through the racks. "See anything you like?" I ask.

She shrugs. "Not really. But there are a couple of other shops here that I like better."

"Awesome."

"But you need shoes first." She smiles again and we're off to the shoe department. It doesn't take us long before we find a pair of shoes that match the blue in the dress perfectly. I nearly had a panic attack when I saw the signature red sole.

I tried to argue about it and Cotah assured me that it was fine, then told me that the dress was going to cost more than the shoes and I thought I was going to have a heart attack.

In an ironic twist of Dex's ability to know when I'm panicking, I got a text message from him.

Dex to Raine: I hope you're having fun. I pray you're spending money. I love you.

I scowl at my phone and somehow push aside my worries. That is until I get a total of over forty-six hundred dollars for one dress and one pair of shoes.

I'm a little sulky about it until we come to our next stop where Cotah drops nearly five grand on several different dresses, though they're not formal by any means.

Finally we came to a store that was more Dacotah's speed and style. She's a very curvy and very sexy girl with a big chest and fabulous hips. When I told her it was my turn to throw her dresses she looked at me and said, "These boobs and these hips do not look good in white." I laughed and went in search of something fun for her to wear.

chapter
32
raine

It was around four-thirty when we returned to the condo with arms full of bags. Well, okay, Derek's personal concierge had all our bags, but still, we pretty much overran the trolley with our load. After helping him sort through whose was what, we found a fresh vase of flowers and a note. I knew immediately that it wasn't Dex's writing because, well, it was legible.

Welcome home girls. We're going out tonight. Be ready to go by six. Dex and I will be back to pick you up.
P.S. You'll find your clothes for tonight laid out on your beds. No deviations and no arguments.

Cotah and I both look at each other and shrug. "What are they planning?" I ask, not expecting an answer.

She laughs. "If I know Orion, it's extravagant."

We both set off for our bedrooms to get ready. When I click open the door there is another fresh flower vase and a card. I open the card.

My Dearest Glowbug,
I hope you enjoyed your day. I missed you.
I love you.
See you soon,
D

My heart melts just a little as I clutch his sweet note to my chest and smell the flowers before walking to the bed to see what's laid out for me to wear.

Laid out on the bed is an electric blue, front zip corset that is accented throughout with rhinestones. It's very long-waisted so I'm surprised when I notice the jeans laid out underneath it. They're a dark blue, worn wash flare legged style. Sitting next to those is an electric blue thong and a big, boot sized shoe box. I lift the lid and underneath the tissue paper is a pair of white and blue striped knee-high socks and under those are a pair of chunk heeled, platform knee high boots in black. They're sexy as shit just sitting in the box. Knowing that he picked this outfit out for me to wear for him tonight makes me smile.

I head into the bathroom to rinse off only to find the counter is now laden with makeup. New makeup for that matter. Various shades of blues, pinks and purples. I giggle. I shouldn't be this giddy about what I'm seeing laid out before me, but I am. There is something Dominant about all of this and I can't help but enjoy it. The last thing that I notice is hanging on the jewelry stand. It's a chainmail style choker with a light blue raindrop hanging down the front. I smile at it before jumping into the shower.

"Raine?"

"In the bathroom, Cotah," I holler back.

"Oh thank god, can you...whoa, look at you." She smiles wide and our eyes meet in the mirror. She's standing there holding a corset, a purple one - similar to mine, against her chest. "Aww see, he got you a zip up one. I need your help." She giggles a little.

I can't help but laugh too. She's so cute. I turn around to face her and she turns around for me. "I don't know how he ever expected me to do this by myself," she chortles. "But he's almost always here to help me."

"This is gorgeous," I tell her as I start to fasten her up.

"I love yours. That color really brings out your eyes."

I get to the top three buttons. "Ready?" I ask. I can already tell this is going to be a snug fit.

She takes a deep breath. "Yup."

I tug and connect the first, then repeat for the second, though I have to tug a little harder, then finally the last one hooks easily. "You good?" I let go.

She breathes in. "Yup, I'm good now." She does a little fluffing on the front side and her breasts are pushed up high. She turns around.

"Dang girl, you look hot," I tell her and she blushes.

"You look pretty hot yourself." She looks me up and down. "Are you about ready? It's ten 'til six and Orion is never late," She tells me.

"Yup, just need to put this on and I'm good to go." I hold up the necklace.

"That's really pretty. Here, let me help you. It's hardly a corset, but…" She smiles and I turn around, handing her the necklace as I go and she wraps it around my neck, clasping it in the back. "Perfect. He's pretty good at dressing you up."

"I wouldn't be surprised if Derek helped."

She giggles. "Yeah, he has some very specific tastes when it comes to clothing. He knows what he likes. I get excited when I get to go shopping for myself. Though ninety percent of what I buy doesn't get worn very much. Part of our relationship is that he chooses what I wear for the day. Though lucky for me, he likes me in sundresses."

"That doesn't bother you?" I ask her.

She smiles wide. "Not at all. In fact, it makes me feel important to him. The fact that before he leaves for work, he takes time to pick out something for me to wear. If he leaves for a few days on business, he decides what I wear before he leaves. He says it makes it easier to fantasize about me being at home waiting for him." She blushes.

"I never thought of it that way."

Just then, off in the distance, we hear the elevator chime as it arrives into the condo.

"Oh, we better go," she says with a smile. "I saved the corset for last." She winks at me and I turn out the bathroom light, I grab my ID, Dex's credit card and some cash, sliding it into my pocket along with my cell phone in the other pocket. "Oh, leave that here." She points to my phone.

"Why?" I raise an eyebrow.

"Derek hates them when he takes me out or we go out at all."

"But I like to take pictures," I tell her.

"Don't worry, he has his and I'm sure Dex has his." She winks. Deciding not to argue about it, I put my phone back on the dresser.

"Little one?" I hear Derek call just as we round the corner toward the living room. Cotah is out front and I follow behind her as she steps into Derek's line of sight. "There's my girl," he says with a wide smile. "Look at you." He gives her a knowing smirk that tells me he set up the corset gig on purpose.

"Holy crap," my very not so elegant fiancé declares when he gets an eye full of me. I blush. He meets me half way and wraps his arms around me. "You look stunning," he whispers in my ear.

Both men are wearing black button up shirts, open at the chest, with black jeans. Derek's is tucked in and Dex has his out. He tucks nothing in.

"So where are we going?" I ask.

I am met with looks from both Dex and Derek. "It's a surprise," Dex whispers and a shiver runs up my spine. "But first, dinner." He chuckles before releasing me. He offers me his arm and I take it.

"Ready?" Derek asks and Cotah and I both nod with excitement as they escort us to the elevator and down into the lobby. We walk straight through the doors and sitting there, waiting patiently, is a massive hummer sized limo.

"Holy crap," I say, repeating Dex's words from earlier. Both he and Derek chuckle. Derek helps Cotah inside and then immediately follows behind her. Dex, finding his gentlemanly skills, helps me up as well.

chapter
33
raine

We spent the evening dining on a five course meal at Twist, an elegant restaurant inside the Mandarin Oriental Hotel. When we finished the meal, we actually had to go down in order to go back up to the Mandarin Bar. I was told it was a Las Vegas Exclusive bar, and while I wasn't able to look at the drink menu, I could tell it wasn't cheap. Couple that with the fact that Dex was not the only celebrity in the bar that night. For being a Tuesday night in Vegas, it sure brought out a few of Hollywood's A-listers.

Dex, ever the gentlemen, introduced me to anyone that came over to chat with him. I think some of it even surprised him when so many of the celebrities he admired himself, recognized him for who he was. Now he's no

Talon by any means, but he isn't a bump on a log in Hollywood either. I was pleasantly surprised when I was treated with the same respect, like I was one of them and not some poor little assistant from Bold International.

It gave me a high unlike anything I've ever felt before. I did my best to curb my fangirl moments, but sometimes Dex had to keep me in line by stopping me from bouncing.

Derek and Dacotah got their fair share of attention too. I learned throughout the night that Derek, though an international businessman, has several ties in Hollywood. Not to mention the fact that he is part owner of several hotels here in Vegas. Which explains his business necessities.

I was a little disappointed when we left, the night was still young by Vegas standards, but the guys had more in store for us. Including my first trip into a casino. Dex and Derek were both determined to capitalize on beginner's luck and they certainly did when we hit a Craps table. Don't ask me how in the hell to play the game, but I freaked out when I was told that one of Dex's bets was roughly a hundred grand. Lucky for me, my lucky blow on the dice meant that he won.

We didn't stay in the casino for long and then we were headed back up to the condo.

When we arrive, I watch Dacotah switch from happy fun to submissive. "Little one?"

"Yes, Master."

"I want you to take Raine upstairs and I would like you both presented, in the playroom in twenty minutes."

My heart starts pounding in my chest and fear starts to creep into my veins. Sensing this, Dex comes to stand in front of me with his hands on my arms, comforting me. "What's wrong, glowbug?" he asks me.

I swallow hard. "I'm nervous."

"About?"

"What's going to happen up there. We've never…" I stop talking when Dex releases me and Derek takes over.

"What is your safeword, sweet girl?"

"Kit Kat."

"Do you understand that you can say no to this right now or at any time?"

"Yes, Sir."

"Do you want to pursue this type of relationship with Dex?"

"Yes, Sir."

"Do you trust Dex?"

"Yes, Sir."

"Do you trust him to keep you safe, no matter what?"

I shiver. "Yes, Sir."

"Good girl, now, what is going to happen tonight is that I would like to show you some sensation play. What this means is that myself, or Dex is going to show you what certain things feel like against your skin. No, I will not take a single tail to you like I do Cotah and I will only allow Dex to take it to a place you are comfortable. Cotah will be with you every step of the way." I nod. "Now, sweet girl, do you want to go with Cotah to the playroom and present yourself for Dex?"

I don't hesitate. "Yes, Sir."

I hear Dex take a sharp intake of breath as I answer Derek's question with a resounding yes. "Good girl," Derek says as he releases me and Dex comes to stand in front of me.

'Look at me, sweet girl." I shiver with excitement and raise my eyes to him. I am met with a loving, reassuring smile from Dex and my heart warms. "I love you," he whispers before giving me a chaste kiss and releasing me. "Now go," he orders and I follow Cotah up the stairs.

She leads me into a smaller, dressing room type of room. Inside this room there are several items of fetish wear, different toys and objects that I have no clue how to identify.

"Don't be nervous," she tells me. "Sensation testing is a great way for you to learn some of the things that you like, and some of the things that you don't. It is also a great learning tool for Dex because you don't want him getting a hold of something and unintentionally using it too hard and really hurting you."

I smile and nod, but I'm still nervous.

"Dex gave these to me and asked me to have them ready for tonight." She hands me a plastic bag. I open it and look inside.

I giggle nervously as I pull out a pair of black boy short panties.

"Do naked woman bother you?" she asks me innocently.

I debate on telling her that I've had bi-tendencies in the past. "Not at all."

She smiles wide. "Good."

"You?" She turns around and presents her back to me so I can help her remove her corset. She catches it before it falls and folds it nicely for the shelf then turns around.

"Not one single bit." She smiles.

Wow, she's...I don't even know what to think, but Jesus, she's gorgeous. I lick my lips. She raises an eyebrow but then smiles at me. I subconsciously lower the zipper on my corset and her eyes dart south. If I said there weren't sparks flying in this room, I'd be lying.

Shaking off the distraction of Cotah's sexy body, I finish removing my clothes and swap out my thong for the panties Dex has provided me. "Take your hair down,"

Cotah tells me and I do and watch as she starts to braid her hair. "It's the best way to keep hair out of the way," she tells me. When she finishes, she hands me a ponytail holder and I too braid my hair. When we are done, she escorts me out of the room and we turn down the hall. There is a door at the end of it and nothing in between the two of us. She inserts the key into the lock and turns it, pushing open the door. She flips a switch and low density lighting flickers on.

"Holy crap," I breathe as I look around. To my left is a full length floor to ceiling mirror, and in front of the mirror are several low dressers, no doubt full of goodies. There is a St. Andrew's Cross, a couple of different benches and all kinds of things hanging from the ceiling. I shiver with excitement.

"We're almost out of time," she says as she closes the door. Behind where the door was, there is a little alcove and she goes to that. "Over here," she says as she turns to face the wall. I move to stand next to her as she lowers herself to the floor. Sitting back on her feet, she lowers her head and then places her palms on top of her thighs. I watch as her submission washes over her and I take a deep breath, closing my eyes, concentrating on breathing and I wait.

chapter
34
dex

"Are you ready?" Derek asks me.

"Yeah, I am. I've been waiting for this all day."

He laughs, "Just remember, watch her body. You'll be able to see if it's too much for her. I will try and show her as much as I can, and we may even find a trigger or two for her, which can be a good learning lesson for both of you. But that's not a guarantee either. I triggered Cotah once and it nearly broke my heart."

"What did you do?"

"Well, we stopped, we discussed it and she added it to her hard limits list. Which is okay because it's not one of my favorite things either."

"Mind if I ask what it was?"

"Not at all. She doesn't like to be gagged. I thought maybe it was because she felt like she couldn't communicate with me, but she said it sent her into a panic attack. Which I could see happening, but the reaction was similar to when we'd try anything new; she safeworded out. That's when I knew because she hadn't used her safeword in a long time. But I need to tell you that this isn't going to happen overnight. You and Raine still have a lot of learning to do about each other. Cotah and I have been together nearly a year and the one thing I know that she truly enjoys is the bull whip. Which is why I used it at the club that night. It was my reward to her for helping show you guys a little of what it's like."

"That was a gorgeous thing to witness. I've discovered very quickly that Raine enjoys pain."

He smiles. "That is great to know." He stands up and gestures for me to follow. "Come on, they've waited long enough."

"I agree."

Derek leads the way up the stairs and down the hall to a cracked open door. There is silence coming from the other side, a positive sign.

Derek stops and turns to me. Whispering he says, "One of the things Cotah loves, and she finds comfort in if things get too rough, is being able to feel my chest against her. Remember the other night, when she seemed to freak out?"

"I was wondering about that," I whisper back.

"I missed, with the whip. I caught her down low, along her thigh and between her legs that no matter how deep into subspace you get, is painful." He continues whispering, "My walking up to her, letting her feel me at her back, was enough to calm her down. Sometimes, it's something simple like that." He unbuttons and removes his shirt and undershirt.

He takes damn good care of his body, putting me to shame. He hangs both up on one of two hooks outside the door. I take off mine as well.

"Nice," he whispers, pointing at my new ink.

"Pain therapy," I whisper back.

"Effective?"

"Very." I smile and he ushers me inside. Once inside, I get an eyeful of his playroom. Hardwood floors, full length floor to ceiling wall to wall mirror on one side, various chests of drawers and contraptions line the walls. He closes the door and there, kneeling on the floor, in near naked glory is Raine. My cock grows instantly hard seeing her like this. Cotah isn't half bad from this angle either.

Derek signals with his hand, pointing at me to approach Raine. I do, standing next to her, gently patting her head, mimicking what Derek is doing to Cotah. Both the girls lean into our touches and the atmosphere charges with sexual energy. "Good girl," I say to Raine who practically purrs under my touch.

"Raine, Cotah, present," Derek orders and I notice Raine sneak a glance at Cotah, who starts to rise, so Raine does the same. "Hands behind your backs and turn around, both of you." I step back, giving Raine some room to turn and she does, her eye downcast, a picture of perfection.

"Raine?"

"Yes, Sir."

"Are you able to take out your nipple rings?"

"Yes, Sir."

I want to pout at his request. "There is a dish on top of the first dresser. Can you please remove them and your ring from your finger?"

"Yes, Sir," she says and without hesitation walks over to the dresser and begins removing her nipple rings.

I look to Derek for explanation. "They can be great fun, especially when they are hooped, but they can also add a lot of added pressure and pain or make using clamps difficult. You can decide which you want for that night, but until you test a few theories with them in or out, I would remove them. And," he says with excitement, "if they're well healed…Raine?"

"Sir?"

"How long have you had your piercings?" he asks her as I hear the clink of the second ring into the ceramic bowl.

"Six or seven years, Sir." Another clink as her engagement ring is set in the dish.

Derek looks at me again. "Since they're well healed, there are some fun little additions you can get that can sometimes heighten pleasure."

She returns to stand next to me and I kiss her cheek. She leans into me and like Derek had said, I can sense her body relax against mine and he nods approvingly. "Cotah, please go get four bottles of water and some towels."

"Yes, Master." He kisses her on the cheek before she goes.

"Dex, I'm going to ask Raine a few questions. The answers she's going to provide are for my knowledge when we're in this room and for you to know going forward." Raine straightens, her confidence grows knowing that I'm here in the room. "Raine, look at me, please." She raises her head and looks at him. "How are you feeling right now?"

"Nervous, but very excited," she answers, and Derek raises an eyebrow at her. "Sir," she adds quickly.

"Good girl, when I am in this room with you and Dex, like we are tonight, I expect to be addressed as Sir. Master is reserved for you to refer to Dex or Cotah to refer to me because that is our relationship. Do you understand?"

"Yes Sir."

"Good, now, do you have any medical conditions that I need to be aware of?"

"No, Sir."

"Any painfully sensitive joint areas, like knees, elbows, wrists, palms, shoulders, hips?"

"No, Sir."

"Excellent, are you currently aware of any triggers that may cause you to panic, freak out or safeword?"

"None that I know of, Sir."

"I am all about pushing limits, Raine, though tonight is not about that. However, if you at any time feel like you're starting to feel uncomfortable with an action, a toy or a tool, I would like it if you would let us know by saying yellow. Do you understand?"

"Yes, Sir. Yellow if I am being pushed too far."

"Perfect."

With each answer she provides, my excitement grows. The more I can feel my desire to do this growing. After the rice incident yesterday, I worried about hurting her and how I would handle it, but knowing that Derek is giving her a way out without her safeword gives me more comfort.

"I also need you to understand that the word no, no longer applies, you have a safeword, it is Kit Kat, correct?"

"Yes Sir."

"Yellow and Kit Kat, either one of those will slow or stop what is happening to you. Yellow will slow for discussion about what is making you uncomfortable. If at that time you choose to proceed with the same item or action and you call yellow a second time, we will stop that action altogether. If you call your safeword, all action stops, no matter what, understood?"

"Yes, Sir."

"Now, does it bother you that I will be helping Dex, that I will be using external only items on you, such as clips, clamps, floggers, paddles, gloves, cuffs, rope, restraints?"

"No Sir."

"Will it bother you, Dex, if I am touching Raine, including nipples?"

"No," I tell him with confidence. I know that his intention is to teach, to show me so that I can learn.

"Raine, does that bother you?"

"No, Sir."

Cotah comes back into the room. She sets down several bottles of water and towels on the same dresser that Raine's jewelry is on and she quickly comes to stand next to Derek.

"Raine and Dex, will it bother you if Cotah touches Raine in any sexual way."

"No Sir," Raine answers quickly but I notice she shivers, and I smile.

"No." I shake my head.

"Raine, does the idea of Cotah touching you turn you on?" She lets out a huff, and shivers again.

"Yes, Sir."

Derek and I exchange a look and simultaneously cock our heads and shrug, we both smirk. "Well then. Cotah?"

"Yes, Master?"

"Does the idea of touching Raine or Raine touching you bother you in anyway?"

"No, Master."

"Raine?"

"Yes, Sir?"

"The same question to you, sweet girl."

"No Sir, it does not bother me."

"Dex, I think we may have a couple of bi-curious girls on our hands."

I chuckle. "You learn something new every day."

Both the girls giggle.

"Alright you two, let's get this party started. Raine, do you like music?"

"Yes, Sir."

"Perfect, Cotah."

"Absolutely, Master." She turns on her heel and goes over to a box on top of one of the dressers, she opens the doors and lying beyond the doors is a small stereo, which Cotah promptly turns on and the room is filled with soft classical music.

chapter
35
raine

"Raine, we're going to set up, will you please return to kneeling by the door?" Derek asks.

"Yes, Sir," I say without hesitation and I return to my position by the door.

Nerves and excitement are playing havoc on my mind as I sit in silence, listening and waiting for what's about to come next.

The energy of the room is unlike anything I've experienced before. Dex is radiant and sexy in just his jeans and I quickly found comfort being skin to skin with him when I needed it most. I would have thought that being naked in front of another person, let alone a man, after saying yes to Dex would make me truly uncomfortable, but there is something about Derek that puts me at ease and ironically, I don't feel naked or exposed around him. I guess a part of me is surprised that Dex seems so open and willing about all of this, though Derek did say that sexual contact was out of the question for him.

But Cotah on the other hand...the thought sends a thrill through me. I'm not a prude by any sense of the imagination, but dang, she's gorgeous and, well, I wouldn't mind her touching me.

There are some hushed whispers going on behind me, and it takes all my self-control to not turn my head and look. I can hear various things being set down and being moved around.

With each passing moment, my nerves give way to excitement.

I know this is about learning, learning what I might like and dislike and even what Dex may like and not like when it comes to me.

A few more minutes pass, my nerves start to come back as the noise behind me settles with signs that they're finishing up. That's when a pair of black jean clad legs and bare feet that come into my field of vision and the hairs on the back of my neck stand up as I know, simply by his feet, that this is Dex.

Then his hand brushes along my hair and I lean into his touch. "You're so beautiful," he murmurs and I can't stop the tremble of appreciation that washes over me. He kneels down in front of me. "Are you ready, my pet?"

I smile. "Yes, Sir," I breathe and he stands, holding his hand out for me to take. I do and he helps me rise to my feet and turn around.

The room is no longer empty in the center. There is a table covered with various things, everything from glove looking things all the way up to a coiled up whip at the end of the table. Standing at the opposite end from me is Derek. His legs are spread, his hands clasped behind his back. His domination is evident and I shiver.

Next to the table is a wooden object. It kind of looks like a prayer bench, the center raised up with two kneeling pads lower down. Though it is not at ground level. Cotah is on her knees at Derek's feet.

"Go, kneel on the bench with your elbows on the cross bar. Do it now," Dex commands and my body surges with warm desire as I take the necessary steps to the bench. I climb up, knees together, and I place my elbows on the cross beam. The padding is very soft, almost cloud like and I'm immediately comfortable.

"Little one?"

"Yes Master," Cotah replies.

"Do you wish to help Raine?"

"Yes Master."

"Then go kneel opposite her, now." His order is felt inside of me as well. I watch as Cotah repeats the process that I've just completed. Her arms lay along mine, giving me a warm contact point, though my hands land between her breasts. I move my hands to her sides, but I hear a small hiss through her teeth as one hand inadvertently brushes her nipple. I watch in wonder as it hardens from my touch. I want to apologize, but I haven't been granted permission to speak and I really don't want to make anyone angry before we get started.

"Lower your head," Dex commands and I do.

"Raine, we're going to begin. I am going to let Dex do to you what I'm doing to Cotah, for now."

"Yes, Sir."

There is some shifting of men, some movement and then like the calm before a storm, everything pauses, charges and ignites the moment that Dex rubs something ridiculously soft up my backside. My back arches as his hand glides up my body. The softness is comforting, soothing.

He runs it up my back, over my shoulders, down my arms, back down my back, down my thighs. Each pass elicits more warm fuzzy. I notice that my heart rate is increasing at a slow and excited pace until the glove comes away.

"That is a vampire glove," Derek announces.

I'm puzzled by the meaning, how something could be so soft...then the glove returns. This time the softness is met with tiny pinpoints of sharp. Nipping into my skin. It doesn't hurt, but it certainly helps to raise my heart rate and the excitement in my veins.

I notice that the same is being done to Cotah when her breathing alters slightly, much the same way that mine has.

Dex follows the same path along my body as he did with the soft side of the glove. The little bites of the sharp are enough to cause my nipples to harden.

That's when I feel Cotah's hand shift slightly downward, brushing along the outside of my tits, just as Dex pulls the glove away. I bite my lip to stop from sighing at the pleasure that is igniting in me.

The vampire glove comes away and is replaced by something cooler and harder, but yet still soft in a way. Dex starts at my shoulder and trails it down my back, then up the other side. I shiver, my nipples harden and my pussy comes alive.

"Hold up your hand, pet," Dex commands and I raise my right hand. "Lay it open." I do, then before I know it, my palm is being smacked. My hand instinctively closes and my fingers rub along the area that was hit. "Does that hurt?"

"Mm..no, Sir."

"Put your hand down," he orders and I comply before he starts with the implement in his hand. At this point, I'd wager to guess that it is some type of flogger or crop, trailing up my arm, over my shoulder and down my back.

Then he comes to my ass. Trailing gently along the lower swell, along the line of my panties, then it disappears completely.

"Ah," I breathe out as the crop makes contact with the last place he left. The flick and bite of the hit melts away quickly and I instantly want to feel it again. My unspoken wish is answered when he connects with the opposite side. Sending a shot of sharp tingles that quickly disappear. I pull in a deep breath through my teeth just in time to be hit with the crop again. This time, he connects a little harder, with a panty covered part of my right cheek. "Ah," I moan. This one takes a little longer to process, but the feeling disappears quickly before he strikes again on the other side.

At this time is when I start to hear similar sounds, but no bite. Cotah's little jumps tells me that it's her turn to feel what I'm feeling though the noise is far more intense than mine. But Dex continues along various parts of my back, my ass and then finally down onto my thighs. Though it hurts more down there than my ass, it feels fucking fantastic.

That's when his hand comes into my hair. "Raise up," he commands in my ear and I do at the same time as Cotah. I brace myself on the bench and her hands are intertwined with mine. The contact gives me comfort, gives me strength and I rub my thumb along her hand as a show of support for her.

"Raise your eyes, both of you," Derek orders and I open my eyes to meet Cotah's. She gives me a small smile that I return. Then Dex's crop is sliding along my chest, I shiver and moan. He caresses the swells, rubs it over my nipples and then continues moving it around.

That's when it comes away from me and smacks right into the lower side of my breast. I moan, fuck, that was fantastic. I meet Dex's eyes, begging him to do it again. He smiles widely at me and quickly connects with the other breast. I maintain eye contact with him, trying desperately to convey to him how it's making me feel and the overwhelming arousal that is now flooding my insides. My blood is racing, warming and finally pooling where I desperately want him most.

He catches the desire, the lust, and the desperation in my eyes as he continues making contact along my chest and even my ribs below my breasts. Then he pulls it away from me and I can no longer see it. Then his hand wraps itself in my braid and he tugs my head back. "You're so fucking beautiful," he growls before his lips land hot and hard against mine. I moan into his mouth and shiver when he pulls back from me.

The lust and love in my eyes is reflected back in his steel grey.

chapter
36
raine

After Dex managed to let go of the crop, I think he was enjoying that nearly as much as I was, he moved on to other types of paddles, five or six, I lost count. Each one having a greater impact than the one before it. By the time he got to the last one, I could feel the warmth of my skin from the blood rushing to the surface. The last of the paddles was far from my favorite. It was heavier and while it sounded harder than it really felt, the bite of the strike was felt across a broader area, allowing my mind to process the pain different. By the third strike across my ass, I'd cried out in pain. Though I didn't call out yellow, I may have if Dex hadn't recognized that it was becoming too much.

He put the paddle down and came back to me, gently caressing along my back and butt gently. The warmth of his hand was a maddening comfort. His hand caressed all the sore spots, but then found softer, less reddened flesh and it became more comfortable. He lifted my head up once again, but my eyes were closed. "Look at me, glowbug." The softness in his voice and the use of my nickname sent a thrill through me and I opened my lust heavy eyes to look at him. The look that came after was all I needed to see to know that he too was enjoying this as much as I was. His lips landed on me hard and with a possessiveness I've never felt from him before. I moaned into his mouth and his hand gently caressed along my breasts, making my nipples harden and my pussy weep with a desperate need to come. I moaned again before he released me, eliciting a whimper of sadness at the loss of his touch. He smirked wickedly at me. He knows exactly what he's doing to me and I fucking love it.

"Now, Raine, it's my turn," Derek says after our moment with a hint of amusement, but more of a, hey-we're-entering-new-territory kind of way.

"Yes, Sir."

Dex gently lowers me back to the bench and Cotah's head rests along mine. Her hands rub gently along my arms and I tremble from her soft touch.

"Sirs?" Cotah asks.

"Yes, little one?" Derek replies.

"May I have permission to touch Raine, please?"

"Dex?" Derek asks.

"Thank you for asking, Dacotah. Yes, you may touch her."

I can sense her shift of excitement. "Thank you, Sir. Master?"

"You may, little one."

"Thank you, Master."

My body ignites, my pussy clenches hard around nothing and my nipples tighten into hard peaks with the knowledge that Cotah now has permission to touch me.

I do as Cotah has done and ask them both if I have permission for the same.

"You do, sweet girl. However," Derek's voice lowers to a whisper next to my ear, "What I am going to be doing to you will make it difficult to give pleasure."

There is no menace in his voice, but a promise of something wild and intense.

"Yes, Sir," I reply.

Dex and Derek talk momentarily, but I can't focus on what they're saying because Cotah is nuzzling her head against mine, coaxing me to raise my head. When I do, our eyes meet. "I'm going to kiss you," she breathes, stealing my breath as her lips land softly against mine. Her kiss is gentle, but intense in a way that could never be matched by Dex. Desire pools and I note that the men have stopped talking. Their change in breathing tells me that they're enjoying this kiss nearly as much as I am.

I moan into her mouth and she slides her tongue along my bottom lip, then pulls it between her teeth. That's when he starts.

There is a heavy thud against my back, though no pain accompanies the thud. I can feel the falls of a flogger bouncing. It is soft, the tips of the flogger stinging slightly on the second shot and Cotah steals my cries of pleasure when she slides her tongue along mine.

Derek strikes again and again, and my eyes look past Cotah and straight into Dex's wide, excited eyes. Again and again the flogger falls against my back. There is a cloudy fog that overcomes my body, weightless and nearly motionless. After a couple more strikes, he stops.

I whimper and Dacotah pulls back from our kiss.

"Master?"

"Yes, little one?"

"Master, can we stand her up?"

I watch as her eyes dart to the ceiling.

"Raine?"

"Yes, Sir?"

"Stand up."

"Yes, Sir."

It takes me a moment to get my wits about me enough to find the balance I need to stand. My knees were not sore on the bench but as I straighten them, I can feel their stiffness. "Cotah, the black cuffs please."

"Yes, Master." Cotah stands quickly and goes to one of the dresser drawers and removes a pair of heavy black cuffs with short metal rods with hooks on the end of them and brings them over to Dex. Dex takes them and eagerly comes to me.

"Your wrists," he says with a command and I lift my arms in front of my body and watch as he first secures one and then the other.

"Thank you, Sir."

I watch him light up and his lips are again on mine. "I can taste her on your lips."

I moan as he raises my arms over my head. I am sandwiched, skin to skin between Derek and Dex and I practically melt as Derek secures my cuffs over my head. He lowers whatever is above me so that I can lean forward, exposing my back and ass. Making me available to Derek and his flogging. Cotah is standing patiently not too far away from me and Dex caresses my breasts in the palms of his hands, rolling my nipples between his fingers as Derek starts to once again bring the flogger to my backside. "Ahh," I cry out and Dex releases me. "No," I whine as he steps back, then he nods to Cotah who promptly takes his place.

"It is taking every ounce of self control I have not to fuck you right now, pet. Let sweet Cotah pleasure you," Dex says in a way that gives me goosebumps and Derek strikes once again across my ass.

"Gah," I cry out.

Cotah moves to stand in front of me. "Still good?" she asks me and I moan, nodding my head. Derek strikes again and again.

Being confined, unable to move and unable to touch Cotah, leaves me a little disappointed, however Cotah is not idle. Her soft fingers trail along my shoulders, down my arms, and occasionally she drags her nails across my skin. Her hands brush down my swaying breasts and Derek switches floggers.

"This one may sting a bit," he tells me gently, giving me warning, but I think it was more for Cotah than me because the moment the flogger lands against my backside is the same moment she sucks one of my nipples into her mouth.

My legs start to shake. My pussy is ready to explode. Cotah's other hand comes to my free nipple and rolls it between her fingers. "Fuck," I cry out as Derek strikes me again.

Dex, knowing all my tells, comes to my ear and whispers, "You do not have permission to come yet, pet."

I whimper and Cotah releases my nipple with a pop. I look down into her eyes. "Kiss me, please." She stands, putting her hand at the back of my head before her lips land on mine and Derek strikes again once, twice, a third time, then he pauses.

"Dex?"

Cotah goes back to running her hands all along my body, releasing my mouth. I kiss down along her neck and she tilts to give me access. I continue south, trying to adjust, without hurting myself, so that I can return the favor. She, sensing what I'm after, helps me by cupping her large breasts in her hands. I quickly suck a nipple into my mouth and she moans softly above me.

The men are still talking, but I can tell they're watching us closely. I switch from one nipple to the other and she throws her head back as the pleasure radiates through her body.

I notice a shift in the men, and now Derek is standing next to Cotah. Feeling like a little girl having been caught with my hand in the cookie jar, I smile and release her nipple from my mouth.

Derek quickly replaces her hands under her breasts and she leans back into him, grabbing a hold of his jeans to steady her against his touch. She moans when he takes her nipples between his fingers and he pulls, letting the weight of her breasts pull downward. She cries out. I practically start to drool.

Dex joins us then. He's holding a few different things in his hands, though I can't see a whole lot more than the tiny chains falling through his fingers. "Thank you," Derek says as Dex opens his hands. I hiss when I catch a glimpse of a pair of clover clamps, nipple clamps and even a few clothes pins. I stand up a little straighter when Derek grabs the clover clamps. He smirks at me. "These, sweet girl, are for Cotah. They are heavy and intense, something I would highly recommend working up to."

I watch as Cotah's eyes gloss over as she takes in the sight of the clamps.

I watch with rapt attention as Derek stretches one nipple and Cotah leans back into him for support. He then takes the clamp and secures it to her nipple and tightens it. "Ahh..mmm," she groans as the clamp takes hold. Derek makes quick work of setting the other nipple before gently lowering the chain. "Ahh," Cotah cries out again as the full weight of the chain is felt in her nipples, keeping them taut and pulling them downward.

Derek gently nudges her forward until she is literally in my face. "Lick," he demands and I very eagerly start licking at her nipple. She moans in pleasure as my tongue dances along her nipple then I gently move over to the other one. I continue licking until I feel Dex's hands on my breasts. I know they're his because of the callouses. He begins tugging and pulling at my nipples, hardening them, lengthening them.

I switch nipples on Cotah and her pleasure is evident in her eyes as I lick and suck on the exposed tips of her nipples. That's when I feel the tug and pinch of a clamp against my own nipple. The pain bites only for a moment, then settles. I feel my second nipple being pulled and clamped and my legs tremble. Then comes the weight of the chain, though it isn't truly heavy, the weight tugging on my nipples is intense and I release Cotah's from my mouth and cry out, hard and loud.

That's when I feel a gentle touch slide under my panties, below the soft flesh of my stomach. I look down. Her hand is framed by my breasts and clamped nipples and my legs start to shake uncontrollably the moment her finger makes contact with my clit. She moans at my wetness. "Fuck," I cry out.

"Are you going to come, pet?"

"No Sir," I respond, biting my lip and fighting the desperate need to explode.

That's when something, a flogger, lands against my back. "Oooohhhh," I cry out, shaking, twitching, the chain bouncing, tugging pulling, too much. "I'm going to come," I cry out. "Please, fuck, please Sir may I come?"

My eyes open briefly to see Derek behind Cotah. The flogger strikes again. "Please," I beg.

I notice Cotah's breathing has changed and look to see Derek's hand down her panties, bouncing and flicking against her clit. "Ahhh, please, please please." My legs are uncontrollably shaking as Dex strikes me again.

"Come, now," he growls from behind me as he brings the flogger down harder and in rapid succession across my back.

The world dips and turns black, ignited by white hot fireworks as I explode into the most intense, powerful orgasm I've ever experienced before in my life.

chapter
37
raine

The next thing that I'm truly conscious of is being wrapped in a robe and picked up by Dex and carried from the playroom, down the steps and then laid out in our bed and the robe removed. I watch through heavy eyes as Dex strips out of his jeans and climbs into bed with me, covering us both up.

His hands begin roaming over my body and I arch and moan into his touch. "I need you," I moan out as his hand slides between my legs, his fingers caressing my sex.

"I'm all yours, glowbug."

That's when his lips land on mine, heavy and desperate. I wrap my arms around his neck, push him onto his back and I straddle him. His cock pressed between us and my pussy, warm and wet, sends shivers rocking through him. He wraps his arms around me and rolls me onto my back, lifting his hips, he lines up and slides inside me. I cry out. My body comes alive and that warmth of love spreads through my veins. "I love you," I breathe right before I pull his lips to mine.

He doesn't speed up or slow down, content to make sweet gentle love to me after all that I've experienced tonight. It's a stark contrast to the paddles and floggers that were on my body a little while ago. "I love you too," he says gently as he continues to make love to me until we're both exploding our release and collapsing into sleep.

When I wake up the next morning, it's to Cotah waking me up. Both the men have already left. I couldn't even begin to imagine what it was that Dex is doing here in Vegas, being away for so long during the day, but I realize that in due time, he will tell me himself.

We take off quickly for the spa and as she and I sit in the sauna before really getting started, we talk, both about last night and going forward. She, like me, has never had a desire to be with another woman before me, and while the experience was liberating in a way, she was sort of eager for another night with the four of us in the playroom and I had to agree, I was desperate for it too.

After the sauna, we spend time being mud bathed and pampered like crazy, then finally fall onto massage tables. It is intense, and amazing and awesome all at the same time. I've never been pampered like I have been today and it is an incredible feeling.

After the massages are over, we are pulled into the salon where I meet a couple of awesome people named Michael and Sherry. Dacotah seems to be well acquainted with them and I gather this isn't the first time she's hung out with them.

Michael is working on my hair. He's eager and it's infectious. We swap out the pink in my hair for blue, something to match with my dress and then when he gets around to cutting and styling it, he turns me around, away from the mirror. I pout teasingly at him. "Honey, you can't mess with perfection." He flips his hand and goes to work. I giggle and so does Dacotah.

Once we're finishing up, hair and makeup done, Michael turns me around.

I am met with sexy smoky eyes, gorgeous cherry lips, my hair is swept in the front from left to right, just a little down my forehead and all my hair is curled into a gorgeously controlled chaos on the back of my head. It's fucking beautiful. I nearly start to cry. I've never been made up like this before and it's fucking stunning.

I look over at Cotah who is facing me. Her hair is pulled up on one side and swept into curls over her right shoulder. A perfect look for the wide strapped, large floral print maxi dress she's wearing tonight. Her makeup, though visible, is more subtle than mine is. "You look gorgeous," I tell her with a big wide smile.

She grins. "Not as pretty as you."

"Hardly," I tell her.

"Yeah yeah, you're both fucking gorgeous," Michael teases as he throws on a few finishing touches before releasing us.

We head upstairs to finish getting ready. We have about half an hour before we will be collected for the party. When we return to the suite, there is a small spread of antipasto and petit fours. Giggling we both grab a plate before heading to our rooms. Once inside my room, I see three very large bouquets of flowers spread throughout the room in various flowers and colors. The room smells divine. There are no cards to accompany the flowers. Obviously they are from Dex.

I take a few bites of the wonderful food that was left for us and then carefully slip into my dress and shoes. Having only to touch up my lipstick, which was given to me before leaving the salon, I'm ready to go.

When I go into the living room, Dacotah is coming down the stairs. "Look at you," I tell her and she smiles wide.

"You look amazing," she tells me as she comes over to hug me.

Arnold, whose name I learned this morning, comes into the room. "The gentlemen have asked me to escort you downstairs to the limo. They will meet you at the party."

"Oh, okay." I raise an eyebrow but shrug it off as Arnold escorts us downstairs and into the gorgeous white limo waiting to take us wherever we're going.

We chat, but before we really settle into anything, we're stopped and the driver gets out, opening the door for us. I find it odd that no one else is dressed as we are and exiting cars for this said cocktail party, but I shrug it off and we head for the elevator. The door arrives and we step inside. "Shoot. I forgot my purse," she says as she steps out of the elevator. "Go up, I'll be right behind you," she tells me as the doors start to close.

Well, okay then. I ride up in the elevator by myself. I notice now, in the elevator, are pictures of the Eiffel Tower in Paris and I wonder if we're in the Paris hotel. I didn't pay any attention.

The elevator stops and the doors open. The floor is empty and I wonder if I'm in the right place. Out ahead of me is a wall of glass overlooking the Strip below in the setting sun. It's gorgeous and since the elevator isn't closing its doors and there are no button options, I step off and walk toward the glass to wait for Dacotah to come up with her purse.

"Hello Glowbug." I hear Dex and I turn to face him. He's dressed in a black tuxedo, looking stunning and elegant and fucking sexy as hell.

"Hi you," I breathe. "What's going on? Where's the party?"

He smiles wide. "It's one more floor up."

I look around. "So what are we doing here?"

"Well, I wanted to tell you how fucking gorgeous you look right now." He takes a few steps closer to me. His eyes are alight with excitement. "And I wanted to tell you that there is no cocktail party tonight."

"Then what…" I turn my head slightly, confused and unsure of what's going on.

"Tonight, I want to celebrate with you."

"What are we celebrating, Dex? I don't understand what…"

There are a series of things that click into place…

The white dress…

The tuxedo…

The overly made up hair and make-up…

"Tonight I want to make you my wife."

chapter
38
dex

"Dex, this is crazy."

I laugh and close the gap between us. "I know, but there was only one other time in my life where I was absolutely sure of what I wanted."

"Which was?" She nervously picks something off my jacket.

"When I decided to get sober." She gasps. "And I am more sure about this than I was then. This I know I can do without the struggle I face on a daily basis. This, you, are more real to me than anything else I've ever felt in my entire life. I want you as my wife, my friend, my partner, my submissive," I say with a smile. "My forever."

"What about our friends?" she counters.

"I promise you, I will say vows to you again in front of all our friends when we're ready, but I need to know that you're mine."

"Dex, I am absolutely yours and no one else can stake a claim on me, no matter what..."

"Good, then marry me, tonight."

"I..."

I press my lips to hers and she melts into my touch, my embrace. I pull back and look her in the eyes. "Please?" I beg.

She smiles. "Is this really what you want? Right here? Right now?"

"More than my next breath."

"Then yes, Dex, I will marry you right now."

I start to laugh and hug her and hold her. I feel tears of happiness welling in my eyes and I can tell she too is on the verge of tears.

I kiss her again, and again, and again before she's finally laughing. "Come on, glowbug," I say and take her hand in mine. I lead her around the observation tower to the elevator that will take us up.

raine

"This is utterly insane, you realize that, right?" I ask him as he presses the call button for the elevator.

He laughs, "I know, but why not? Why not give in and just do it?"

"Because we hardly know each other," I tell him.

He turns on me then, wrapping his arms around me. "I've told you everything about me. You know my demons, you know my past, you know my history, and yet here you stand, dressed in a gorgeous white dress. What more do you need to know?" I shrug. "I have been lost for so many years, wandering this earth with very little purpose until the day that I found you. Now I know who I am and where I belong. I will likely never feel worthy of a princess like you, but you make me desperate to try harder. You make me want to be a better man. Every moment I'm with you is a treasure to me and I will do anything to hold on to that forever."

By the time he's finished his speech, my eyes are leaking. "You sure know how to knock a woman off her feet, Dex Harris."

He smirks and kisses me at the same time as the elevator arrives.

We step inside and he holds on to my hand, giving me little squeezes to remind me that he's there and each little squeeze reminds me that he will always be here.

The elevator chimes and the doors open into a little sanctuary of sorts, or at least that's the appearance of it. We are met with clapping and cheers of excitement and I want to cry when I see one person I never expected to see. She approaches me and Dex releases my hand. "How did you know?" I ask as she wraps her arms around me.

She shrugs. "Derek has a big mouth," she laughs. "I wouldn't have missed this for the world," Cami tells me as she releases me from my hug. "You're like a sister to me, Raine. You've been there for me through everything. The least I could do was be here to see you marry the man of your dreams."

I am crying harder now.

"Oh, don't cry. I know that your friend pool is very limited and your family pool is nonexistent, but you will always have a friend and a sister in me. No matter what."

She smiles at me and takes my hands in hers as Tristan comes up behind her.

"You look gorgeous," he tells me with a smile.

"You're not so bad yourself," I tease him and he shoulder checks me. Something he has done practically from day one.

"I'm gonna kill you all," I say a little louder and everyone laughs. She kisses my cheek and is replaced by Cotah and Derek. "And I'm going to start with you two," I tell them as they both hug me. "Now I see why you only kept handing me white dresses yesterday, missy." She laughs.

"It was all my fault." Derek actually blushes.

"I don't doubt that for a second, Sir," I tack on and he smirks.

"Alright alright...so I guess I'm getting married." I laugh nervously as Dex comes over to take my hand and we walk toward the makeshift altar. "Where's Elvis?" I tease and everyone laughs, including the justice of the peace.

"He's unavailable, so you're stuck with me."

I laugh, "Sounds great to me."

Our ceremony was a no frills, cut to the quick kind of ceremony but it was awesome nonetheless. Dex had never given me back my engagement ring after taking it off last night and suddenly it all made sense when he slipped it, along with a wrap, back onto my finger when we exchanged our rings. His ring was a gorgeous black gold band, simple and nothing fancy, but completely Dex.

After Dex and I were married, the whole lot of us, Derek, Dacotah, Cami, Tristan, Dex and myself went out for dinner to the MGM and Joël Robuchon's restaurant and were promptly seated. Derek handled the ordering in perfect French, it made me envious. I sat next to Dacotah, who like me, seemed a little uncomfortable in this setting.

"For a small town girl, this is…" she whispered to me at one point.

I gently nodded my agreement with her. We had a lot more in common than I thought and this night proved exactly that. The food was exquisite, by far the richest food I've ever eaten in my life. The wine, to die for, and the conversation was phenomenal.

After dinner had concluded, some three hours later, we all retired to Derek and Dacotah's condo where we had more drinks, changed into more comfortable clothes, or lack thereof in swimsuits as we all hung out in the hot tub, chatting, telling stories, and having an all-around good time. I haven't laughed this hard in a long time and I was constantly catching myself peaking at Dex. He was so fucking sexy when he was unguarded, when the world lies at his feet and he is ready to conquer it with a swipe of his hand and not give a damn about anything.

It is during this night that I notice the dramatic change that has been happening with him since I met him in New York. Sure, the assholian he portrayed himself to be is nowhere to be found and I take great comfort in that and I realize that counting down the years, months, weeks, days, hours and minutes to his next breakdown is never going to get us anywhere.

It's also in this moment, with his head thrown back laughing, that I understand what his sobriety really means to him. What it means to be healthy and happy and in love. His subtle winks, kisses and touches always send a shot of excitement straight between my legs, each one raising me higher and higher, more wanton with each little pass.

I have to say that tonight turned out pretty amazing, even if it started on a whirlwind of Dex and I getting married...I'm freakin' married to Dex Harris...Holy shit!

I stand up from the hot tub. "If you guys don't mind, I have a husband to break in." I giggle and everyone whoops and hollers. Dex smiles wide and takes my hand to help me from the hot tub.

"Surprised you guys stuck around this long," Tristan teases and I know I blush.

Dex gives him a smirk that says it all for me. "We didn't want to be rude."

They all start laughing as Dex and I disappear into the condo and toward our bedroom.

When we get to the door, he stops me, then sweeps me off of my feet. "I know it's not home, but..."

I wrap my hands around the back of his head and pull him in for a kiss. "It's home, as long as you're with me," I breathe against his lips as he steps over our bedroom threshold.

"I promise, once the tour is over, we will have a proper honeymoon," he says softly as he sits me down on the bed and kneels before me.

I smile, "I look forward to it, Mr. Harris."

"So do I, Mrs. Harris." The grin on his face is astounding. It steals my breath away with the utter happiness that is rolling off of him in waves as he grabs the string of my bikini top, setting it free and tossing it aside. Next comes the string of the bottom, causing it to fall away, exposing me to him with the flick of a few fingers. The air is cool, causing me to shiver, both with the chill and the glorious look of utter love and devotion in my husband's eyes.

chapter
39
dex

While staring into my wife's eyes, I lay her back on the bed and push her legs up, pulling her bikini away from her sex so that I can see all it's beautiful pink glory. I lick my lips and lean in. Her sex tastes like heaven on my tongue and her hand fists into my hair, holding me there as her back arches. Our eyes never lose their contact as I lick and suck at her clit. She moans and grinds her pussy against my tongue, causing even me to moan.

She shivers as the vibration overcomes her and she arches once again for me. I slide one finger inside gently. "Ahh, bubba," she cries out and my cock twitches. Fuck, I need her, but I am determined to make a meal out of her as best as I can.

She doesn't let up, in fact, I know I'm pushing her to the brink when her hand fists and her legs tremble around me. I scrape my teeth gently against her clit and she explodes. Coming undone with a little help from my mouth. I tease her gently before removing my finger, then finally my tongue. I kneel up and remove my trunks, freeing my raging erection, barely before she tackles me, knocking me back onto my feet.

Her sweet wet cunt slides along my shaft. I can feel the remains of her orgasm sliding down over my balls. "Fuck," I growl and we lock eyes once again. She shifts her position, lining me up and sliding me home before I even register what she's done. "Fuck, glowbug, go slow, baby, please."

She smiles and slowly moves her pussy up and down my cock.

Our eyes stay on each other, the connection and depth I feel with her is unlike any high I've ever been on before. She doesn't stop. Her arms are wrapped tightly around my neck, holding on, pulling me closer, like I can't get close enough and my arms wrap around her equally as tight. "I love you," I whisper. "More than life itself."

"Ahh," she cries out at my declaration and I can feel her tighten around my cock. "I love you," she says before closing her eyes and stealing a long deep passionate kiss. I hold her still. Holding her to me, desperate to prolong this moment as long as possible. She doesn't fight me. She is simply content to sit here for the moment, with me buried inside of her.

I somehow manage to find the strength and flexibility to lift her and myself up off of the floor before laying her out on the bed. My cock, miraculously still settled inside her.

Once she's laid out, she releases my lips and our eyes meet once again.

I am determined to devour every inch of her before I come, and I do just that.

Licking, kissing and sucking my way along her body, up and down, front and back before sliding back inside of her and bringing us both to the orgasm we so desperately need.

The next morning we don't get out of bed until nearly noon. When we do, Dacotah is lying out in the sun on the patio and Raine joins her while I order us all some lunch. I watch through the window as Dacotah and Raine talk and laugh, having a good time until Raine comes inside. "I'm going to put my suit on," she tells me as she passes me with a chaste kiss. I smile at her and off she goes.

I shoot Derek a text.

Dex to Derek: The girls are up and it looks like a lazy pool day is in order. When will you be done?
Derek to Dex: Maybe an hour.
Dex to Derek: want lunch?
Derek to Dex: no, I'm good. Plans for tonight?
Dex to Derek: Not in the mood for crowds.
Derek to Dex: Playroom?
Dex to Derek: Sounds fabulous to me.
Derek to Dex: Done.

In the midst of texting with Derek, Raine went back outside and I watched her lather up with sunscreen and sit back with Cotah. Sometimes I wonder what it would be like to be a fly on the wall when they talk.

Derek to Dex: C, T & Jaden will be over shortly to hang out before they head back to PHX.

Dex to Derek: Awesome, thanks.

I slip into the bedroom and throw on my trunks and finally join the ladies outside. Though they're lying in the bright Vegas sunshine, I take a seat at the table with an ear to the suite for both our lunch and Cami and Tristan. I watch with rapt attention as the girls giggle and talk. Though I can't quite tell what they're talking about, I notice that I haven't ever seen Raine so happy and animated like she is right now. Then I realize that a good portion of that may have been my fault.

God, I was such a dick when I first met her and look at me now. I subconsciously twirl my wedding band. Fuck, I never told the guys.

When lunch arrives, Arnold, Derek's concierge, butler, whatever the hell he's called, sets up our lunch and pours drinks. The girls come out of the sun and sit with me at the table. "Cami, Tristan and Jaden will be here shortly."

"Oh yay," Dacotah says with excitement. "I haven't seen J-man in forever." She smiles wide.

"You really like kids?" Raine asks her.

"Oh, I love kids, I can't wait to have some," she tells Raine with a smile.

"Does Derek want kids?" I ask, trying to join in the conversation.

She smiles. "You know, I don't know. We've never talked about it. Maybe because I know I'm not quite to the point of wanting them." She shrugs and takes a bite of her salad.

Raine looks at me and smiles. "What about you?" she asks me and I raise an eyebrow at her. "Do you want kids?"

"Kind of a funny question since you married my ass yesterday." I laugh and so does she. "But eventually, yes, I'd love to have a little you running around." As I tell her those words, I realize that my answer is honest and without hesitation.

Raine gasps before sitting up straighter.

"What?" I say, my own surprise ringing out.

"Not an answer I expected from you."

"Why does that surprise you so much, glowbug?"

She giggles. "Oh, there are countless reasons why that surprises me, bubba. The easiest of which is the fact that you're very much a 'me me me' kind of person. I guess I have a hard time picturing you with a baby on your hip."

Cotah snorts a laugh, "I'm pretty sure she's not the only one."

"Hey, what the hell, are you two ganging up on me?" I tease them and Raine leans over, kissing me quickly on the lips.

"Never. It's just, well, I don't know, surprising I guess."

"Well princess, lucky for you, I'm full of surprises."

She snorts. "You can say that again." She raises her left hand and pointedly looks at her ring.

"Hey, you're the one who said yes."

"Aliens made me do it," she says with a straight face then bursts into one of those deep belly laughs, something I've never heard from her before. Cotah and I join in and then we go back to eating our lunch.

Hearing that laugh makes me start thinking about how much I really don't know about the woman I married less than a day ago. I don't even know what her hobbies or habits are and I'm a little bothered by it. And no, I do not regret marrying her. It's just enough to push me to the point of finding out more about her, making her laugh like that more often.

chapter
40
raine

Today was awesome. I got to play with Jaden in the pool for a while when Tristan and Cami came over. After our kid conversation earlier, I noticed Dex watching me closely while we played before Cami and Tristan took off back to Phoenix.

I don't know why, but as we finish up dinner with Dacotah and Derek, I start to feel a little nervous. No one has said anything about going out tonight, which is fine. I think I'd rather stay in and chill, but it is Vegas.

As I finish my food and put my silverware down, Derek looks at me. "So Raine, when we were in the playroom the other night, what was one thing you absolutely hated?"

I swallow. "I can't say that I hated anything, though the last paddle was um," I squirm, "not my favorite."

He smirks and Cotah shudders. "That's no one's favorite."

"Well, that's debatable," Dex says with a smirk.

I gape at him and he laughs. "Well, okay, it's a Dom's favorite." Derek winks. I, like Cotah, shudder. "So with a least favorite comes a favorite, what is one?"

I look at him. "Only one, Sir?" I know I blush. He and Dex both smile and perk up a little bit. I look down at my wringing hands in my lap, trying, unsuccessfully, to hide my blush. "It's really a tie, Sir."

"And what would those be?" Dex asks eagerly.

"The crop." Dex smiles wider. "And the clamps."

"Good girl. Cotah and Raine?" Both of us raise our head to look at Derek. "You have fifteen minutes."

"Yes, Sir." "Yes, Master." Cotah and I say together and we both rise from our chairs and immediately head upstairs.

dex

"She's eager," Derek says once the girls are out of ear shot. "That's a good thing."

"I'm worried that she's eager for the wrong reasons," I tell him honestly, and he cocks his head, so I explain. "Her submission gives me a high unlike anything I've ever felt before and I worry that I'm replacing a drug addiction with dominance."

He sits back in his chair, in a nonjudgmental way appraising me, "I think it's different than that. You're afraid of replacing one addiction with the other?"

"Yeah, in a way I guess I am."

"Is that so bad?" he states firmly.

"I don't know yet. We get away from here and it is going to be difficult to foster this side of our relationship," I tell him.

"How much longer are you on the road?"

"Just a couple weeks. But I have a tiny studio apartment. She, for all intents and purposes, is homeless at the moment."

"Whoa, what happened?"

I fill him in on everything that happened in Atlanta, and when she got back to LA.

"Well, you're married now, so your home is her home. Whether a tiny studio apartment or a mansion, it doesn't matter, but I see what you're saying. I think this is a great starting point to opening up a discussion with Raine about what kind of submissive you want. Sexual or full on lifestyle. Figure out your rules, guidelines, limits, hard and soft. Figure out if she's willing to surrender everything to you, allow you to handle everything. If she is, then you start to take care of everything for her, help her emotionally and physically. If she wants bedroom submission but to retain control of her own life, then you know that too. There is no easy answer to this question, but it is a door that really needs to be opened. She's amazing as a sexual submissive. I'd be very interested in how she'd fare as a lifestyle sub. She's feisty, but yet she indirectly seeks approval from you for just about everything she does. She also has no problem with protocol when it comes to me and especially with Cotah. I think she knows a lot more about this lifestyle than you or I are aware of."

"She said that Nashville was her first club experience and that she's never been trained by anyone. But that she's always had the burning desire in her. Much like me. Though I acted on it. But it became a time thing, between the band and everything. It made it hard to commit to attending regularly and I couldn't exactly use a website to find someone."

He snorts a laugh. "No, you can't. Which is why I value the clubs anonymity. No one knew unless I decided to tell them and even at that, there are two Tops in Nashville that openly know my identity. If the others have figured it out, they haven't let on."

"If she'd let me, or her job for that matter, I'd move East, or at least get a second home out there. I can't exactly live on the other side of the country from the guys."

"This is true. It's not just you. Like with Tristan, they live in Phoenix, but yet Cami works in LA, though for her position, same with mine, we can do that." I finish off my beer. "So tonight, the reason I asked her what her favorites were was because I was certain the clamps would have come into play. I'm going to clamp her, get her nice and warmed up, let her feel her submission while I show you Shibari on Cotah. She's been a good girl, ropes are what she loves, so I'd like to reward her."

"I'd like that. With Raine's desire for cuffs, rope might be something she'll devour."

He laughs. "I'm going to agree with that statement." He sets his napkin on his plate. "Shall we go find them?" He looks at his watch. "They're been up there for at least ten minutes waiting."

"Why make them wait?"

He smirks. "It's all in the head. It's psychological torture. For Cotah, because I generally give her no indication of what's coming, she conjures up the worst of the worst and it makes her more contrite. It will take some time for Raine to reach that point and with her penchant for pain, you're going to have to be very creative with punishments. Orgasm denial is an amazing tool to remind her of who she belongs too."

"I like the sound of that."

chapter
41
raine

Nervous excitement courses through me as Cotah and I wait in the playroom. I know it's been longer than fifteen minutes since we left the dinner table but I get the impression that this is on purpose. Before I can dwell on it too much longer, the door opens. I notice Cotah straighten, as do I.

Neither one of them come over to us when they enter the room, but I can hear a clicking and what sounds like a drawer opening, then finally footsteps approaching us.

"Hello, little one," Derek says and Dex, not needing to say anything, runs his hand through my hair and I lean into him.

"This is for you," he says as he bends down next to me and he hands me headphones. I look at him and he smiles. "Put them on."

"You too, little one."

"Yes, Master."

"Yes, Sir," I say and place the headphones around my neck and into my ears. Soon there is music piping directly into my ears, washing out all other sounds and with a gentle brush of my cheek, Dex stands and moves off away from me.

The music in my ears drowns out all noise, though it's not extremely loud. I can only make out, vaguely, when they are talking, but not what they're talking about.

The music morphs into another song, and they continue doing whatever it is that they're doing.

With each passing beat of the music, I get more nervous. Last time it was torture listening to the three of them move around the room, now not being able to hear them is worse. Leaving me to imagine the worst possible thing.

My nerves are shot when the familiar strains of a 69 Bottles' song comes on and I let out a nervous giggle, quickly covering my mouth, praying like hell they didn't hear me. But the moment the music cuts off, I know I'm busted and in trouble. Shit.

"Raine," Dex snaps. "Stand up."

Shit, he's pissed. Crap, crap, crap. I slowly rise to my feet. I can feel the support that Cotah is silently giving me. My legs are shaking as I stand up and I feel him come up behind me. He doesn't touch me, but he stands in front of me, pulling the headphones from my ears. "Something funny, pet?"

"No, Sir."

"But you were laughing."

'Yes, Sir. I didn't..."

"Why?"

I lower my head a little further. "I'm sorry, Sir," I breathe. "I...I let my nerves get the best of me, then..." I take a deep breath.

"Then what?"

"Then one of your songs came on in my ears, I...it was...it wasn't funny, Sir, and I'm sorry."

"The headphones were a reward," Derek says behind me. "We gave them to you to help you relax. Now, I think you need to listen to us making noise." He comes up behind me. He leans in and whispers something to Dex then they exchange something.

"Raine?"

"Yes, Sir," I answer Dex.

"Come." He side steps me and leads me into the corner, away from Cotah.

"Kneel, facing the wall."

I lower myself to the floor and onto my knees.

"Closer to the wall," he tells me and I step forward on my knees until they are practically touching the wall. He then slides something along the wall. "Put your nose on it." I lean forward until the tip of my nose touches the coin. He lets it go and then kneels next to me. "Hands behind your back," he orders and I obey. Something gets passed to him again and I hear metal scraping on metal, then I feel the coolness against one wrist and the flip of a handcuff as it wraps around. The process is repeated for the other wrist. "If that penny hits the floor before you have permission to let it go, you will be sent downstairs to your room for the night. Understood?"

Fear, anger and determination washes through me.

"You cannot safeword out of this. No harm is coming to you, is it?"

"No Sir," I answer Derek.

"If you safeword, you will go downstairs," Dex says.

"Yes, Sir."

"Good girl. Don't drop that penny," he says in such a way that my fear and anger quickly morph into a desperate need to please him. Because I am fully on my knees on the hardwood floor, it only takes a few moments before my knees are sore, but I take a deep breath and press my nose harder against the penny. Determined to please Dex and to take my punishment for my behavior.

I knew the moment the giggle bubbled past my lips that I'd messed up and now I have to listen to the thuds and sounds of what Derek and Dex are doing behind me. A couple of the thuds make me jump and I fight to maintain control of the penny and now I understand why he cuffed me. I can't stop the penny from hitting the floor.

Jesus, this fucking sucks. I don't like this at all.

"Present yourself, little one," Derek says to Cotah but no one is anywhere near me. Now I know and understand why this punishment sucks.

I listen intently as Derek explains to Dex what he's doing. It's almost like reading a good book and I desperately want to look, but I can't even so much as shift my eyes away from the wall. If I do, I will lose the penny and....it slips slightly but I manage to catch it before it slips too far and I'm able to bring it back up so that I'm even with the wall. But now I notice idly that there is no more talking going on in the room. I feel eyes boring into me.

Shit, shit, shit. No, damn it. I will not fail at this.

After a few heartbeats, they go back to talking and ignoring me and I'm happy about that. Knowing they were watching me was seriously a lot of pressure.

It feels like it has been hours since Dex put me over here, but in reality, it's only been a few minutes. My knees are really starting to hurt and my legs are beginning to shake. Finally, Dex returns to me. Only he doesn't say anything, he just grabs gently onto my fingers. Again, I want to look at him, but I can't. I can't drop this penny.

"Drop it," he orders and I breathe a huge sigh of relief and pull my face away from the wall. The penny slides to the floor, it sounds like a brick hitting the hardwood. His hand comes up to pet my head and I lean into his touch. Desperate for him. Desperate to feel some sense of reward.

He gives it to me when he leans over and kisses my forehead. "Good girl, I'm proud of you."

The blood in my veins warms. "Thank you, Sir."

"Tell me, pet, what did you learn?"

I take a deep breath. "That punishment sucks and that it's disrespectful to laugh when I am being rewarded."

"Well done. Now, stand up."

I hesitate, my hands are still cuffed behind my back and my knees are very sore from being on the floor. He doesn't help me. He wants me to figure it out on my own and I manage to do just that. Once I am standing up, I feel warm hands, his hands, massaging my thighs, knees and down my calves. "Thank you, Master," I tell him. The response doesn't go unnoticed by him, but it also slipped from my lips without a second thought. I hear his sharp intake of breath and I look at him, straight in the eyes.

"Well, Dex, I think you have your answer," I hear Derek.

"I think you're right," Dex says with a wide smile and I wonder what the question was. Dex rises up and he cups the back of my head, pulling me in for a deep hard kiss that sends sparks of electricity across my skin and straight to my sex. "I love you," he breathes against my lips.

"I love you, Master," I say and he growls before capturing my lips once more.

In reality, Sir and Master seem no different to me, however, the title, for Dex, is far more fitting than I could have ever imagined. In my head, a Master is rougher, more commanding, more demanding and while I'm not sure I can sit naked at his feet, the desire to serve him excites me in ways I've never imagined I'd feel. He pulls back from our kiss and then leads me to the center of the room.

Cotah gives me a small smile and I can see that her wrists are bound in bright red rope and I shiver while my nipples harden.

"Do you like what you see, pet?"

"Yes, Master," I reply like the endearment was meant to be there all along.

He smiles and slides behind me to release my wrists from the cuffs before massaging them gently. I notice now that the thuds I heard were bundles of rope being tossed in various positions around the room. There are bright and dull red ones along with blue. I notice Cotah is wrapped in red so when Dex grabs a blue bundle from the floor, it makes perfect sense to me.

"Your wrists," Dex orders and I present my wrists to him, similar to the way Cotah has hers, with the insides pressed together. Derek steps in front of me, next to Dex, and the two of them go to work binding my wrists.

chapter
42
raine

Feeling rope slide along my skin sends shivers up my spine and my pussy floods with my arousal. I watch with rapt attention as Dex, following Derek's lead, wraps my wrists just like Cotah's are bound. I notice now that he's creating a loop that is hanging between my hands. I wonder what the loop is all about, but don't ask. I have a feeling I will understand sooner rather than later. Soon Dex finishes and I'm disappointed that he's done and I hope he mimics whatever else Derek is going to do to Dacotah in here tonight. I'm eager and anxious to explore the warm fuzzy feeling I got when Dex started.

When he's done, he runs his hand along one breast, then the nipple and then the other. My breathing hitches at his touch and my pussy clamps down hard on the empty space. "You removed your jewelry, good girl." He continues tugging and pulling on each nipple in turn, hardening and lengthening them. The sight is sexy as fuck and it causes me to moan again. He reaches into his back pocket and produces the nipple clamps from the other night and I whimper. Dex gives me a salacious smile and I shiver when he pulls hard on my nipple before clamping it between the rubber headed prongs.

"Ahh," I groan as the bite of the clamp registers.

He slides his hand over to the other nipple, repeating the process. Knowing better what to expect, my breathing hitches with the contact. He only lets the clamps settle for a couple of seconds before he tugs gently on the chain. "Argh," I cry out as the sharp pain flies straight to my sex. He releases the chain and then cups my cheek.

"So fucking beautiful," he breathes. "Now, take a seat," he points to the bench from last night, "on the floor, next to it."

"Yes, Master."

The second I start to walk, the chain on my nipple clamps bounces and my steps falter as the pleasure and pain rock through me. My eyes roll up, but I quickly gain my composure and go to sit next to the padded bench as Derek attends to Cotah.

I watch as he gently lifts her arms and hooks her hoop into the carabiner hanging from the ceiling and it all makes sense. I watch as Cotah's body flexes and stretches, her breasts rising up, her torso stretching out. Her gorgeous body is on full display with one exception. She's still wearing her boy shorts, much like I am. My breathing falters as I watch Derek caress her arms after hooking her up. His nails run along her arms, down her body and over her breasts, then down her stomach and finally onto her thighs. Her head lazily falls back and her eyes close. Observing the pleasure elicited by his hands causes envy to wash through me.

Dex comes over to me, checking my hands, checking the circulation and when he's satisfied with that, he gives the chain on my clamps a tiny tug. My eyes meet his, hooded and desperate, and he grits his teeth. Unsure if it's pleasure from the fact that I raised my eyes to him, I lower my head and he tugs again, harder this time, sending stabbing pleasure through my nipples and into my core. I moan. His hand then cups and caresses my cheek before joining Derek next to Cotah.

He stands off to the side and Derek gets behind her. He has fresh rope in his hands and I watch with eager anticipation when he brings the rope around her front, under her breasts and he slides it purposefully against her skin and her eyes roll and then meet mine. She doesn't smile, but I can see the pleasure in her features and my envy rises to jealousy, I want to feel what she's feeling.

Derek continues to wrap the rope around Dacotah in various ways. He now has rope above and below her tits and he proceeds to box them in as he winds the rope between the rope that is on top and below her bust.

I watch as her breasts grow bulbous as the rope tightens. I've seen this before in porn and I've always thought it was sexy as shit. Gradually her breasts grow rounder and firmer with each tightened pass of the rope against her skin. With each pass, each tightening, I can see Cotah's eyes glazing over with lust and I wish I could help her.

"Raine," Derek says and I sit up. The chain between my nipples bounces and my eyes roll slightly. "Come here," he orders and I stand up gently, fighting the bounce of the chain, trying to not let the sensation get the best of me, at least not yet.

I come to stand before Cotah. "Yes, Sir?"

"Help her out, will you?"

I hesitate for a moment wondering how I can help with my hands bound but I answer, "Yes, Sir."

"Good Girl," Derek praises and I watch Cotah shiver.

With her breasts pulled tight, the areola surrounding her nipples is darker, more pronounced, and her nipples are, yeah, they're just fucking lickable. Which is exactly what I do. I flatten my tongue against her swollen flesh and I slide it up, fat and wide, wet and warm, right over the peak of her nipple and she moans loudly. I repeat the process, only this time with just the tip of my tongue. She fights her bindings but manages to arch into me, encouraging me to continue. Taking my cue, I suck her nipple into my mouth, flicking it with my tongue until I get it hard enough to bite gently on it. She cries out. I look up at her for reassurance and she nods. I lick the sting away before moving to the other nipple, which is now hard and wanting as well.

I repeat the process against her other nipple.

That's when I see Derek's hand slide around her side. He reaches out and finds my chain. He tugs on it and my knees nearly buckle from the pleasure he's eliciting from me. When he's done, I watch as his hand slides in under Dacotah's panties. I wanted to do that, but my hands being bound make it nearly impossible for me to be able to do so.

"Ahh, Master," she cries out. Her whole body is shaking with obvious pleasure. That's when I feel Dex come around behind me, his hands sliding along my back, joined by his other hand. He rubs both along my shoulders before wrapping around the front of my body. I feel his denim clad erection pressing into me and I moan. He tugs on the chain once more.

I release Cotah's nipple from my mouth as I cry out. Pleasure and a desperate need to come overrun all other thoughts. "Fuck," I growl.

That's when I feel Dex's hand smack hard against my ass. "Argh." I feel his hand on the back of my head, pushing me towards Cotah's nipple and I pull it into my mouth. Derek's hand continues to move slowly beneath her panties and her breathing becomes more and more ragged. She's getting close. I switch nipples, back to the one I haven't bitten yet.

"Do you want to come, my precious slut?"

"Yes, Master."

"Do you want Raine to keep sucking your tits?"

"Please, Master."

"Or would you rather have the clamps?"

"No, Master. I love Raine's mouth on my tits."

Her declaration spurs me to pleasure her the best way I can and know how. Dex isn't helping with my own pleasure as his cock rubs against my sex. His hands roam over my body, caressing, loving and devouring me.

Dacotah starts to tremble and Derek's pace increases on her clit.

"Please Master," she cries out.

"Please what, precious?"

"Please Master, may I come?"

I switch nipples and prepare to help her over the edge.

"Please Master," She cries out, her body trembling with each pass of his finger over her clit and I can only imagine how hard it is right now. I lick and suck on her nipple. I'm trying to be gentle, trying not to tip her over the edge before she has permission. I notice some shifting, though I can't see exactly what happens, but Cotah's cries become more desperate. "Please, please, please, Master. Please let me come," she begs harder.

"Come, now," he growls and I feel Cotah's orgasm rock through her entire body, shaking and convulsing, her hips thrusting. I let up my licking and sucking of her nipples, knowing my own personal irritation with over stimulated nipples. When I release her nipple from my mouth, Dex pulls me to stand up straight and he lifts my arms over my head. Before I know it, I am hooked up, just like Cotah. I whimper. I am desperate to feel what she's felt.

I watch as Derek extracts himself from her, placing his fingers into her mouth and she eagerly licks her juices from his fingers with closed eyes. When he's satisfied with how clean they are and he's walked around to her front, he removes his fingers from her mouth and then I watch as he slaps one of her breasts and then the other. She cries out, loud. "Again?"

"Yes, Master," she answers and Derek repeats the process and I watch as Cotah's breasts start to turn red with his slapping. Then he produces clamps similar to the ones I'm still wearing. I watch as lust and a cloudy haze washes over Cotah's eyes as Derek attaches the clamps to her nipples. He walks around her, pressing his chest to her back and she melts, whimpering into his touch.

"Good girl. Do you want more?"

"Yes, Master," she answers without hesitation.

Dex has come around me, watching them and watching me watch them. His hands gently caress my breasts, occasionally tugging on the chain. It's getting to be too much and just as I start to think that, I feel his fingers on one of the claws. I watch as he releases it, then watch as the blood and overwhelming burning sensation radiates as the flow is restored. "Fuck," I cry out as he unclamps the other one and I fight my bindings as the pain is nearly too much to handle.

He softens the pain with a gentle flick of his tongue across one nipple followed by the other one. "Fuck...Master," I cry out. I start scissoring my legs together, desperately seeking relief.

"She's going to come," Derek says.

Dex smirks and licks across the other nipple before plunging his hand under my panties.

"Please Master, please, I need to come, please. Oh god." I fight it, hard, but I'm losing. "Please," I beg again and his mouth comes to my ear.

"Come for me, now, princess."

I fucking explode, everywhere. Literally. Shattering into a million tiny fucking pieces as his hand pulls back on my braid, raising my lips to his. He swallows my cries of pure pleasure.

chapter
43
raine

That was the first of three orgasms from me in the playroom that night. We extended our scene to Dex and Derek wrapping me in the same way as Cotah, giving me a chance to experience something so far beyond intense that I didn't know what was happening at first. That was until I heard Derek tell Dex that I was floating. Once I'd gotten tied up, determined to test the limits of what I could handle, Derek brought out a flogger and proceeded to flog my back for a few minutes until Dex had seen enough to give it a go. By that point, I was slipping deeper and deeper into what I now know was subspace. When I was untied, I was completely shattered.

Dex took me back to our room and made sweet love to me, extending my high even higher.

In the middle of the night, I crashed and I did it hard. Cold shivers wracked my body, but what never faltered that night was Dex's rapt attention to me and my needs, comforting me, and making me feel like the most important person in the world. It was that feeling that I knew I was going to grow addicted to.

We left Vegas that Saturday, at the same time as Derek and Dacotah headed back to North Carolina. They were off to Paris on Monday, and again I was very jealous of Cotah getting to hop the pond. Derek promised that Dex and I would join them one trip and that excited me and reminded me that I needed to get a passport.

By Sunday, I'd moved out of the hotel and into Dex's tiny little studio apartment. It worked great for the few days that we were there.

Monday and Tuesday, I worked from the office. Actually, I used Cami's office because they hadn't gotten me set up anywhere yet. Trinity told me that with everything that I'd done so far that Addison was going to be mine. When I called Addison to tell her the news, she was over the moon and told me to bring Dex to dinner at her place.

We went to her condo that night and man was it gorgeous. I'd almost wished I'd taken her up on her offer to move in. Funny thing was, Kyle and Talon kept ribbing her about getting rid of the condo so that they could all move into their own house. The idea comes to me later, what if I rented it, or Dex bought it?

I expressed my idea to Dex and he just smiled at me.

When we got home from Addison's, Dex and I sit down for a long talk. It was rather business like. Though we don't actually have that type of contract, we discuss many terms that would be included in said contract. The main thing we discuss is what we both want from a Dom/sub relationship.

"Do you want someone to sit at your feet and cater to your every need?" I ask him candidly.

"No, I don't. In fact, I want a partner, an equal, though there are certainly things. For example, if we had a house, I'd do the yard work." I snort a laugh, he ignores me. "You'd do the cooking and laundry."

"That's a bit sexist, don't you think?"

He smiles wide, "No. Do you want to mow the grass, weed the yard, mend the fences?"

"You sound like you fell out of the 1920s. No, I don't want to do that stuff."

"Do you really want me to cook?" He raised an eyebrow at me.

"Can you cook?"

He laughs. "Have you looked in the cupboards around here?"

I laugh too. "I'm pretty sure there is more dust than food, but you've been gone and you weren't here very long before you left." I try to make an excuse for him and he just shakes his head.

"No, glowbug, it's empty because I know where the takeout menus are and I know how to drive a car to take my happy ass to a restaurant."

"Figures."

"But you cooking and feeding me pleases me."

"You're not a baby, you can feed yourself. But cooking, I can do the cooking." I smile a Cheshire grin at him.

Our banter continues for a little while longer and eventually morphs into more serious conversation.

"I want you to surrender yourself to me."

I cock my head. "I do that already."

He shakes his head. "In the bedroom, absolutely you do and I treasure every minute of it, but I want you to surrender everything to me."

"I won't quit working and I refuse to give up my friends," I state matter of factly.

"Glowbug, I would never ask you to stop working, in fact, I like the idea that you work, though you don't need to on a financial aspect, but it gives you something to do. I cannot picture you sitting at home like Dacotah does."

"But she's not idle."

"No, she's not, but I can't imagine anything, with the exception of kids, that could take up that much of your time every day. When and if we decide to have children, we'll re-evaluate the working thing." I start to protest but he talks over me. "Children and working are not up for discussion right now. That is sometime down the line and there is no point in us wasting this night discussing something that isn't even a reality right now."

"Okay, true."

"But, I have control when it comes to you and work."

"I'm confused."

"For example, if work is too much, too stressful, taking up too much of your time and energy, I will step in and force you to step back..."

I start to protest, "Ahh, wait..."

"How many clients do you have right now?" he asks and I hold up one finger. "Addison, right?" I nod. "How many potential clients could you have?" I shrug because I honestly don't know. "Okay, well, if it ever comes down to where you're working twenty-four seven and I see it taking a toll on you, I will force you to step back."

"But I'm not self-employed," I tell him.

"Ahh, but do you really think Cami would deny you if you went to her and said it was too much and that you couldn't handle it?"

I pout, "No."

"That's my point."

"Okay," I say. "What are my rules?" I move on since having him take over is pretty much what I've wanted all along.

"You're agreeing to surrendering yourself to me in all things?"

I smile. "Dex, it's what I've wanted all along. I don't want to be your sex slave, I want to be your partner and I truly do want to give you my submission. I can't say that it will be easy, I know I will fight you on certain things, that I will probably get a little bratty about other things, it won't be perfect, and I know I will struggle, especially with independence. Because I have been so independent my whole like. But you have to be willing to work with me too. You can't get all high and mighty without a good reason."

"Understood. That all works both ways."

I smile at him. "Agreed."

"You want rules?" he asks and I nod. "Rule number one, communication. I can't fix issues that you may be having if you don't tell me about it. Rule two, honesty, I expect you to be honest with me at all times, failing to do so will result in punishment. I will not tolerate lying."

"Both of those aren't really rules, those are mandatory guidelines. I need to know what I can and can't do, what my restrictions are, what I should do, things like that."

"I don't have those answers yet and I won't know until something comes up where I can address it as such. But I do know one rule that falls in line with respect."

"Go on," I say softly.

"Yelling, screaming, snotty attitude, especially when we're talking, disrespecting me, my directions, choices or decisions."

"Understood."

chapter
44
raine

I'd give you the rest of the details, but in short, we discussed what it was that we want from the kinkier side of our relationship. I think he had an orgasm in his pants when I told him that the night in the playroom, while I had a penny stuck to my nose, I realized that disappointing him was my only concern. My drive to please him was so strong that it overruled the pain in my knees. I also told him that I could not and would not wait on him hand and foot, but that I would be more than willing to work on a relationship similar to that of Derek and Dacotah.

My declaration was almost enough to send Dex to tears. When I asked him why, he said simply that he wanted to be responsible for taking care of me, my life and every aspect of it.

We also decided not to tell the band that we'd gotten married in Vegas. Not wanting to make everyone angry that we'd married without them. Ultimately, we'd plan a wedding later and treat it like our first, just for our friends, if nothing else.

When Wednesday rolled around, Addison, Talon, Kyle, Mouse, Peacock, Dex and I boarded Bold's plane for Denver and the first show of the last two weeks on tour. Everyone looked refreshed, but yet tired and weary at the same time. I couldn't do a whole lot about that, but I tried my best to raise everyone's spirits. It seemed to work because we were all laughing and joking by the time we touched down in Denver.

The security detail shrunk over the break. The band is now left with Mills, Rusty, Beck, Casey and Tori. Tori was still assigned to Addison, but also to me as well. It makes sense when Addison and I are probably going to be glued at the hip as we work out some things for the band, as well as for her career. I don't know whether or not she's decided to sign on with anyone, but there are strong negotiations going on for her to duet with Bryan Hayes after the tour is over.

With marijuana legal in Colorado, I was petrified over how Dex was going to handle being assaulted by something so familiar to him, especially at the concert. Instead, I was rewarded with his Dominant side, glares, stares and commanding orders. I soaked it up and loved every minute of it. Especially when he needed me. He'd just walk right up and wrap his arms around me, burying his face in my hair. Each time I would catch him inhaling long and hard. I knew then that my presence was a complete and total comfort to him, and that my presence alone was enough to curb his appetite for drugs and increase his desperation for me.

When the show finally got started, I noticed that Dex slipped into a zone, the same zone he always does when performing, and the rest of the night went off without a hitch and included a three song encore. The fans weren't ready to give up just yet, but the band was literally running out of songs to play.

The band went out that night and we all had an amazing time. I can't even begin to describe the euphoria the guys felt after another great show. Only to have it squashed by a twenty plus hour bus ride to Seattle. We took off mid-morning on Friday. The band wanted to spend time in Seattle versus Denver and I was glad. I wasn't sure how much more Dex could handle. I was naive in thinking that pot wasn't going to be an issue for him when clearly it was.

Once we were on board, Dex's switch flipped to his Dominant side and I fucking loved every minute of it. We were on the bus, so yeah, it was nothing like Derek's playroom, but he found ways to make me feel small and contrite without any issue.

When we got to Seattle, we checked into the Marriott Waterfront. Putting us in the heart of Seattle with an amazing view of the harbor from our room was the icing on the cake. It was early Saturday when we arrived, so we had a good portion of the day to do just about anything we wanted and we did. We all went to Pike Place Market and wandered around, had lunch and then the band and crew had dinner.

By the time we returned to the hotel, we were wiped out.

Until my phone rang at four in the morning…

"Hello," I answer, my voice heavy with sleep.

There is no one there…

"Hello?" I say again, and again there is no one there. I look at the phone, the number is private. When I put the phone to my ear, I get the disconnected beep.

"Who was it?" Dex asks, wrapping his arms around me.

"No clue, no one was there."

"Turn it off."

"What…"

"Princess," he says in that voice that makes me weak in the knees. This is truly the first time he's used his position to control something about my life.

I hesitate, not wanting to miss anything important. He senses my hesitation and looks at me in the glow of my phone, his eyes are stern. I frown but power it off. "If anyone needs you, they have my phone to call or the hotel room," he grumbles before settling against me and dozing off again.

Something about the call bothers me and I have no idea why that is. It takes me until almost six to fall back to sleep.

chapter
45
dex

I'm pleasantly surprised when Raine is still asleep next to me when I wake up Sunday morning. It takes me all of ten seconds to slide my hand down her stomach and start massaging her clit. She moans and stretches but doesn't wake up. I smirk and slide under the covers. She has her one leg straight and the other is bent and off to the side. I slide over her straight leg and move the other one slowly, making room for me between her legs.

I grin with satisfaction as I swipe my tongue along her sexy pussy. She moans above me again, but she still doesn't move. Being under the covers, I can't tell whether or not she's really awake. I suck her clit into my mouth and her legs tremble and her back arches. Her hand comes to rest on my head. Then it moves, sliding in under the covers and into my hair, holding me to her. I breathe against her clit.

"Please don't stop," she whispers.

I nibble on her clit, intending to make it hurt, but she moans. I move my mouth over to her thigh and bite down.

"Ow!" she squeaks.

"Please Master, please lick my clit, and finger fuck my pussy until I come."

"I fucking love it when you talk dirty, you little slut." I smack her pussy and her back arches as she cries out. "But who's in charge here?"

"Mmm, you are Master, always you," she breathes out.

"Good girl."

I tease her again with a single swipe of my tongue across her sex, then stop. Her hand fists harder into my hair, trying to control my head to her pleasure. It makes me smile to know that I've gotten her so worked up already.

I lick her again.

I pause, her breathing is more ragged.

I lick again...

Then pause...

She groans in frustration and I smirk under the covers. I slide my hands up her stomach and find her nipples and I tug on the barbells. She groans in pain and I know I'm winning. Finally. I bury my face in her juicy cunt and I lick and suck at her clit while I roll her nipples between my fingers until her back arches, her hips buck and her legs begin to shake with an impending orgasm. She hasn't asked permission yet, but just when I know she's on the verge I pull my mouth away, removing my hands and I sit up, bringing the covers with me.

"Wha...no...why?" she whines as she looks at me.

"That's for this morning, and wanting to argue with me about your phone."

"But I..." I give her a warning look and she sinks back into the sheets. "Yes, Master. I'm sorry," she whispers.

I watch as rejection washes over her and she fights to roll over, but I'm in her way. "No, Raine," I tell her.

I see tears welling in her eyes and my heart breaks, but if I learned anything from Derek, it's to remain strong. "Talk to me, pet."

She brushes the tears away from her eyes. "This morning was the first time you've asserted yourself in something that directly relates to me or my job, by requesting I turn off my phone. The request took me by surprise and...I hesitated only because you'd never done anything like that before. Then this morning, I wake up to you between my legs and your soul intention was to deny me an orgasm. I'm trying to wrap my head around how that is fair."

"It's not," I state simply. I move from between her legs and lay back down on my pillow, she tries to roll away from me. "Raine," I snap and she reluctantly rolls back to face me. "It's not fair, but it is also not fair for you to think that you can question what I tell you or ask you to do. I told you to turn it off last night because, well, I did not want it waking you up again. Wrong numbers can do that, because they keep calling until they're satisfied. Or it was something else entirely. Either way, you are not unconnected from the world. Anyone who needs to reach you has my information and if they're here in the hotel, they have our room number to call or someone will pound on the door until we're up. Also, it was four in the morning. There is absolutely no reason for you to still be working at that time."

"I understand that. But I..."

"That is why your orgasm was denied this morning. You're arguing with me."

"No, I'm trying to talk to you," she snaps and throws the covers off, climbing out of bed. "Communication, Dex," she snaps again as she walks around the bed, but I'm quicker and I cut her off before she can hide in the bathroom. She tries to move around me and I move with her. "Damn you," she growls.

"Give me one good reason why someone needs to reach you in the middle of the night?"

"The press."

"How so?"

"Story confirmation."

I shake my head. "You and I both know damn well that they will run a story regardless of whether or not you confirm it. Try again."

"My boss."

I shake my head again. "She has my number. Try again."

She stomps her foot in frustration, I bite my tongue, hard, to stop from laughing. "I..." She stops, and I watch as she fights for a good, logical reason for her phone to ring and she keeps coming up empty.

"Starting tonight, at midnight, your phone goes on do not disturb, understood?"

She deflates and concedes with the lowering of her head, contrite. "Yes, Master."

"Good girl." I reach out for her and she doesn't move. "Raaaine..."

"Am I not allowed to be upset, Master?" By the end of her question her voice is condescending and it outright pisses me off.

I lean into her. "You know that tile, by the door? Get your ass over there, on your knees, now," I snap.

"I have to pee…"

"Tile, now."

I watch as she turns red with anger before stomping off to the door. Then she lowers herself to her knees and sits back on her heels. "Nope, up, on your knees."

She doesn't hesitate. I go to my jeans pocket and pull out a quarter and walk over to her and place it on the wall. "I'm sorry, Master," she says.

"No, you're not, you just don't want to hold the quarter. Try again," I tell her and she leans forward, pressing her nose to the quarter. "If you drop it, I will deny you pleasure for the next twenty-four hours. Understood?"

"Yes, Master," she breathes and I stand, turning on my heel and going into the bathroom and into the shower.

Not sitting there watching her is a test of her honesty. If she truly values this relationship, she will tell me if she dropped it or not.

I dry myself off and wrap myself up in a towel and walk out of the bedroom. "Did you…"

She jumps and squeaks, the quarter falling to the floor. She immediately starts to cry as she scrambles for the quarter. I walk over to her, grabbing her wrist gently. "Calm down."

"I'm sorry, I'm sorry, I didn't hear you coming. You scared me." I release her wrist and cup her cheek in my hand. She settles and leans into it. "I'm sorry, Master, I'm sorry I got cross with you, I'm sorry I did not accept your decision to take control of my phone, I'm sorry I snapped at you…" She continues to sob.

"Glowbug." She stops and stares at me. "Breathe." She takes a deep breath, then another one. Her panic tells me that she didn't drop the quarter before now. She is so utterly freaked out right now. But, needing to trust her I have to ask, "Did you drop it?"

She sniffles, "Not until you scared me, Master."

I smile softly at her. "Good girl. Now, go to the bathroom and take a shower."

"Yes, Master."

I lean in and kiss her and her body hums right back to life. I regret kissing her only for the fact that it is not my intention to fire her back up. She whimpers when I pull back and release her. She doesn't stay and argue, she simply stands and walks off to the bathroom.

While she's in the shower, I text a quick rundown of what happened to Derek.

Derek to Dex: are you telling me because you feel guilty or because you're afraid you crossed a line?

Dex to Derek: both

Derek to Dex: feeling guilty is normal, I do with D, a lot, especially if the punishment doesn't exactly fit the crime. Crossed a line? Not at all. Cotah has very specific rules when it comes to her phone and electronics. I don't monitor her on them, but she's incapable of lying to me.

Dex to Derek: I feel a little bit better.

Derek to Dex: Who called at 4a.m.

Dex to Derek: no clue.

Derek to Dex: Open the communication lines, ask her to show you. Don't just look.

Derek to Dex: Well done. You may feel guilty - but truth be told, you should be proud of yourself. It's not always easy to lay ground rules, sometimes better with a lesson to accompany.

Dex to Derek: I feel like I still have so much more to learn.

Derek to Dex: you'll get there.

The water turns off and I move into the bathroom doorway to watch her towel off. When she catches me staring at her, she stops while holding the towel over her body, like she needs protection from me. "I apologize for scaring you," I tell her gently. "It was not my intent."

"I know, Master," she replies before finishing toweling off. I'm still naked, having ditched the towel. I watch as her eyes wander south, taking in my erection. I watch as she licks her lips.

"I'm still angry with your tone," I tell her.

"I understand. I am truly sorry I snapped."

"I agree that the lines of communication must never be closed. In this case, it was not up for negotiation. Your phone goes on do not disturb at midnight. Understood?"

"Yes, Master."

I play the debate game in my head. Pleasure her or leave her wanting? I decide to leave her wanting so I get dressed. Her disappointment is evident, but I need her to understand that I'm serious about being angry with her tone. Which is what this has switched to versus the whole phone thing.

That's when she does something completely and totally unexpected.

She comes into the sitting room, naked as can be and she moves the coffee table out of her way, then grabs a pillow from the couch, tossing it on the floor next to me before kneeling down and leaning in, sitting at my feet. My cock throbs and my heart nearly explodes. I never knew I would find this attractive until she actually came in and did it, on her own, without my asking her to do so.

My hand slides into her still damp hair and I caress her head. I start playing with her hair as she lays her head on my thigh.

chapter
46
raine

Dex leans forward. His hand comes around to my chin and he lifts it up to look at him. "Why?" he breathes.

I shrug. "It seemed like the right thing to do. I guess it's my way of apologizing to you, again. You didn't deserve my tongue, you didn't deserve to have me react the way that I did. I guess it was a gut reaction."

"I forgive you," he tells me softly.

"I know, but I'm not sure I forgive myself."

"So sitting at my feet is you punishing yourself?" he asks.

"No, it's more repenting for my actions. I know that this isn't going to be easy, for either one of us. At times, I wish you'd take control and then other times, I feel like I'm losing my grip on who I am when you're taking control. Like last night. Rather than feel relieved that you took over, told me to shut it off, I stewed about it. I was up for almost two hours."

"I know." His voice is very matter of fact. "I could tell you weren't sleeping." He gives me a small smile.

I smile in return. "It just seems so trivial. Something as tiny as a phone call is the first thing you assert your domination on."

"I didn't plan for your phone to be the first thing, believe me, but it is appropriate. Part of my being your Master is ensuring that you're taken care of and that you are taking care of yourself and that means that I see absolutely no reason why a cell phone should ring after midnight. In fact, I really think ten should be the cutoff, however, given where we are and what we do for a living, midnight seems more appropriate."

"I understand," I tell him and I do. "I understood it when you told me to turn it off, but I just couldn't quite wrap my head around it. Then you cut me off and I saw red. Communication is important and I felt like I wasn't being heard."

"Then that is my fault. I did not let you finish what you needed to say and for that, I am sorry."

Wow, that must have taken a lot for him to do that. "Apology accepted."

"Good, now kiss me." He smiles and I lean in, pressing my lips to his and my body ignites, my pussy pulsing, back on the verge of the orgasm he's denied me, and I hiss in a breath and pull back. I lower my head.

"I'm sorry, Master, it's just…"

"Come up here, pet." He leans back and pats his lap. I go to sit on one thigh. "Straddle me," he commands and I do because it's what he wants, regardless of my discomfort.

His hands slide up my thighs, over my hips, along my sides to cup my breasts. His touch obliterates me, sending shockwaves of desire everywhere. I whimper. "What's wrong?"

"I'm scared."

His eyes grow concerned. "About?"

I want to cry. "That you're going to deny me again. That you're going to work me up just to let me crash back down."

"I should deny you again, and again, but you've been punished for your hesitation, then for your mouth toward me. You've served your punishment with good grace and until I scared you, you hadn't dropped the quarter, so..." His hands move along my breasts and over my nipples, my back arches, pressing my tits into his palms and he takes my nipples between his fingers. "I think you've earned it," he breathes before replacing one hand with his mouth.

My body ignites, white sparks flying though my veins. His free hand slips down between my lips and flicks at my clit.

"Ahh!" I cry out as he flicks and slides past, sliding his finger up into my pussy. I can't stop the flick of my hips against his hand, it is certainly not his cock, but it is so much better than nothing at all. "Please..."

He releases my nipple. "What, princess, what do you want?"

"I need you. Please."

"Lift," he says and I lift off of him and he slips his shorts from his hips, exposing his erection that slaps back against my ass. I moan and take his shaft in my hand and begin to stroke him up and down while rubbing the head of his cock against my wet sex.

I notice his hips start to minutely thrust upward and I take the hint, lining his cock up with the entrance of my sex as he releases my nipple again. "Take me," he orders and I shiver as I slide down his cock. "Ohhh," I groan as he takes my nipples between his fingers and I claim his mouth with my own. Holding on to him, I start to slide up and down his cock, his little thrusts up with my downward slides are the perfect balance and my orgasm is so close, sitting just under the surface.

Desperate to please him, to make right my wrongs today I call out, "Please Master, may I come?" He smiles against my lips as he wraps one hand around my neck, holding me to him.

"Yes," he growls and I explode, his mouth swallowing my cries of ecstasy.

"Bring me your phone," he orders as I return to normal from our exploits.

I clamber off of his lap and go to the bedside table and grab my phone. I don't turn it on. I don't do anything but bring it back to him and he pats his lap. This time I sit sideways and snuggle into his shoulder while he turns on my phone.

When the passcode comes up he strains to look at me, I giggle. "Guess?" I tease and realize that could go one of two ways, either he'll laugh or demand that I tell him.

"Hmm," he murmurs. "If I get it wrong will it wipe out your phone?"

I giggle again. "No, I don't trust myself to remember. But then again, my thumb works too."

"Well, then give me that," he laughs. I tuck my hands under my chin.

"If you think about it, you'll figure it out."

He smirks and I kiss his prickly chin.

I watch as he hits 548528 and I giggle. "You're missing a number and that's the wrong combination."

"I see," he says like he's really thinking about it.

"What was that anyway?" I ask.

"Kit kat." I smile wide because he's on the right track.

"Dex's girl is too many letters."

"Well, it could be shortened to D, e, x, s, g, r, l," I tell him so he tries it and I giggle.

"Wrong answer," he laughs, then he types in 4 5 6 9 2 8 4 and my phone unlocks. "Glowbug, huh?"

"I like the nickname."

"Why not bubba?"

"Too boring, 28222?"

"Okay true." He looks back at my phone and points to a picture. "Where was this taken?" he asks me.

I smile. "Addison took it after Nashville."

He pokes me in the rib. "Why don't I have this picture?"

I shrug. "She didn't send it to me until we were on our way to Orlando. We weren't exactly on speaking terms if you recall, then I just kind of forgot about it."

"You're forgiven," he teases as he pokes me again and I squirm.

My being poked in the ribs turns into an all-out tickle war where I'm on the bottom being mercilessly tickled until there is a knock at the door. I raise an eyebrow at him.

"Brunch," he smirks and gets off the couch, pulling me with him. He sends me on my way with a smack on the ass. "Clothes, now," he orders and I melt as I walk into our room.

chapter
47
raine

As I walk toward the bedroom and Dex the door, my phone starts to chime repeatedly. I turn back to look at it vibrating on the table. "What the hell?" Dex says, then I hear the door click open and he starts talking to the gentleman who brought us food and I duck into the bathroom to change. We have a sitting room and a bedroom in this room but there is no door to separate the two.

I throw on a t-shirt and a pair of cotton shorts. Checking myself in the mirror, I look like shit. My hair's a mess and the whole just fucked look isn't working for me today. When I come back out Dex is setting our food out on the coffee table. "What was all over my phone?" I ask.

"I don't know. I didn't and I won't look at your phone, not like that," he says with a genuine smile.

"I'm impressed," I say as I pick it up off of the coffee table.

"Why is that?" He's looking at me, honest curiosity in his eyes.

"Well, I figured the whole 'lifestyle' thing..."

"That's not what it's about. Me looking into your phone, with or without your permission, is a violation of trust and the last thing I want to do is lose that. You've freely given so much to me already, the last thing I want to do is put that rift between us." I sit down on the couch.

"Well, I appreciate that."

"Now, I do expect to know what the blow up was all about, however."

"Yes, Master," I say sincerely and press the button on my phone, my thumb print does the rest and I can see several calls popping through, a few voicemails and lastly a couple of texts and only a few new emails since I last checked it.

I start with the texts.

Addison to Raine: we're taking a harbor cruise, you and Dex want to join us? Leaves at one.

I look up at the time, it's only about 11.

"Addison wants to know if we'd like to go on a harbor cruise?"

"When?"

"She says it leaves at one."

"Let's eat first, then see what we feel like doing."

"I'm game." I smile and move on to the next message.

Cami to Raine: Morning Sunshine, wanted to let you know that Tristan and I will be heading to Tarah in May. Discuss it with Dex, you guys should come. We'll talk more about it later, unfortunately, commercial flight is required. Bold won't make it that far.

Cami to Raine: Give Dex Tristan's number. They can discuss it.

"Well, what is it with all the invitations?" I tell Dex.

He gives me a puzzled look. "Cami and Tristan are going to Tarah in May."

"Where's that?" he asks, clueless.

"It's a private island near Tahiti."

"Now there's a honeymoon spot." He winks.

I decide to fill him in on the details later.

I flip over to my emails, nothing to out of the ordinary, just the usual Google alerts on Addison, 69 Bottles, Dex's name and my own. Nothing to worry about. Upcoming concert news etcetera.

There is one that confuses me.

"That's odd," I say out loud.

"What's that?" Dex leans over, looking over my shoulder.

"Unknown Sender, but it looks more like that's the name of the person, not a mailer demon." I debate on opening it.

"No subject." He reads over my shoulder. "Delete it."

"It's in my work email…" He doesn't let me finish the thought.

"Anyone emailing your work email should have proper credentials on their email, correct?" I nod. "Then it's probably spam that the filter missed."

"Good point." I delete the email and then finally flip over to missed calls.

Seventeen of them.

"Well hell," I breathe before turning the phone to show Dex. There are seventeen missed calls from unknown number.

"One voicemail."

He shrugs. "Play it."

I flip over to the voicemail, press play and hit speaker.

All that can be heard is heavy, sick breathing. I nearly drop the phone in disgust.

"Ugh, fuckers," Dex growls, stands and goes into the bedroom. He grabs his own phone, presses a couple of buttons before putting the phone to his ear. "Hey Rusty, can you come to our room?…Great, thanks." He ends the call.

"Why do you guys always call Rusty for this kind of stuff?"

He smirks as he comes to sit back down, handing me a plate of breakfast awesomeness. "Because he has friends in all the right places. He's ex-military for one, ex-cop for two, and I think he even did a tour in Sing Sing before hooking up with Mills."

"Well, that about covers it." There's a knock at the door and I stuff a piece of bacon in my mouth. Dex chuckles as he stands up to get the door, letting Rusty inside, Beck follows behind him.

"What's going on?" Rusty asks. "Hey Raine."

I swallow my food before answering, "Hi."

Dex grabs my phone. It's turned to black again and he grins as he types in glowbug. Then he plays the voicemail.

"Ugh," Beck says. "What the fuck, Dex, don't you breathe…"

291

"Stuff it, dick, that ain't me. She got a call at four this morning, no one was on the line, they hung up and I had her turn off her phone. We're just now turning it back on and that was there. You know, come to think of it, Raine?"

"Yes M..." Lucky for me it came out as more of a yes'm than what I was going to say.

Dex unsuccessfully tries to hide his smirk. "Can you pull up that email? The one you deleted?"

I frown and shrug. "Maybe." I reach out for my phone and he hands it to me. I try going into trash. I frown and scowl at my phone. "No need to, it's still here..." I look a little closer, "or rather was sent again." I click on it, opening it up. I look at it, squinting, trying to enlarge it slightly, but I don't need to, the image changes, it's a gif, "Oh Jesus," I squeak and drop my phone. Dex goes to reach for it and I practically shout, "No!"

He gives me a hard look and I flinch back. He picks up my phone.

He watches the gif. "Fuck," he growls as he hands the phone over to Rusty and he looks at me. I'm trembling at what I saw. I hear the buttons on my phone as Rusty types something in, then grabs his phone as it chimes. But rather than looking at the email, he dials something. "Zach, hey it's Rusty..." Zach, why would he be calling him? "I'm good, yeah, the band is fine, but, listen, can you put a tracer on an incoming email?...Raine's account. She got a strange email this morning, but she deleted it, only to have it resend again." He looks back at my phone, pulls down with his thumb and says, "Yeah, it's back in there as new, there are now two, one opened one unopened...you see it? Perfect, can we send back a tracer on it?...yup, yeah, no, let me know, forward over the report once you have it, I'll get it over to Ryan. Perfect, thanks." He hangs up his call. I only heard half of the call, but I gather I got the gist.

"So they can do that?"

Rusty shrugs. "Sometimes it works, sometimes not. He said he would reroute the email to him automatically so you shouldn't see any more of that email. It will make it easier to trace."

"Do we take that seriously?" Dex asks the same question I was thinking.

"Yes and no."

"That is a gif of me getting my head cut off...naked, thank you very much."

"Well, unless Dex is sending you the picture, who else would have pictures of you naked?"

"I'm not entirely sure that was my body," I tell them, Dex takes back my phone and looks at it.

"Pre-tattoo, pre-piercing...no, it's not her body."

"Well, that's good to know," I say sarcastically. "But still..."

"Well, other than giving you a stranger danger pep talk, Raine, I don't see when you will actually have a chance at being alone. So..." Rusty looks to Dex. "Here, let me put something on her phone." He reaches for it and Dex gives it to him.

"What are you putting on my phone?"

Rusty gives me a wicked little 'I have secret toys' grin, then he does something on his phone and my phone chimes. "I need the password."

"Here," Dex says and he puts it in and hands it back to him. Rusty pushes a few buttons and then after a minute he pushes a few more and then hands me back my phone.

"What did you do?"

He presses a number on his phone and suddenly my phone rings, making me jump. "Jesus, what is it with you guys scaring me today?" I say, trying to be funny and I look at my phone. It has Rusty's name, but also his location and phone number on it. There is also a kill button. I look at him in confusion. "I don't understand."

"I put an app or program on your phone that decodes callers. It catches on to their signal, and radios back where they are calling from and unmasks their identity."

"And the kill button?"

He smiles. "That's fun, but be careful. It will actually require your passcode to actually activate that. It obliterates any chance of that number ever calling you again. In this case, if you manage to capture the information, phone number, location etcetera, let me know and I can pull it, and get it to Ryan. Let him investigate and we can go from there. There is also a redirect button that will pop up with most numbers, the redirect button allows you to trace the caller for the next twenty minutes."

"Why didn't I see that when you called?"

He smirks. "You'll never see it with mine, any of the security guys, Addison or the band. They all have the same program installed and because you have it now too, they can't trace you, but they can permanently block you." He rolls his eyes. "Okay, permanent isn't entirely true, you can bring them back with a new phone. Basically all calls in and out of your phone, though dialed through the standard methods, are directed through that app."

"So can't I just delete the app?"

He gives me a knowing grin. "No, you can't, it's hardwired into your phone."

"Ya. Broke. Ma. Phone," I tease and the guys laugh. "Thanks," I say with a smile.

"You're welcome. I'll let you guys know if I hear from Zach."

"I hope Ryan is on someone's payroll," I say.

"Oh he is," Rusty says. "Yours."

I scowl. "I don't have anyone on my payroll."

Rusty laughs. "No, he's on Mills' and the band's payroll. He bills us for hours worked and we pay him."

I sulk and the guys leave. "I need to figure out how to pay for Ryan staying at my apartment."

Dex just shrugs and sits back. "Already taken care of."

"Dex," I scold him.

He gives me a stern yet playful look. "Eat," he orders and I sulk my way through my breakfast.

chapter
48
dex

"If it makes you feel any better, I didn't pay for it until after we were married," I tell her as she puts her plate on the tray.

She gives me a sideways glance and a smile, then surprises me by leaning in and kissing my shoulder. "Thank you, Master."

My breathing hitches in my throat. "You're welcome, princess. Why no argument?"

She sighs. "Because I've already learned that I can't win when it comes to you and money and I agreed to let you handle things."

"Wow, is that really how you feel?" I ask her with a chuckle.

"It's debatable," she says with another sideways glance. "But truth be told, I really do appreciate it. Just please don't go throwing a bunch of money at me or anything like that. I need to handle this one step at a time, in my own way."

I lean over and kiss her hair. "That I can handle."

"Good. Now what are we going to do today?" Her enthusiasm is infectious.

"What would you like to do today?"

"Hmm, let me think…shopping…nah…go to a movie…nope, too boring…" She looks so fucking cute while she's pretending to think about what to do. I'm pretty sure she already has an idea or two in her head. I sit back, then in a cute, almost cat like motion, she climbs on top of me, straddling me. "How about we lock ourselves away in bed all day?" She blushes at her own boldness.

"Oh, I don't know…I thought maybe we could go shopping, go to a movie, grab dinner…"

"I bet I can change your mind." She gives me a hooded look filled with lustful promises.

I turn my head in mock thought. "Hmm, I bet you can't."

She wiggles her eyebrows at me and pulls her shirt up and over her head in one quick motion. I sigh heavily. "You're going to have to work harder than that, you insatiable slut."

She shivers at my words, then leans back, cupping her breasts in her hands and I watch as she very carefully twists her tit in such a way that she's able to take her own nipple into her mouth. My mouth falls open and I let out a rush of air. She moans as she sucks it into her mouth deeper. "I'd imagine my mouth would feel better."

She lets her nipple go. "Oh, I don't have to imagine, I know it feels better." She smirks at me then leans forward. She brushes her nipple across my lips, but I don't move.

"Topping from the bottom?" She pouts prettily.

"I remember a time when I could make you melt."

I lean up and kiss her quick on the lips. "You still can." I cup her breasts in my hands and squeeze, pulling her nipples hard between my fingers and I feel her entire body tremble with pleasure, letting her know who's really in control. I release her tits from my grip and she whimpers.

"Not fair," she groans as I stand up, carrying her with me and then tossing her onto the bed before I climb on top of her, licking and kissing down her chest, then her stomach, making my way to the waist of her shorts. Just as I'm about to pull them off, there's a knock on the door.

"Go away," I growl but climb off of the bed. Before I open the door, I toss her t-shirt at her and she's pouting. One downside to being in a hotel with a rock band, you can't leave without the world knowing you're gone.

Standing on the other side of the door was Addison. She begged and pleaded with Raine for us to come along. She pulled the pregnancy card on us. "Come on, pretty soon I'm gonna be as big as a house and cool fun things like this won't be fun anymore." She actually pouted.

"How's that our fault?" I teased her and she shot me a look.

"Probably because I wouldn't sleep with you, you put some weird Dex voodoo on me and I got knocked up."

Raine bursts out laughing and I just stand there in dumbfounded shock. "Can we go?" she asks me sweetly.

"You know, Addison, you interrupted us, I was just about to get busy with my girl." I watch as she visibly shivers. "Thanks so much, sweetheart."

She laughs and begs some more.

"Alright, let us get dressed," I tell the girls and they get giddy. I would have rolled my eyes if it wasn't so fucking cute.

So we ventured out with Addison, Talon, and Kyle. When I asked where Peacock and Mouse were I got a sideways look that told me I should ask more later. Of course Rusty, Tori, Mills and Beck came along. Though they were very inconspicuous, I was impressed.

We spent the nice weathered Sunday afternoon trolling around the Sound, island hopping and just having a good time. We came across a house for sale and I joked with Raine that we should buy that one. My joke backfired when she agreed with me. That was until she saw the sticker price when I pulled it up on my phone. I laughed, she panicked.

We found a nice quaint little place to eat on one of the islands. The food was amazing and the companionship was even better. I could tell that Raine and Addison were getting along really well and it warmed my heart.

I'd honest to god wanted to invite the band and Addison to Vegas when we got married, but I was more worried about Raine freaking out and saying no, at least with Derek, Cami, Dacotah and Tristan it wouldn't have been a big deal, just old friends getting together.

By the time we got back to the hotel, Raine had passed out with her head on my shoulder, so I carried her to our room and put her to bed. I grabbed her phone, remembering that I hadn't set the do not disturb on it yet and when I put in the passcode, I was met with a shit ton of missed calls. All unknown until I clicked into the information. The number stayed the same, but the location kept changing. I'd made her leave her phone behind, not wanting to ruin the day with crazy phone calls and wild emails. She'd easily agreed and I'm glad I did. I turned on the do not disturb and scheduled it to come back on at six each morning. Not wanting to make it too complicated and knowing that whoever was calling her was calling constantly, I decided to program individual numbers for me and the rest of the crew, but not tonight.

I slipped into bed and wrapped my arms around my woman, my wife, the girl of my dreams.

We spent most of Monday in the hotel room. Raine worked from one of the chairs in the sitting room. The unknown caller didn't call at all on Monday.

I took her out for dinner at SkyCity - atop the Space Needle. For someone anti-romance, I sure as hell pulled this one off. Tomorrow is our Seattle show and then we're on the bus to Portland and finally on to Los Angeles, home and two final shows to end the tour. Four more shows then I can get started on our house and our lives. I never felt like being a drummer was ever a burden before, but right now, all I seem to want to do is devour Raine every chance I get.

chapter
49
raine

There is nothing sexier than that gasp of breath in your ear on the first thrust.

That's how I was woken up on Tuesday and what a fucking way to wake up. Dex buried inside me, though I think we fell asleep that way last night.

"Ahh," I cry out as everything comes alive. My heart is racing, my body is humming and Dex is pounding mercilessly inside me from behind. His body is a blanket over mine, holding me to the mattress as he thrusts in and out.

He licks and bites at my shoulder and I cry out. "I'm going to come," I practically scream.

"Come, princess, come for me."

I call out his name as I explode around him, but he doesn't slow, he just keeps pounding into me through my orgasm, desperate to build me back up quickly. I can sense his urgency, he too wants to come and I know he won't do it without me. "Give it to me, harder, please," I beg him and he complies without hesitation and I love it. He shifts so that his right hand is on my left shoulder and his left is on my left hip, altering the sensation and depth. "Fuck," I cry out. He releases my shoulder and smacks my ass, hard. "Argh!" I know why he smacked me and I fucking love it. "Fuck! Fuck! Fuck!" I cry.

He continues to smack my ass, once for each cuss word.

"You're cussing on purpose, aren't you, pet?"

"No Master, it feels so fucking good, I can't fucking help myself."

He growls, "I love it when you fucking challenge me." He smacks me again and again.

"I'm so close."

"Then fucking come." His hand wraps into my hair, pulling my head back, immobilizing me completely. His other hand wraps around my neck. He doesn't squeeze, but he's testing himself and me.

"Oh my god," I cry out as I explode all over his dick inside me. Just the feel of his hand against my throat is enough to send me toppling and spiraling over the edge.

I wake up again a little while later and he is snoring softly next to me. My phone beeps. I grab it off of the nightstand to see that there is a text message and I notice that it's now nearly eleven.

Talon to Raine, Dex, Calvin, Eric: sound check at two.

I roll over and snuggle into Dex. He wraps his arms around me. "Gotta wake up, bubba."

He grumbles and it's so fucking cute. "Come on, bubba, you have sound at two. Do you want food?"

He grumbles some more and nods. I kiss my tattoo on his chest and climb out of bed to use the bathroom and order him some lunch.

The rest of the day flies by and before I know it, it's show time. Dex walks right up to me, dips me backward and kisses me hard and fast. He elicits some whooping and hollering from the guys and it makes me blush like an idiot and causes me to giggle. He lifts me up in an embrace. "Break a leg, bubba." He smiles wide and takes the stage.

I stand there with Kyle and Addison watching the show. We chat a little between songs when we can actually hear our own thoughts. When the band's break comes, Dex charges off of the stage, pushing me against the wall, holding me close and kissing me with fervor, much like he's done every show and I fucking love it. He's is sweaty and gross, but I don't care.

The band finishes their set and their encore which sends Dex right into the shower for the greenroom. Like all the other shows, with the exception of Orlando and Miami, I wait for him with the rest of the guys who do their fair share of ribbing on me about being with Dex. I have to admit, it's kind of fun and they do it with the utmost love and affection, it's obvious that they have a soft spot for their brother.

When Dex joins us, I repeat our routine of beer and sitting on his lap. Tonight is especially insane. More VIP tickets were sold than usual because they're based on a percentage of attendance, and Seattle is one of their biggest shows. It's around eleven thirty when Rusty comes up to me, leaning in, and he whispers in my ear, "You guys should get your stuff ready to go and I need to talk to you."

"Oh okay," I say with a smile, not wanting to alarm Dex. He looks at me and I kiss him on the cheek. "Be right back, bubba. Gonna go wrap up in the dressing room so we can bolt when you're done."

"Good girl," he breathes into my ear and I shiver.

I climb off of his lap and follow Kyle out of the room; he's going to clean up too. When I step out of the room, I follow Rusty into one of the other rooms. Mills is inside, on the phone.

"I understand that, but she no longer lives there and she's turned in her keys, terminated her lease, she is not...no, I will not allow it."

"What is going on?" I whisper to Rusty but my eyes are on Mills.

"Give him a minute."

"I can assure you, she is not now, nor has she been anywhere near that place in more than two weeks and I have a mountain of people who can attest to that." There is a lengthy pause. "No, and I'm one of them. Least of which is the fact that we have a hotel receipt, plane tickets, confirmations and what not to verify her whereabouts." Again he pauses, listening to whoever is on the other end. "Why are you focusing on her? You have two fucking witnesses that can place two people at your scene, running away, you told me flat out one was distinctively male and the other a small male or female, and if you'd bother to look into Ms. Montgomery's license information, you'd see that she does not meet your requirements. If you want to keep pursuing this, I will get more lawyers involved in this and bury your ass in paperwork for the next fifty years."

My heart starts pounding, hard. I sit down in a chair, listening to his conversation. There are a number of things that are starting to click together and click into place...the emails, the phone calls, the... the...two weeks, I haven't been there, I turned in my keys...my apartment, my old apartment...Jesus. I sob into my hands.

"That's what I thought, now if you'll excuse me." I hear some shuffling but I can't quite look up. "So help me god, I am going to have that detective's balls for lunch tomorrow." I've never heard Mills so fucking aggravated before and it scares me even more. "Raine, do you want me to get Dex?"

I shake my head. "Just tell me what happened." I'm afraid of Dex sugar coating, not telling me something or excluding me altogether, I shouldn't feel that way but his overwhelming need to protect me is too much sometimes.

"Your old apartment..."

"I gathered that." I look up at him, he's a little wary.

"Your apartment was determined to be the starting point of a fire that broke out early yesterday morning. There are witnesses that place two people, though unidentifiable, at the scene shortly before the fire broke out."

"Was anyone hurt?" I ask, unable to breathe.

"No, but the fire destroyed three apartments and damaged four others."

"Am I responsible for this?" I ask.

"No," Rusty answers. "You'd already turned in your keys, and if I have any understanding of a psychotic's mind, it's that seeing the apartment empty was probably what set him or her off. Unable to continue with their harmless harassing."

I snort. "Harmless? They destroyed my fucking apartment," I snap, looking at Rusty.

My snapping causes me to hear something in the back of my head, Dex barking at me for getting snippy. Shit.

"So why do you guys know about this? I gave over my keys what...two weeks ago?"

"That's why you're here. I just got off of the phone with an LAPD detective who was determined to have you for dinner tonight. I was not going to allow you to be brought through the mud when you've obviously been here the whole time since the fire and your whereabouts since turning in your keys are likely accounted for."

"They are," I whisper. "Dex and I were in Vegas, I was staying in a hotel in downtown Los Angeles until I moved in with Dex before flying to Denver."

"Can anyone outside the two of you corroborate your presence in Vegas?" Rusty asks.

"Derek Hunter, Dacotah Miller..."

"What about that first Wednesday night after Miami?" Mills asks.

I look up at him. "Why Wednesday?"

"Because apparently there was some prior vandalism in and around your apartment Wednesday evening, Wednesday night," Mills tells me.

I start laughing. "Yeah, those two, plus Cami and Tristan and a legally binding piece of paper that is date and time stamped."

"A what?" Mills says with honest shock and curiosity in his voice.

"Yeah, it's called a marriage license," I giggle.

Mills' jaw drops to the floor, then he looks from me to Rusty and back and forth a few times.

"No way?" Rusty says. "You guys got married?"

Mills' shock and the dropping of his overall hard exterior has me laughing really hard. "Yeah, we did."

We all burst into a fit of laughter, then I turn serious. "Beyond that, Derek, Cotah, Cami and Tristan were with us until at least two in the morning before we crashed. I think that night is covered pretty well. We stayed in Vegas with Derek and Dacotah until Saturday, then I checked out of the hotel and moved what stuff I had left into Dex's apartment. We went to Addison's condo Tuesday night for dinner before we got on the plane for Denver and as you know, I've been here ever since. The one and only time I was in my apartment, Ryan was there. They handled the rest of the cleanup. When I turned in my keys, I walked to the apartment with the manager for an inspection. It was still missing the appliances, but other than that, Ryan and his crew had painted and cleaned up what they could. That was the last time I was anywhere near that building. I thought they were supposed to have security there?"

Mills shrugs, "Well, that's where this fire will fall back on them. If they cut security after you moved out, they left it wide open. They were told by Ryan several times to keep an eye on the place until new tenants moved in, obviously they didn't do that."

"Are they going to go after Raine for this?" Rusty asks.

Mills looks at me with a genuine smile on his face. "Not if I have anything to say about it. There are too many people that put you too far away at the time both crimes were committed."

"The first phone call..." I look at Mills. "What time did the fire start?"

"They believe between four and four-thirty, the nine-one-one call came in at four thirty-two," Mills tells me.

I look at Rusty. "The first phone call came in at three fifty-nine."

chapter
50
dex

"Dex?"

"Yo?" I holler back at one of the crew members.

"Hey, sorry to bug you, but we've got a bit of a problem."

"What's up?"

"You might want to see for yourself." I look down the hall where I've been waiting patiently for Raine to come out with our stuff.

"Yeah, alright." I follow him out the back of the venue and Kyle is coming in. "Hey man, is Raine on the bus?"

"I didn't see her, she still in the dressing room?"

"I don't think so. I'll go check in a minute. I gotta go with him," I tell Kyle.

"Yeah, I heard some commotion with the crew, I just let it go, figured they were comparing dick sizes again. Let me grab Talon and Addie and I'll be right out."

"Yeah, okay." I go back outside, wondering where Raine could be, but I forget all about that when I get out to the bus area. There is a large pile, looks like... "What the fuck happened?" I bellow.

"We don't know. We were loading up stuff, and we left them here like we always do, they're last on first off. When we came back they were like this."

"Why didn't you get the security team?"

The dude just shrugs and I stare at my now spray painted drums and the words- manwhore, asshole, scumbag. But I don't give a shit about that, every single head has been slashed with a knife.

raine

"Give me fifteen minutes, or less and I'll be ready to go," I tell Rusty as I step inside the dressing room.

The minute I close the door, a hand wraps around my mouth. Dex? Then a light flicks on and there is a woman sitting in the chair before the mirror. I want to scream, I do scream, but I am held hard and unable to make a sound that projects loud enough to be heard. "About fucking time you showed up here, you slut." Michael's voice in my ears sends an icy chill through my veins.

"You should have answered your phone. I could have told you all this over the phone, but instead, you had to be a stuck up little cunt and ignore my calls."

I struggle in his arms, fighting to get myself in a position to at least stomp down on his foot with my own, but he's holding me at a distance, making it difficult.

"You have something that belongs to me," the woman in the chair says. "You see, I tried to do this as amicably as possible, but you wouldn't listen, you fucking whore." I watch as she twirls a knife in her hand, pressing the tip to her finger, letting the light reflect and flicker around the room. The word whore on her lips gives me a clue that maybe she was the one to trash my apartment. Sam, perhaps?

"You see, slutbag, I am his and he is mine, and I will no longer let you get in the way of what he and I have. You see, things are finally starting to get back on the right track with us and I will not let you derail that. I know he's a manwhore, but you mean absolutely nothing to him. He does this all the time, he finds some woman to make him believe he's in love with her, just so he can get what he wants, though you're a mystery because I have absolutely no clue what he sees in you. You have no money, and frankly, you're a fat slut willing to throw herself at someone just to get attention. And well, with Dex, it worked, because as soon as the tour is over, he will drop you like a bad habit and come back home to me."

"You're fucking insane," I growl into the hand holding my mouth.

"But you see, sweet Michael here loves you and he's more than willing to take you back, despite you cheating on him. So you go with Michael and I'll get my man back." She stands up and comes over towards us, knife in hand, poised and ready to strike. "Or I'll just kill you." She smiles a sick sadistic smile and I try to kick her, that's when I feel a hard punch, right to my kidney and I double over in pain, crying and screaming into his hand. "I bet that felt pretty bad." She leans over, and puts the knife in my face. "By now, Dex is getting my little message, which means the hallway is now clear of security staff, so which is it...Michael or death?" I don't answer, I just stare at her. "I will not let my unborn child's daddy go trolling around with a dirty little slut like you, so I will only ask you one more time, Michael or your death?"

dex

"Where the fuck is Raine?" I shout as the security team comes running out of the venue, Addison, Talon, Kyle, Mouse, and Peacock in tow. "Where the fuck is Raine?" No one answers. "Where the fuck is my wife?" I shout and I'm met with a shit ton of baffled faces but I don't give a shit about that right fucking now.

"Shit...the dressing room," Rusty says, turning on his heels, everything in slow motion. I feel like I've slipped into that god awful dream where I'm running an endless hallway. Mills and Beck join us, I'm assuming everyone else is ushered onto the bus.

Raine...

Raine...

Jesus fucking Christ, what the hell is going on here?

Finally I make it to the door and run inside, down the hall, toward our dressing room, the door is closed. I slam into it before I manage to get my hand on the knob. I turn it but the door is locked. I step back, kicking at the door. God damn it. "Raine," I shout, kicking and shoulder checking the door.

"DEEEEEEEEEEXXXXXXXX!" I hear a scream, but it's not behind the door. Just then the door opens.

"Welcome home, baby."

"Sam," I growl. "What the fuck have you done?"

"I was just making sure we could be together forever. I'm having your whore of a fuck buddy taken care of as we speak."

I get in her face. "She's my wife," I growl before grabbing her wrist and pulling her from the room and right into Beck's hold.

"I fucking knew you were trouble," Beck growls as he pulls her arms behind her back and cuffs her.

"HHHEEEEEEEELLLLLPPPPPP!"

I turn and run toward the arena, heading up onto the stage, Mills and Rusty in tow.

I am flashed in the face with a spotlight. Blinding me, making it impossible for me to see anything.

"Raine!" I shout.

"She's right here, asshole." Just then the color in my eyes shifts and changes and starts to move like a video.

I turn around and on the backdrop of the stage is a video of Raine, tied up. "Fuck."

"What the fuck do you want, asshole?" I shout.

"I just want you to watch," he says over the sound system.

I watch as he cuts away the strings of her corset. "No!" I scream. "Fucking find her, right fucking now," I tell Mills and Rusty. Mills starts talking into his handset and off they go.

"Oh, don't bother trying to find us, you see, I've been planning this for weeks. I needed to find a way to get my woman back, and well, your fiancé gave me the perfect opportunity. You see, she was tired of your games and bullshit so we got together and found a way to flush her out. And look, here she is." He cuts away the last of her corset and it falls open.

"Don't you fucking hurt her," I scream.

"Oh, I can't possibly hurt the woman that I love." I see his face come right next to hers. "I'm just going to take what she's been flaunting all night."

I watch as absolute terror slides over her face…those words…the words…

He licks her cheek. "That's right, baby, we've been here once before, haven't we? I thought for sure it was never going to work, but then that night, in the dingy bar, you came right up to me, smiled and wiggled your ass, taunting and flaunting it in front of me. Then you started talking to me and ooooh wow, I couldn't get enough, so I decided that maybe I could finish what I'd started what was it, four years ago at the time." He licks her cheek.

Her eyes are filled with absolute terror. "I'm coming for you, glowbug," I whisper and stand up, turning around. I jump off of the stage and run across the empty space directly under the projection light.

"Where you goin'? Aren't you going to watch me take what's mine?"

"She wasn't yours then and she isn't yours now. So help me god, I will kill you when I find you."

He laughs. "You'll never find me in time." I hear her crying and the metal chair scraping the floor. I turn around just in time to see her being knocked over onto the floor and the video goes to snow.

"Goddammit!" I growl as I nearly run into Talon. "Find her."

"We're looking, we're all looking."

I feel my grip on reality slipping away the longer I search, slamming into closed doors, open doors, doesn't matter, I'm checking every fucking room I come across.

Hopping concession counters, doing everything I fucking can to find her.

I run into Kyle, then Peacock along my path to finding her.

When I come back around to where I started, I climb the steps, headed for level two.

With each passing minute, my mind starts playing out the worst.

She recovered once. She'll never recover a second time.

"Raine?" I keep shouting as I go. I run into Addison. "No, no, no, get out of here. Go back to the bus."

"I can't sit idle," she says near tears.

"I will never forgive myself if something happens to you too, please sweet girl, go," I beg her.

"Alright Dex, alright." Something passes between us in that moment. I felt our entire relationship altering, and if it wasn't for my desperate need to find Raine, I would have apologized to her right then and there for all the times I've been a dick to her, treated her like she was nothing but a piece of meat. Been an assholian, as Raine would put it.

"Raine!" I scream again, listening, amazed at how empty this place is. Where the fuck is security? Where the fuck are they? "Raine!" I scream again. The longer this takes, the more scared I get. I can't fucking lose her, I'll die without her.

chapter
51
dex

My phone rings.

"What?" I snap.

"We've got them."

"Where?"

"We're coming back to the floor now."

"Is she hurt?"

"No."

That was all I needed to hear and I hang up, running back toward the door I'd just passed a moment ago.

I run down the steps, looking around, looking for them. No one is there. I spin around, trying to see them, find them. "Dex." I hear the voice that saves my life, brings me my sanity in a single word, my name. I turn toward the sound and see my glowbug coming down the steps. My heart shreds when I see she's wrapped in a blanket, but relief replaces pain when I realize she's walking on her own steam next to Rusty. Behind him, Mills has that fuckwad, Michael.

I run toward them, skipping three steps at a time. When I get to her, I throw my arms around her, harder than I should. "Oh god, oh god," I breathe. "Are you okay?" I sob into her shoulder.

"Physically, I'm fine," she sobs.

"Thank fuck."

I release her, looking her over. Her mouth is red where the tape was, her eyes are black and puffy with makeup, but she looks relatively unharmed. But looks don't stop me from trying to examine her. "I'm fine," she whispers, thank god.

The fucker who assaulted her is squirming in Mills' grasp. "Go with Rusty, baby," I say to her but I'm looking at him.

"No, Dex, don't. Let the police handle it."

"Yeah, because they've done a bang up job so far."

"Dammit, Dex, don't. I need you. I don't need you going to jail."

"Go Raine," I command her. I know she won't be able to resist and I know she's going to be so fucking pissed, but she's not going to stand here watching me beat the shit out of this douchecanoe.

I hear Rusty whispering in her ear, "Do you really think we'd let that happen?"

I don't bother to look back, I just hear them going down the stairs. I stand there, staring at the motherfucker.

"Are they gone?" I say through gritted teeth.

"Yes."

"Uncuff him."

"Dex."

"Do it. Let him fucking fight back. Makes it easier for me." I cock my head menacingly at him and I can see the fear creeping into his eyes. Oh buddy, you ain't seen nothing yet.

I can't see what Mills is doing but I can see the wheels turning in Michael's head. He's planning his escape, until I grab his hair and pull him down the stairs as Mills releases the last cuff.

"You're fucking insane," he squeals as we hit the last step and I throw him down onto the arena floor.

"I'm insane? You're fucking kidding me, you're the son of bitch that not only raped my wife once, but tried to do it again. Who falls on the insane spectrum?"

raine

"Damn it, Rusty, take me back."

"No, you don't need to see that."

"Like hell I don't." I spin in his grip and head back toward the stage.

"Dammit," Rusty growls behind me, but I am not the only one in the hallway anymore. Behind me are Casey, Beck, Talon, Kyle, Addison, Mouse, Peacock, and Tori. I can feel the force of them coming up behind me as I step back onto the stage just in time to see Dex throw him onto the floor from a couple steps up.

"Come on, you son of a bitch," Dex growls. The look in his eyes is absolutely terrifying.

I watch as Michael, or whatever the fuck his name is, gets up and tries to run toward me and the stage, the fastest way out of here. That's when our entire collection of friends and family hop down off of the stage. It's a massive presence that sends Michael sliding to a stop, but not before Peacock gets a solid grip on his t-shirt. I watch as his fingers shred the shirt before he releases one side and connects with his face. I watch Michael stumble backward, running straight into Beck. "You fuck with one of ours, we fuck you up." Beck cranks his arm back, sending him careening toward the floor face first. That's when Mouse connects with his ribs. Beck pulls him back up. "You see, there are eleven of us here, do you think your story will stand up, that you were attacked?" Beck whips him around to Dex. "He's all yours, brother." Beck pushes him forward, right at Dex who connects with his right fist, right in the side of Michael's head.

I watch as rage fills him as he spits blood all over the floor and he charges back at Dex.

Dex is prepared, waiting for him to strike at him, and Michael doesn't disappoint, connecting one right into the side of his face.

"Thank you," he growls and he lets loose on Michael, kidney punches, throws to the face and finally one shitkicker to the balls that finally brings Michael back down to the ground, groaning and rolling around.

"Dex, stop," I cry out.

His eyes meet mine. I watch as the menace, the rage and the fierce need to have control morphs into all the love and devotion that the man I love has for me. It's beautiful to witness.

"Cuff him," he tells Mills. "Get this son of bitch out of my sight. Where's the other cunt bag?"

"She's locked away. The cops are on their way'" Mills says and Dex lands one more kick to the dude's stomach before walking past him, walking past our friends, up the stage and slamming into me.

I break down into body wracking sobs as he picks me up. He nuzzles his nose into mine before carrying me toward the back of the venue and the bus. "I've got you, bug. I got you. I will never let you go. You're the sweetest, most perfect person I know…" His sweet nothings continue as we walk through the back of the arena, through the parking lot and straight onto the bus.

Once he's on board the bus, he bypasses our room for Talon, Kyle and Addison's room. I don't question him. He sets me down on the bed and I get a good look at him.

"You're bleeding."

"Fuck that." He drops to his knees, wrapping his arms around me, holding me to him.

I manage to get an arm out of my blanket and I stroke his hair. "Are you hurt?" he chokes out.

"Physically? No." I brush my hand through his hair again. "Did they get her too?" I whisper.

"Yes, I found her in the dressing room."

"Who is she, Dex?" My voice comes out harsher than I wanted it to.

He looks up at me, his eyes wary and worried. "I met her in San Diego, you know this. Addison's told you this."

"She said she was your fiancé?"

He pulls back and gives me a little half smirk. "Well, you're my wife, so I think that trumps anything else, don't you?"

"She said she was pregnant."

He hisses through his teeth. "That's impossible." He stands up defensively and starts to pace in the small area. His defenses are up.

"Really?" I question and he scowls at me.

"It's impossible because I never stopped using condoms until I met you."

"Condoms are not foolproof, Dex." I try not to snap, but I'm angry, hurt and I need answers.

"No, they're not, but not coming is pretty foolproof."

"What do you mean-" I don't finish.

"I faked it, I faked it with her, much the way I've faked it with a lot of women. I fucking made them get me off with their mouth before I'd fuck them. Sometimes I'd come, sometimes I wouldn't. When I wouldn't, I'd play it off like I had, tie off the condom and bail as fast as I could. I didn't orgasm with her, at all. She was horrible at giving head and even worse at getting laid." He runs his hand through his hair. "Do you really need the details?"

"Yeah, Dex, I do."

"With her, she started spouting bullshit about love and … I freaked the fuck out and ran as hard and fast as I could."

"So you fucking knew then that she was fucked up."

"That's not fair," he snaps at me. "I never fucking knew she'd go this far."

"She fucking destroyed my apartment." He looks at me. "Yeah, she's the one who trashed my shit, the one responsible for destroying my entire world. She gave me a choice. Either she killed me, or I went with Michael. I chose Michael, I thought that I would at least have half a chance of surviving versus being stabbed to death. Either way, she was going to get rid of me so that she could get you back. She was convinced that you would stop fucking around when you got off the tour, so that you could go back to your life, that once the tour was over you were going to drop me like a bad habit, that she was the only woman you loved…" I keep rambling as I completely melt down.

"Dex! Raine!" a female voice shouts from the front of the bus. Addison.

"Back here," he hollers back.

Addison comes bounding around the corner. "Raine?"

I look at her, tears and all. "What?" I mouth.

"The cops are here. They need to talk to you and Dex."

"We'll be out in a minute," Dex tells her. "Give us a minute."

"Absolutely," Addison says and she leaves the room.

Dex turns to me and once again kneels at my feet. He takes my hand in his. "Thank you." Before I can ask for what, he continues, "For choosing him. She's fucking insane. I swear to god, glowbug, I never knew she'd even consider this kind of behavior. I've met some crazy women in my life, but this is beyond the pale. I swear to you that she is not pregnant. I am not that stupid, trust me on this, please. She was ready and willing to do anything she took to plant the seed of doubt in your mind, to push you away from me. Once this tour is over, I am buying a house with you, I am going to build a life with you, I will marry you again. You, Raine Montgomery are the only woman I've ever fallen in love with, have loved and will love for the rest of my life. Without you, I am not whole, I am not human. I cannot live without you."

I cup his face in my hands, the blanket falling away. "I know," I tell him.

His eyes grow wide with shock as I plant my lips on his, he unthaws, melting into my kiss, I stroke my thumbs against his stubble covered cheeks. "I know," I breathe again and again as he captures my mouth, bringing me into a soul scorching, heart devouring kiss that sends shivers all over my body.

chapter
52
raine

Dex helps me into our alcove and finds me a t-shirt. I can't help but smile when he pulls out my white 'Superman' t-shirt. I just wish I felt more like him. More invincible. I flinch when his hand touches along my side. He freezes. "What's wrong? Raine?"

"He...he got me in the kidneys."

"Let me see."

"Dex, I'm alright."

"Really? Because you're bruised. We're taking you to the hospital."

I sigh. "For what? I'm perfectly fine."

He cocks his head at me. "Let's at least have the paramedics look at you, please? Let them decide if you need to go to the hospital."

I realize there is no longer a point in arguing with him. "Yes, Master."

He wraps me in his arms and he kisses my forehead before releasing me and helping me change into a pair of shorts. "Come on, let's go get your face cleaned up," he tells me as he leads me out of our alcove and into the bathroom. I wash my face with shaky hands as the adrenaline starts to fade.

He notices. "Sit down," he says sternly and I do. That's when he takes the washcloth from me and he gently cleans up my makeup mess. In the face of something that could have been worse, he's being tender and gentle and being the caring man I always knew was buried in the tough exterior that is Dex.

I start to cry. He stops what he's doing and kneels down in front of me in the tight space of the bus's bathroom. "What's the matter, glowbug?"

I gently wipe the tears from my eyes. "I don't know how to explain it," I tell him.

"Can you try?" His hands are resting on my thighs and I feel a gentle squeeze and I close my eyes a little tighter. "I just realize that," sniff, "that you really do care, that...that hiding under your tough guy exterior is a soft, gentle person. That there is a caring Dom under all that."

His hand cups my cheek. "I will never stop taking care of you. No matter what the circumstances. This is why I asked you to surrender yourself to me, to let me take care of you."

"She burnt down my old apartment."

"What?" he breathes. "How do you know that?"

I sigh, I have to tell him. "When I left the greenroom tonight, Rusty pulled me into one of the other rooms and Mills was on the phone with a detective from LA. They were trying to pin the vandalism and fire on me, despite the fact that I'd turned over my keys already."

"Why didn't you tell me?"

"Because, I didn't see you until Mills and Rusty brought me back into the arena. The phone call, the first one, was right before the fire was set. Mills put up a pretty big fight with the cop, he has a solid alibi for me, for you, for all of us, but the cop was being a douche. Apparently, Wednesday night, our night, there was another vandalism event at my apartment. Mills and Rusty know we got married."

He smiles. "So does the band."

"What? How?"

"She trashed my drums and I realized the similarity in the spray painting to what I'd seen in your apartment. I panicked, looking for you, I sort of shouted, 'where the fuck is my wife?'."

"Oh Dex, you didn't."

He laughs. "Yeah, I did. It slipped." He wipes the tears from my cheeks. "It's all good, but I'm sure we're going to get an earful."

I snort a little laugh. "Well, then we better face the music."

He cocks his head. "I really want to step in and stop this from happening."

I smile then and cup his face between my hands. "This is the one time your Dominance cannot step in the way. I've got to talk to the cops, and so do you. It's the only way we can get it over with, pack up and get the fuck out of here."

"And get you checked out."

I kiss his lips gently. "Honestly, I'm fine."

"I know you are, sexy as fuck, but I will not have my glowbug getting sick, or worse."

I release him. "Alright."

"Good girl," he says and I know I light up a little on the inside.

The minute we step off of the bus, we're met with everyone, literally, surrounding the bus, though seemingly casual to an outside observer. Dex and I look at each other, knowing better. They weren't going to let anyone on the bus before we were ready.

"Is he still here?" Dex asks.

"No," Mills answers as he comes over to us. "They took him off in an ambulance. He's probably got a broken nose at the very least, maybe a few ribs."

"Am I in trouble?" Dex asks the question I'm thinking.

Mills snorts. "No, Beck all but took the blame for the incident, stating that Michael had attacked Raine, then you, then lastly him. The cop that interviewed him could clearly see that Beck was a bodyguard and that he more or less was doing his job. Though they may ask you about it." He looks pointedly at Dex.

"No problem there."

Mills turns to me. "Come on, the paramedics are waiting for you."

"But I'm fine," I protest and Dex glares at me. "Oh for the love...fine," I grumble as Mills escorts me to the back of the ambulance.

"Hi guys, this is Raine." That's all he has to say before the female paramedic comes to the end of the bus.

"Will you come on up here?" she asks me.

"I'm not leaving these grounds on this thing," I state.

"Let us decide that, but for now, we're just going to examine you and ask you a few questions."

I look at Mills who nods his head toward the gurney lying in the back of the ambulance.

"Do you guys take lessons is bossing women around?" I tease him, and he jerks his head again.

As I go to climb up he leans in and whispers, "You have no idea." There is a tone in his voice that instantly reminds me of Dex and Derek. I look at him and he smiles, jerking his head toward the bus again.

"I'm going." I climb up and sit down on the gurney.

dex

"What's your relationship to Samantha Gill?" the cop asks me.

"Who?" I say and the cop frowns. "Oh Sam, uhm, yeah, there isn't a relationship there."

"She's under the impression that there is."

I snort. "You can add that to her list of delusions. She has several of them. That being the first, the second being that she's my fiancé, the third being that she's pregnant with my child."

"So you have a relationship with her?"

"Fuck no."

"Calm down," the cop says.

My blood boils. "Look, she attacked my wife with a knife, vandalized twenty-five grand in equipment, set my wife up to be attacked, nearly raped, or killed. She's also responsible for severe vandalism to my wife's apartment back in Los Angeles, harassing phone calls, among other things and you want to accuse me of having an affair with her? Go to hell."

"Dex, don't." Addison comes up.

"No, goddammit, these sons of bitches are out to fucking make Raine look like she deserved what she got and that Sam, Samantha, whatever the fuck her name is, is in the right."

Addison smiles and turns to the officers. "Let me tell you who Sam is. She's a deranged woman who threw herself at Dex nearly three months ago. She was denied, rejected and she slipped her cork. I have a phone call history with more than a thousand calls on it because at one point, before all this bullshit happened, she was my friend. She thought that through me she could get to Dex. We also have picture proof of her outside of Raine's apartment in LA, after it had been vandalized the first time. We have concrete proof that she's been calling and harassing Raine for the last forty-eight hours and we have concrete proof of where everyone was and what they were doing tonight and every night of the attacks and destruction back in California. Now, do you have any more questions for Dex that are not going to accuse him of being responsible for what happened here tonight or is that all you're here to do?"

Holy shit...well, fuck I always knew this chick was feisty, but hot damn. I look over the cop's shoulder to see Talon and Kyle grinning wildly from ear to ear over what their girl has just done and all I want to do is hug her.

"What she said," I say to the cop who is momentarily off his guard compliments of Addison's rant.

"Got it!" Rusty calls from behind us. We all turn to see Rusty running out of the back of the arena, with something in his hand.

"Got what?" I ask as he approaches me and the cop.

He smirks. "Oh, just a little video action going on."

"Is that...oh god." I feel like puking, watching it once was enough, I pray to god I never have to watch it again.

"It is. See, I knew he was stupid, it's all right here." He hands a disc to the officer. "Oh, and there is a feed from inside of the dressing room. There's no sound, but I'm pretty sure you'll get the idea."

"Well, we will review it and..."

"And nothing. The only thing we want to hear from you is when and where we need to be for court for both of these assholes." I tell the cop who looks positively railroaded by all of us.

"Alright, I'll be in touch." He finally shoves off.

I turn to Addison and wrap my arms around her. "Thank you and I'm sorry."

"You're welcome, though you don't owe me a thank you for anything. I just did my job and I haven't a clue what the hell you're apologizing for. Unless of course it's for the fact that you married her and didn't invite us."

I know I blush. "The thank you is for handling the cop, and for your help in trying to find her. The thank you is also for putting up with my bullshit and I'm apologizing because you've had to put up with my bullshit. I've been a dick for far too long."

"Dex?" she says.

"Yes?" I hesitate.

"Shut the fuck up or I might start to think you're actually a human being."

I laugh. "Blame her." I cock my head toward Raine who is approaching us from the back of the ambulance.

"Blame me for what?" she says as she snuggles in under my arm.

"For taming his ass." Talon nods in my direction.

She smiles. "He devoured me."

"Are you free to go?" Kyle asks.

"For some reason the cops no longer wanted to talk to me and the paramedics gave me an all clear."

I look down at her, tucked under my arm. We're surrounded by friends, family. Me and the love of my life, my wife and my best friend. I lean down, capturing her lips with mine and hold her tightly to my side. Vowing to never let her go, to never leave her side, to always care for her, take care of her, and devour her every chance I get.

"I love you, glowbug," I whisper against her lips.

"I love you, bubba."

he collars
me...

We wrapped up the tour later that week with a big shindig in Los Angeles. The shows were incredible and the parties even more fun.

Dex and Addison finally seemed to get along. Whenever I asked him about it, he'd shrug it off, telling me that he was repenting for being an asshole. I'd just smile and let it go.

Derek, Dacotah, Cami, Tristan, and Erica all came to the show. I made good on my promise to Erica, bringing her as a thank you for all she did for me while I was away on tour with the band. Dex was excited to meet her and he looked forward to seeing her again soon. I vowed to keep her in my life, no matter what and Dex agreed. He told me that I was required to go out with her at least once a month when we were in town.

Following the tour, Dex and I followed Talon, Addison and Kyle to Nashville while Addison recorded her duet with Bryan Hayes.

Dex surprised me with a membership to The Box. I was so excited, I could barely contain myself when Derek and Cotah showed up at our hotel, dressed appropriately for The Box, and we took off for dinner and of course a night of playing and more training. I was in submissive heaven.

Derek was impressed with the leaps and bounds Dex and I had made in our D/s relationship and even Cotah praised me, after gaining permission of course, for my improvements as a sub to Dex.

We'd passed on Cami's offer to go to Tarah, which bummed me out when Cotah got back and called me, telling me her Orion had finally proposed to her. I teased her that it was only because Dex and I'd gotten married first. She laughed. "True," she said. "But he collared me first."

After that conversation, I asked Dex about it, asked him if he wanted to collar me. He said absolutely, but that there were a few more steps in our relationship we needed to hurdle first. That was until I told him that collaring me meant that I would relinquish my safeword. Giving up my safeword is a way for me to show him how much I trust him and our relationship. It means that I trust him completely to not push me beyond the limits of what I can handle. He got eager after that, but leading up until tonight, he'd always teased me with it.

Tonight, Derek and Cotah have come to our condo in Los Angeles. Addison's old condo to be exact. We're christening our brand new playroom with a ceremony. Dex is collaring me and I am over the fucking moon.

I stand, bouncing upstairs in our room with Cotah.

"You're already married to him, so why is this so important?"

I smile wide. "He's claimed me as his wife, now I want to be claimed as his submissive."

"Excellent answer," Derek says as he crests the steps into our loft bedroom.

I smile at him, but bow my head submissively.

"Nah, not tonight sweet girl, please look at me."

I raise my head, looking at him and he hands me something, a box. It's the size of a ring box. "Our gift to you," Derek says. "For finding your submission."

Tears start to well in my eyes as I pinch open the lid. Inside is actually a bracelet, it's a starter bracelet actually. There are two white beads, surrounded on both sides by silver and hanging from the bracelet is a triskelion symbol, the three yin-yang halves making a circle, the symbol for BDSM. "It's gorgeous," I say and look up at him. "Thank you, Sir."

'My pleasure."

"Permission to talk to Cotah, Sir." He leans in, kissing me on the forehead.

"Always."

"Thank you, Sir." I look up at Cotah. "Thank you Cotahbear."

She giggles at my nickname for her and smiles wide. "You're welcome."

"Cotahbear huh?" Derek says with an amused smirk.

"Yup, that's the name I've given her." I smile and he wraps his arm around her.

"I like it." He grins and kisses her forehead before looking at me. "It's time."

"Can I wear this?" I ask him.

"Hmm, yeah, then you can show him, and he can remove it before he does anything." I shiver at the prospect of whatever Dex might be conjuring up tonight.

Cotah helps me put the bracelet on and Derek descends the stairs ahead of us.

Cotah leads the way down and she joins Derek in the playroom ahead of me. Outside the door, I hang up my robe and my new bracelet catches the light and I smile.

This is everything I've wanted and so much more.

When I walk into the room, I lower my head, and walk toward my husband, my partner, the man I love and will love forever.

He's claimed me as his girlfriend, his fiancé, his wife and now, as I lower myself at his feet, he will claim me as his submissive.

He's claimed me, he craves me, he's redeemed me from the roller coaster that is my past.

I've tamed him and he's devoured me.

epilogue

one year
later...

Michael - though not his real name, but we'll keep it there for these purposes - was charged with one count of rape, one count of attempted rape when it came to me. He was also charged with more than fifty other counts of rape and six counts of attempted murder. Michael was a wanted man in more than thirty different states, but somehow he always managed to elude the authorities. It took me, Dex and a team of rock star bodyguards to finally bring him down. Fortunately, he pled guilty to avoid the death penalty and I never had to testify in court.

Sam was found guilty of attempted murder, criminal vandalism, stalking, harassment and a multitude of other crimes I can't quite think of at the moment. She was sentenced to a facility for the criminally insane, a place where she will likely be for the rest of her life. Regardless, she's gone from our lives.

When Dex claimed me as his submissive, he presented me with two collars. The first was my playroom collar. It's a thin, almost dainty leather collar with a hoop attached to it, something he frequently uses at the club. We both like it when he leads me around by a leash. The second was an everyday collar. It was a gorgeous platinum necklace that came together just below my neck. Holding the two parts of the necklace together is a locket that literally needs a key to unlock it. Him unlocking my everyday collar means that I am to go to the playroom.

He started off the ceremony with sweet whispers and murmurs as I sat at his feet, then told me that he did not want my safeword. He cherished my eager willingness to surrender it to him, but said that it might be a good idea to keep it, for now.

Addison's twins were born this last November and we're over there all the time. Whether the band is writing music or we're all just hanging out and having a good time.

After that night in Seattle, Dex never left my side for a very long time. He was petrified that something was going to happen to me. I kept reassuring him that all our external threats had been dealt with. He finally convinced me to seek therapy for what happened with Michael, both times, and I have to say, it's helped a lot.

But I'm not sure what helps me more, talking about my past, or the advancement in our Dom/sub relationship. We've made great strides and Dex, after letting Derek go at me with the single tail, has been diligently taking classes. He was disappointed that Derek was responsible for the first two times I've fully reached subspace. But he's managed to get me there nearly every time we step into our own playroom. Which is where I hope we end up tonight.

He's been in the studio with the guys all day, and he's been there for the last few weeks. Though they're recording a lot of Addison's music and not 69 Bottles stuff, Dex is happy because he gets to do the things he loves. Drumming and me.

I hear him come into the condo. "Glowbug?" he calls out.

"In the kitchen, I'll be right out. Have a seat on the couch," I tell him. I have a surprise for him tonight.

Now I don't do this very often, ironically, it's usually when I want something from him. In this case, it's a discussion.

I grab him a beer and walk toward the living room.

He scowls at me. "Servitude, on a week night?" He raises an eyebrow as he takes in my nakedness with my playroom collar on my finger and a beer in the other hand.

I just bow my head and hand him his beer before folding myself on a floor cushion I'd found online. His hand comes into my hair and I nuzzle into his leg. Truth be told, I actually love doing this, but I think of it as a gift and it needs to be earned, so I don't do it often.

"What do you want, pet?"

I try not to laugh. "Can't I just serve my Master?"

He wraps his hand in my ponytail, pulling my head back, forcing me to look at him. "Always, but this is your own little way of topping from the bottom." He gives me a chaste kiss.

"We actually need to talk," I tell him softly.

He cocks his head before releasing his grip on my hair. I put my head back where it was and I start fingering his shoe lace.

"What do we need to talk about, glowbug?"

"We have a decision to make."

"Oh."

I take a deep breath and I get onto my knees and turn around, putting palms on my thighs. "May I look at you, Master?"

"Please do," he says softly.

"I have an appointment coming up next month. It is my annual exam and with this exam, I have to have my IUD removed and replaced." He raises an eyebrow. "I don't want to have it replaced."

I watch as his face lights up and he leans forward. "Are you sure?" he asks me softly.

"The only other thing I've ever been more sure of in my life was the day I married you, the first time."

"So all of this was to tell me that you're ready to start a family?"

"Yes, Master."

"When's your appointment?"

"Four weeks from now."

He smiles wide. "That's too far away. Reschedule it, tomorrow would be perfect."

I can't even begin to describe the excitement that is coursing through my veins. Throwing protocol out the window, I throw my arms around his neck, pushing him back against the couch, crashing my lips to his. "Thank you." I kiss him again. "Thank you, Master."

He kisses me back and laughs before wrapping his arms around me and engulfing me into the warmest, sweetest hug I've ever felt from my husband.

After a few heartbeats, my husband disappears and my Master appears.

"Playroom. Now!" he snaps and I jump off of him and head straight for our little room of happiness.

Zoey Derrick is a Best Selling Author of Contemporary, Erotic, Erotic Romance and Paranormal Romance from Glendale Arizona. She was once a mortgage underwriter and she now writes full time.

She writes stories as hot as the desert sun itself. It is this passion that drips off of her work, bringing excitement to anyone who enjoys a good and sensual love story.

Not only does she aim to take her readers on an erotic dance that lasts the night, it allows her to empty her mind of stories we all wish were true.

Her stories are hopeful yet true to life, skillfully avoiding melodrama and the unrealistic, bringing her gripping Erotica only closer to the heart of those that dare dipping into it.

The intimacy of her fantasies that she shares with her readers is thrilling and encouraging, climactic yet full of suspense. She is a loving mistress, up for anything, of which any reader is doomed to return to again and again.

Stalk Zoey on Social Media

Zoey Derrick